PENGUIN BOOKS

The Good Wife

Praise for *Revenge of the Middle-Aged Woman*

'In Buchan's witty hands, it is fate, the most satisfying, entertaining mischief maker, which proves the undoing' *Sunday Times*

'Buchan is brilliant at creating memorable characters . . . poignant, oddly uplifting and intelligent' *Sunday Mirror*

'This perceptive, beautifully written book brings a fresh perspective to an age-old situation . . . For women of all ages, a poignant, unforgettable novel' *You Magazine*

'Extremely readable, well-written, funny and sad' *Daily Mail*

'A compassionate and thoughtful portrait of a marriage in crisis and a woman bent on survival' *Woman & Home*

'Buchan's portrayal of Rose's emotions – from shock, betrayal and anger to a gradual acceptance of her situation – sets this novel apart from other tales of midlife crises' *Good Housekeeping*

'Intelligent and uplifting' *Sainsbury's Magazine*

'Miss Buchan skilfully sets the serendipitous scene where hungry Nemesis hovers . . . This is a compelling read' *Country Life*

'Bitter-sweet charm' *Sunday Tribune*, Dublin

'The Revenge is not about cutting up his suits or pouring away his collection of vintage wines, for Elizabeth is much too subtle a writer for that . . . a resonant and excellent novel' *SW Magazine*

Praise for *Secrets of the Heart*

'Celebrates human resilience and flexibility . . . confirms her skill as a storyteller' *Independent on Sunday*

'In this latest of her acutely intelligent novels, Buchan proves she is not only a powerful romantic novelist, she is a nice one too' *The Times*

'A finely written, intelligent romance' *Mail on Sunday*

'Beautifully observed and richly detailed, the writer's powerful prose has the ability to move emotions' *Evening Herald*

'A finely balanced, superior love story' *Sunday Mirror*

ABOUT THE AUTHOR

Elizabeth Buchan lives in London with her husband and two children and worked in publishing for several years. During this time, she wrote her first books, which included a biography for children: *Beatrix Potter: The Story of the Creator of Peter Rabbit*. Her first novel for adults, *Daughters of the Storm*, was set during the French Revolution. Her second, *Light of the Moon*, took as its subject a female undercover agent operating in occupied France during the Second World War. Her third novel, *Consider the Lily*, hailed by the *Sunday Times* as 'the literary equivalent of the English country garden' and by the *Independent* as 'a gorgeously well-written tale: funny, sad, sophisticated', won the 1994 Romantic Novel of the Year Award. An international bestseller, there are over 320,000 copies in print in the UK. Her subsequent novel, *Perfect Love*, was called 'a powerful story: wise, observant, deeply felt, with elements that all women will recognize with a smile – or a shudder'. *Against Her Nature*, published in 1998, was acclaimed as 'a modern day *Vanity Fair* . . . brilliantly done' and *Secrets of the Heart* was praised by the *Mail on Sunday* as 'a finely written, highly intelligent romance, without any of the slushiness usually associated with the genre'. *Revenge of the Middle-Aged Woman* was described by *The Times* as 'wise, melancholy, funny and sophisticated'. Her most recent novel is *The Good Wife*.

Elizabeth Buchan has sat on the committee for the Society of Authors and was a judge for the 1997 Whitbread Awards and Chairman of the Judges for the 1997 Betty Trask Award. Her short stories have been published in various magazines and broadcast on BBC Radio 4.

For further information on Elizabeth Buchan and her work go to www.elizabethbuchan.com

The Good Wife

ELIZABETH BUCHAN

PENGUIN BOOKS

PENGUIN BOOKS

Published by the Penguin Group
Penguin Books Ltd, 80 Strand, London WC2R ORL, England
Penguin Putnam Inc., 375 Hudson Street, New York, New York 10014, USA
Penguin Books Australia Ltd, 250 Camberwell Road,
Camberwell, Victoria 3124, Australia
Penguin Books Canada Ltd, 10 Alcorn Avenue, Toronto, Ontario, Canada M4V 3B2
Penguin Books India (P) Ltd, 11 Community Centre,
Panchsheel Park, New Delhi – 110 017, India
Penguin Books (NZ) Ltd, Cnr Rosedale and Airborne Roads,
Albany, Auckland, New Zealand
Penguin Books (South Africa) (Pty) Ltd, 24 Sturdee Avenue,
Rosebank 2196, South Africa

Penguin Books Ltd, Registered Offices: 80 Strand, London WC2R ORL, England

www.penguin.com

First published 2003
1

Set in Monotype Garamond by Intype London Ltd
Printed in England by Clays Ltd, St Ives plc

For Margot

Her price is far above rubies
Proverbs 31, 10

Acknowledgements

Many thanks are owed to Vanessa Hannam and Deborah Stewartby for their kindness, generosity and patience in answering my questions about life as an MP's wife. Any mistakes are entirely mine. I am also extremely grateful to Emma Dally for sending me *Complete Wine Course* by Kevin Zraly (Sterling Publishing, New York). I borrowed details for (my) Casa Rosa and the visit to the Etruscan tombs from Frances Mayes's *Under the Tuscan Sun* (Bantam Books), from Iris Origo's *War in the Val d'Orcia* (Cape), and from Tim Parks's *An Italian Education* (Vintage). Also information and anecdote on being a Member of Parliament from Gyles Brandreth's *Breaking the Code* (Phoenix). With apologies also to Jane Austen. A huge thank-you is also owed to my brilliant editors Louise Moore and Christie Hickman, to Hazel Orme – as always – to Stephen Ryan, to Keith Taylor, Sarah Day and the rest of the Penguin team. Also to my agent Mark Lucas, Janet Buck and, of course, to Benjie, Adam and Eleanor.

I

It is a truth universally acknowledged that one person's happiness is frequently bought at the expense of another's.

My husband Will, a politician to his little toe, did not entirely get the point. He maintained that sacrifices in the cause of the common good were sufficient in themselves to make anyone happy. And since Will had sacrificed a significant slice of his family life to pursue his ambitions as, first, a promising MP, then a member of the Treasury Select Committee, then minister, and – latterly – as one who was tipped to be a possible Chancellor of the Exchequer, it followed that he should have been supremely happy.

I think he was.

But was I?

Not a question, perhaps, that a good wife should ask.

If you ask some people what it means to be 'good', they reply that it is to tell the truth. But if you are asked by the huntsman which way the fox went, and you tell him, does that mean you are good?

On our nineteenth wedding anniversary, Will and I promised each other to be normal. To this end, Will carried me off to the theatre, ordered champagne, kissed me lovingly and proposed the toast: 'To married life.'

The play was Ibsen's *A Doll's House*, and the production

had excited attention. Although I could see that he was aching with tiredness, Will sat very still and upright in the seat, not even relaxing when the lights went dim. An upright back was part of the training he had imposed on himself never to let down his guard in public. Although I am better than I used to be, I am still laggardly in that department. It is so tempting to slump, hitch up my skirt and laugh when my sense of the ridiculous is tickled – and there was much in our life that was ridiculous. Politicians, ambassadors, constituents, coffee mornings, chicken suppers, state occasions ... a wonderful, colourful caboodle replete with the ambitious and the innocent, the failures and the successes.

Of necessity, Will laughed with circumspection – so much so that, once, I accused him of having lost the ability through lack of use. There was only a tiny hint of a smile on his lips when he explained to me that one small error of attention could undo years of work.

I sneaked a look at him from under eyelids that still stung from the morning's regular date with the beauty salon. Dyed eyelashes were a necessity because, when I do laugh, my eyes water. In the early days Mannochie, Will's watchful and faithful political agent, had been forced to come up to me at some constituency do and whisper discreetly, 'Train tracks, Mrs S', which meant my mascara had smudged. There was no option but to laugh off that one, and whisk myself to the nearest mirror for a quick repair job. Increasingly, I burn inside at the daily reminder of one's physical imperfections – the evidence of slide, which is recorded by the mirror. It is such a bore having to resort to such stratagems, but body maintenance is a must, particularly when a girl is . . . *especially* when a woman is forty, plus a tiny bit more.

Dressed in pale, shimmery blue, Nora made her entrance on to the stage and her husband asked anxiously, 'What's happened to my little songbird?'

Will reached over for my hand, the left one, which bore his wedding ring and the modest ruby we had chosen together. It was small because, newly engaged and glowing with love at the prospect of shared happiness and mutual harmony, I had not wished him to spend too much money on me. Hindsight is a great thing, and I have come to the conclusion that modesty is wasted when it comes to jewellery. The touch of his hand was unfamiliar, strange almost, but I had grown used to that too, and it was not significant. Beneath the unfamiliarity, Will and I were connected by our years of marriage. That was indisputable.

At the end of the play, still in her pale blue, Nora declared, 'I don't believe in miracles any longer.' The sound of the front door opening and closing as she left the house was made to sound like a prison gate clanging shut.

'Fanny darling, I'm begging a favour . . . I know, I know, I owe you more than I can count but just say yes – please.'

It was the following day and the ministerial car had picked us up from our mansion-block flat in Westminster to drive us to the church in Stanwinton for Pearl Veriker's funeral. Stanwinton was Will's Midland constituency, neither decadently café-society south, nor professionally only-real-people-live-here north but hovering, geographically and metaphorically, unthreateningly between, and

Pearl Veriker, former chairman of the Stanwinton party association, had once been the bane of my life.

I reached for my notebook. 'Do I need this?'

Will snapped his armrest to attention. 'You sound very formal. Are you all right?'

I could have replied, 'I feel as though I have been stretched as thin as possible and now I'm almost transparent. Stop and look through me: you will see my heart labouring under the strain.' Instead, well trained in the art of preserving appearances, I replied, 'I'm fine.'

The car stopped at traffic-lights. I glanced out of the window at a poster that depicted a bride in white with a long, misty veil through which a pair of diamond earring studs shone. The caption read: 'Eternity'.

When I married Will, I had no idea of how the little evasions and dishonesties shore up the everyday. Our partnership was to have been a translucent stream into which we would both gaze and from which we would both draw nourishment. This had been fine, but I had no idea that casting my net into that sparkling water would also yield . . . not the plump, pink-fleshed truth but a shoal of tiny white lies and, occasionally, a sharp-fanged black one.

The car accelerated away from the lights and I said, 'Will, what did you want to ask me?'

He looked uncomfortable. 'You couldn't sit in on the next two Saturday surgeries, could you? You do it so brilliantly.'

Naturally, the excuse was the ministerial diary, which ranked above everything else. All I was required to do in surgery was listen to small histories of disquiet and everyday injustice – hospital negligence, an intolerable

4

neighbour, a wrong gas bill – and report back. Very often, it was a question of contacting the right people. They were at the top of the pyramid and Will had made it his business to know plenty of them, which was only sensible.

'Will you, Fanny?'

'Of course.'

That was that. When Parliament sat, Will lived in London during the week. When Chloë, our daughter, had been younger it had been weeks sometimes before I joined him but now that she was eighteen, I went to London regularly. The Savage dinner parties were considered something of a talking-point, which I put down to the good wine. In the old days, Will travelled to Stanwinton every weekend to nurse the constituency and his family, in that order. Now that he was a minister, his visits were less predictable: if he had a micro-squeak of spare time it vanished into the red boxes.

Confident and assured in his formal clothes, he smiled at me. 'Thank you so much.' It was his official voice.

'I'm not one of your constituents,' I informed him. 'I'm your wife.'

Will did one of his lightning changes and stepped out of the politician's mould into the person he really was. 'Thank God,' he said.

The coffin must have been heavy, for the undertakers had difficulty manoeuvring it down the aisle. An arrangement of red roses and green euphorbia rested on the top and the vicar was robed in gold and white. This was good. Pearl Veriker, a born bully, was going to meet her Maker in a suitably colourful manner after being felled at party headquarters by a heart attack – which, as deaths go, she might have chosen. I was certain she would have appreciated this outward show, especially the strict order of precedence observed in the seating. In my experience, the natural order of things was for the sitting MP and consort to walk at least ten paces behind the town dignitaries, but since Will had orchestrated his way into ministership the hierarchies had been hastily reshuffled and, today, we were accorded first-pew status.

Above the altar there was a stained-glass window of a procession of pilgrims making for a distant Paradise. The halos on a couple of men suggested they were already saints. Others, women, looked both exhausted and surprised that there was any hope at all of reaching the final destination. Over the years of – necessarily – close examination, my favourites had changed. As a bride, I had liked the strong, bold-looking knight who led from the front. Now my attention tended to focus on the tiny dog that lagged behind a nun in trailing black draperies. But I worried about all of them. It must have been so hard without clean clothes, a favourite pillow, a goodnight milky drink.

My hat, large-brimmed, black and not *too* witty – purchased in Harrod's especially for these occasions – was a little tight. 'Darling, your head has swelled from all the praise,' said Will, as I struggled to put it on. The comment was not quite as light-hearted as it sounded. Even now, having been the sitting MP for almost two decades, Will could be jealous of his constituency. There was a silence as I struggled to smooth over a ruffled surface as I would have done in the past. But lately I had felt less flexible, less accommodating, sadder. 'I've earned it, Will,' I snapped.

Will was taken aback. 'Yes, of course you have.'

Aware that I was being scrutinized, I adjusted the brim, which brought my view of the opposite pew into better focus. It was part of my function to be scrutinized and I had chosen my outfit with care. A slim-fitting black suit that did not shriek 'Extravagance!', modestly heeled shoes, and a warm, friendly lipstick. The effect was smart, clever (but not *too* clever), worn by a woman of confidence and conviction who had been broken in to the job. A Good Wife. I knew this because it had taken several attempts, and not a few discarded outfits, to get it right.

Will nudged me to attention. It was kindly and affectionately, rather than imperiously, meant. We functioned on nudges, my husband and I, little jabbing reminders of our duty, our tasks, our partnership. In the early days, I gave the nudges too. Now, for various reasons, I was more of a nudgee – but I reckoned that, in time, that would change too.

I let my hand rest briefly against his thigh, knowing that with this subversive, suggestive touch I would unsettle him.

On the other side of Will sat Matt Smith, the new chairman of the association, who sported degrees from Warwick and Harvard and had a lot of experience in think tanks. He dressed in linen suits, collarless shirts and lace-up boots, and talked about shifting voting patterns and focus groups. He was, he maintained, a professional.

On the other side of me Chloë picked at the cuticles of her left hand, which, at the last count, sported five silver rings, including a thumb ring that Sacha, her cousin, had brought back from his last gig up north. 'It's your job to attend funerals for old bats, not mine,' she had stormed at Will. 'Besides, I don't believe in God.'

'That puts you in the majority,' Will pointed out, not unreasonably, then cracked the three-line whip.

I suppose every shared life, every separate life, has bloodstained patches and tattered remnants of compromise. Sometimes, too, the dull ache of small martyrdom.

Chloë now fixed her gaze dreamily on the pilgrims. She was a smaller, infinitely more delicate version of her father with fair hair and dark eyes. One day, she would be beautiful, and that promise gave me deep, unqualified pleasure.

The congregation sang, 'I Vow To Thee My Country', and Will delivered the address with good grace. I listened with only half an ear – his private secretary had already rung and asked me for any contributions. 'She had a great heart,' I said for I had grown fond of her.

'Darling,' Will commented later, '*Not* quite the right term.'

Again, I had turned on him without warning: 'Shut up, Will. Just shut up. *Please.*'

'What *is* the matter with you, Fanny?' he asked, a little bewildered, a little rattled.

After the service Chloë vanished. At the reception, Will and I consoled a shell-shocked Paul Veriker then went home, and Mannochie came too. This was normal. Along with everyone else, Will's agent had been absorbed somehow into the running of our household. 'He's your *real* wife,' I had told Will, more than once.

On the way upstairs, I paused on the landing. It was

growing dark, the lovely mysterious moment of the day when I played the game of not-turning-on-the-light-until-the-very-last-minute. In that transition between light and dark, an observer becomes extra-sensitive to objects and to the textures of light and shade, of peace, happiness, disappointment, restlessness . . .

Like many things, the view out of the (*faux*) Gothic window had changed. One of the two fields we overlooked had been sold for development and was now home to twenty four-bedroomed houses. The second field had survived and the rooks still cawed and swirled above the beeches.

I leant on the sill. I knew myself better now and I had learnt that if I was quite still something surprising might swim up out of the spaces in my head. Sometimes a fleeting thought. Sometimes a revelation or a conclusion. Its chief element was always of surprise and I found myself craving the delight of discovery. One of the saints, I think it was Teresa, wrote that the soul has many rooms. So does a life, and a marriage. Motherhood too. I was increasingly curious to shine a light into each one.

But there was nothing tonight, except a faint sensation of despair, which made my eyes fill with tears. Why, I did not know.

I wiped them away and continued upstairs to our bedroom where I stepped out of the suit, brushed it, hung it up and put on some jeans.

Our bedroom was a depository. It was the sort of room that invited dumping and the dumped included a stool with a tapestry seat featuring two kittens that Will had felt obliged to buy at a jumble sale in aid of a cancer charity.

Whenever I looked at it, it looked back reproachfully: first, because I hated it, second, because I had not done anything with it.

In other worlds, into which I occasionally peered, mainly in Chelsea and the Shires, interior decoration was taken more seriously. There, the houses were the frames for rich, rare materials that breathed expense. The walls gleamed with the sludge of authentic paints and no one would dare to dump into those rooms a stool with tapestry kittens. Our house was plain, straightforward fare. (Economical, argued Will, with the grin that, when I first married him, made my heart soar.) A last-minute stab at Victorian Gothic, ugly in places, painted in colours from the local DIY store, it was utilitarian and solid. I had never loved it, never sought to pretty it up or make it smart. We jogged along, the house and I.

A departing backbencher's wife, Amy Greene, had once lectured me on economy. In order to survive (the words had dropped from her defeated-looking mouth), it is necessary to be economical with expectation. I had not discussed with her – or, for that matter, with Will – the little economies of spirit that creep into the everyday. They were whisked out of sight and never mentioned.

I pulled the bedspread straight. That, at least, was lovely. A traditional American quilt, sent by my mother, Sally, it was aged and faded, sewn with exquisite stitches and care. That never failed to delight.

Down in the kitchen Mannochie was making a late tea and Will was talking on the phone. On Sunday mornings, Mannochie often joined us for breakfast, tiptoeing into the house, and when I came down, still sleep-mussed, to the kitchen, it was to the inviting smell of frying bacon. It was no surprise, then, when he offered me cake from my own tin. 'Brigitte made it specially for you two,' I said. Brigitte was our au-pair-cum-housekeeper for the summer. I cut two slices and dropped the knife into the sink, well out of reach. I watched Mannochie eat, and imagined how the sugary crumbs would dissolve on his tongue.

'How's your son?' I asked.

Mannochie failed to repress his smile. 'Turning out to be a gymnast. And the fastest runner in the school.'

Information on the Mannochie home-life was not often released, even after the unexpected late marriage, which had produced a pallid, thoughtful child who fetched up, occasionally, at our house to be fed fish fingers at the kitchen table.

Will put down the phone. 'Do you think Matt Smith will do a good job? Pearl Veriker's a hard act to follow.'

A suggestion of humour softened Mannochie's features. 'He's keen on putting forward women and minorities.'

I looked at Will. 'You'd better watch it.'

Will sent me his private signal – a tiny lift of the eyebrows – which meant: 'Share the joke.' Or 'You're right.' Or 'Thank you.' Or sometimes all three.

After Mannochie had driven off to scoop up Mrs Mannochie from the swimming-baths, Will retired to his study to work on the red boxes. I moved around the kitchen, checking, making lists, when the sound of raised voices issued from Meg's side of the house.

Will's sister had lived with us in the Stanwinton house for a long time now and there had been plenty of opportunity to argue about most things, including what we meant by being good. Meg was as fair and delicate as I was dark and tall, and looked like an angel. 'I'm a hopeless case,' she once said, 'bad all the way through.' She sighed and shot me a look. 'Poor me. But you're good, Fanny.' She was at her most sarcastic. 'The bit I lack.'

I screwed the top on to a bottle of olive oil with fingers that, suddenly, felt all thumbs. That sort of commotion usually meant one thing – and the house had been free of it for some time. Meg had been drinking. Not now, I thought. And then, why now, Meg? You've been doing so well.

Will would have heard – and his lips would have gone white. It had taken me several years to work out that this meant fear, loathing and love in equal measure, and that it was my job to protect him. 'I'll go,' I called.

I went down the passage that ran the width of the house and let myself into Meg's part of the house. 'Sacha?'

'Upstairs, Fanny.'

I found him in Meg's bedroom, manhandling his mother's inert body on to the bed, and hastened to help. Meg was hunched on her side, and her breath soughed audibly in and out. I smoothed her hair back from her forehead. 'I should have checked on her.'

Sacha arranged her legs into a more comfortable position. 'She's been at it all day.' He added, with an effort, 'Sorry.'

'It's not your fault.' I bent down to retrieve a whisky bottle from the floor. It was still three-quarters full. 'I don't think she's had that much, Sacha.'

'But enough.'

'She's been brilliant lately, and nothing while you were away.' Sacha's nu-metal band was struggling to get off the ground and he was frequently away doing the circuits.

Sacha flinched and I could have kicked myself. 'Sacha, it *isn't* you. It isn't you coming back . . . It's the time of year, an unexpected bill or – '

'I know. She rang my father today. Apparently, he wants to renegotiate the alimony. That's probably it.'

'Yes.' Meg had never got over Rob walking out on her when Sacha was tiny. 'Talking to your father's always tricky for her.'

'I know,' he said again. He spoke far too wearily for a twenty-four-year-old. I slid my arms around my surrogate son. He smelt so clean. He always did, however many smoky, drink-filled places he worked in. 'Don't despair.'

'I don't,' he lied.

'Shall I sit with her?'

Sacha pushed me gently towards the door. This was between him and his mother and he kept it that way – because it was so terrible and so intimate.

Meg's lost battle was marked out in the kitchen by a trail of half-empty coffee cups. The one by the phone was still full, and marked the moment of defeat. 'Tea and coffee are so unattractive to look at,' Meg said. 'I can't fancy them.' But when it came to the rubies and topazes of wine and brandy, *then* we were talking.

How could I, of all people, with my passion for wine, disagree?

'I hate you for knowing when to stop,' Meg had flung at me once.

I harvested the cups and washed them up, scrubbing

13

angrily at their brown, scummy rims. Meg had not only blackened the important moments of her son's life, she had also instilled in him the fear that, one day, he might be like her.

I looked up from the sink and outside, outlined in the dusk, a vixen was sliding along the flower-bed. She was thinner than a London fox. They say that foxes are safest in the city, but I wonder if they have a genetic memory from the past that plagues them. Do they miss the smell of corn in high summer? The sharpness of frosted grass?

In our room, Will was already in bed and I slid in beside him. 'Is she . . . is she all right?'

'Sleeping.'

'What triggered her off do you think?'

I considered it. 'Rob rang her and wanted to talk about money, but I suspect that it had something to do with our anniversary.'

We talked about it for a bit. Will scratched his head. 'I would give much to think that Meg was happy and sorted out.' He turned to me. 'She has a lot to thank you for, Fanny. So do I.'

My feelings for Meg could be ambivalent, but being thanked by Will was certainly sweet.

He stirred restlessly. 'What do you think is best, Fanny,' he said. 'Do you think we should arrange more help for her? Could you manage to do that?'

'I could, but it might be better if you could talk to her. Maybe she needs a bit of your attention.'

He thought about this. 'I haven't got the time at the moment. But I will when I can. I promise.'

2

It was eight o'clock on Monday morning and downstairs line two, the line reserved for constituents, was buzzing. This was not unusual.

'You answer.' Will was thick with sleep. He hunched over in the bed and dragged the duvet round his shoulders. *Go away, world.* He did that rather well.

I had pulled on my jeans but not yet reached the jumper stage. The morning chill brushed my cheeks as I padded downstairs. Many things were required of me but dealing with a constituent before I was dressed was not at the top of the list.

'Mrs Savage . . .' The voice was familiar.

'Hallo, Mr Tucker. Where are you phoning from?'

'From Number Nine Heaven.'

Mr Tucker changed his locations according to which medication he had been taking. 'Mr Tucker, are you alone?'

'You're never alone, Mrs Savage. I want to complain about the lack of angels in Stanwinton.'

This seemed a rather admirable complaint. 'Do you remember, Mr Tucker? We dealt with that one last week.'

Voices in the background urged Mr Tucker to put down the phone and come along. 'Goodbye, Mr Tucker. It was nice to talk to you.'

Mr Tucker resided on a planet of his own but, as Will argued, a vote was a vote. 'You mean, the staff taking care of Mr Tucker will vote for you,' I said. '"That *nice* man Mr Savage . . . never too busy . . ."'

'Exactly. Anyway, an MP should listen to the dotty as well as the sane,' he pointed out.

'Well, that sheds a new light on Parliament,' I said.

In the hall, cleaning materials were distributed over the floor, which indicated that Maleeka had come in early. Maleeka was *my* angel and my saviour, and other wives – especially my friends – hated me for her. I see the point. One can envy another woman's beauty, or her mind, but you only truly hate her if her house is clean and shining. Of distant Arabian extraction, hence her name, Maleeka was a Bosnian refugee who had appeared in Will's surgery and begged for work. Will had a habit of forwarding problems to me, and did so on this occasion. 'Mrs Savage, I have two daughters and four grandchildrens to make food for,' she said. What could I say?

During the first week of her regime, she smashed two china figurines and dropped bleach on to the landing carpet. The navy blue pile now sported three almost perfect white circles. 'Look on them as symbols,' I told Will, 'of our commitment.' Will had been a little slow to see the point, a reminder that he dealt with *theory* so much that the *practical* was often beyond him. Not so for Maleeka: she made it her business to absorb herself into my household, and had turned up faithfully twice a week for ten years to impose order on the piles of laundry, remove tidemarks from the bath and the encrustations that decorated the taps, dust from the landing window-sill and the strange marks that inexplicably appeared in the fridge. If grime, disorder and mess flickered through the rooms like

16

marsh gas or plague, Maleeka maintained a firm perspective on the family chaos that made me catch my breath: 'Izt *safe* here,' she said. 'Good.'

I picked my way through a flotsam of bleach, polish and dusters, and tracked their source to the kitchen, where she was kneeling with her head in the oven – a position not a few political wives (any wife?) had, from time to time, considered. 'Izt bad, Mrs Savage.' Her voice was muffled. 'Very bad.'

She meant the oven but the remark had a portmanteau ring to it.

I boiled the kettle and made toast. 'Come and eat, Maleeka.'

She hauled herself upright and sat down. I gave her coffee and two thick slices of toast: I knew she went short of food so that the rest of the family had enough. *Tengo famiglia*, as Alfredo, my Italian father, would say. 'Hold the family safe, Francesca. We may be sinners and failures but that is the one thing we must do.' On that point, Maleeka and my father were perfectly matched. Not that Maleeka talked about it much – she was ashamed of her transient status and deeply homesick.

'Have you heard from your husband?'

Poitr had been left in Bosnia to fight. Or, at least, to guard the family house. Not that Maleeka minded the separation. 'Pouf, the man izt bad.' Yet, there was no question of divorce. 'He izt my husband. Finish.'

She was eating a third piece of toast when a fresh, shining Will appeared. However late we had been, he always managed to look new-minted and ready . . . to tackle the theory at any rate. Maleeka crammed the remainder of the toast into her mouth and leapt to her feet. 'Mornings, Mr Savage. I get on.'

Will did not fail at many things, but he had failed in his attempt to make Maleeka call him Will. 'Mr Savage' pricked at his principles and made him feel uneasy. Or so he said.

He ate his breakfast rapidly and efficiently, and worked through the papers. Afterwards we did a final check of our respective diaries. Of course, his was full. 'Can you make drinks for the European and Commonwealth finance ministers' convention on the seventeenth?' he asked. 'And on the twenty-first, there's a dinner for the same people. Much smaller, more intimate. I'll count on you, Fanny.'

I turned over the pages. For all sorts of reasons, the convention was important, not least because Will was spearheading the UK end of a controversial European initiative to impose a tax on anyone who owned a second car. Naturally everyone was up in arms: the car lobby, the country dweller, the salesman and anyone who had to endure public transport. But Will believed in it because, as he explained, it was right to tax those who enjoyed a standard of living that permitted them to have a second car. 'We would be setting an example to the world,' he said. 'We should do that. We *must* do that.'

I stabbed my finger on the seventeenth. 'I've got a homeless-persons meeting in the morning. Afterwards, if the traffic's OK, I can hop into our second car and make a dash for it.'

Will tried not to smile. 'Don't be nasty. Will you target Antonio Pasquale? Use your dazzling Italian. I need to make sure that he's on board. But you will go carefully?'

'Will, look at me. What do you see?'

He leant over and cupped my chin with a hand. 'You, of course.' He wore his busy-busy expression but his eyes were soft and, as usual, I melted.

What did I see? His hair was shorter now than it had been when I'd first met him, but he had a much better haircut. His jaw line was rather tauter than his waistline these days . . . but no, I won't go into that. And those dark eyes still lit up, from time to time, with a combination of idealism and a hint of vulnerability that he was careful only to show to those he loved.

Much the same.

'How long have I been on the circuit for you?' He had the honesty to look a little discomfited. 'I do have *some* idea, Will.'

'Yes, but . . . I want to be sure you *understand*.' Will retrieved his hand and launched into an explanation of the whys and wherefores of the tax scheme, which, to be fair, were tricky.

I listened, as I had many times before. On the one hand Will was right: it would strike a blow for a better, greener world and bring in more money for useful projects. On the other, ordinary families would struggle, the bus queues would snake out of sight, jobs might be at risk. Will's smile turned into that of the professional debater and his voice swooped up and down, brightened, sharpened, drove home the points. He leant back in his chair, an embodiment of clear thinking, authority, given edge by his weight of experience, and he knew it.

And I wanted to be there with him – but increasingly I sensed I had lost the almost mystical sense of mission, and the capacity to believe in it. Being married to an idealist was different from being one. I had become dulled by the glue of routine and domesticity, and diverted by the equally passionate imperatives of motherhood.

'So you see,' said Will, and smiled at me.

Not bad, I thought appreciatively. Over the years Will had shed a certain innocence. But so had I – so had everyone. We were warier, more realistic, pathetically grateful for the small triumphs of a policy implemented, a constituent satisfied. We knew our limitations better – oh, much, *much* better. We knew, too, for we had discussed it, that as that innocence slipped away, personal ambition had grown in direct proportion.

There was a pause.

'What's best for those living in a rural area?' I asked, because this side of the argument should have an airing.

Will held out his cup for more coffee. 'Fanny,' he sounded a warning, 'we can't afford any wobbles. Otherwise we get dumped on.'

He meant the press. Not for the first time, I thought how strange it was that treachery and dissent reached so much wider than loyalty . . . or fidelity.

No, scrub that.

That last had caught me unawares, which it did from time to time. I had learnt to deal with any bruising it inflicted.

Will pressed on: 'I know what you're thinking, Fanny, but we have to do something before the world chokes.' He stopped. 'Why are you looking at me like that?'

I shook my head. 'Nothing.'

These days when I looked at Will, I no longer perceived

the golden light that, when I first fell in love with him, had bathed him from head to foot. Now I saw differently and Will was only an element in a larger context: family, home, commitments. At forty-something, I had learnt many things, not least to reshuffle the priorities. Perhaps that was better, certainly more rational. All the same, I mourned the golden light. I missed it, and the intensity of my hunger to find out what Will *was*, my passion to possess him, and for him to possess me.

Again the eyebrows arched above the brown eyes. This time it meant: 'Let's sort this out.' 'Give it a chance, Fanny . . . yes?' He smiled, willing the old intimacy to bind us together. If I played ball, Will would be comforted and assured that we were walking down the right track.

'Trust me?'

'Should I?'

He yawned theatrically. 'Am I being pompous?'

In politics, or anywhere where power was the prize, it was hard to keep the layers of oneself glued together, and it was hard not to run with the hares. I understood that perfectly.

He got to his feet. 'For goodness sake drive a pin into me if I get fat, boring or pompous.' He looked briefly appalled. 'On second thoughts, perhaps you'd better not.'

'Would it be that easy to burst the bubble?'

He bent over and whispered, 'Only you know the answer to that.'

Outside in the drive, the ministerial car nosed to a halt with a discreet toot of the horn. Will shoved his papers into his briefcase. 'See you Friday.'

I sat quite still. Will's hand pressed into my shoulder. 'Fanny . . . the question of Meg.'

'Is she a question?'

Meg had never been a question. She had always been a fact. A hard fact that sat at the centre of our marriage.

The pressure on my shoulder became almost intolerable. 'No,' he replied. 'No, she isn't.'

Meg and Will's parents killed themselves in a spectacular car crash. The tangle of wreckage made it almost impossible to say who had been driving but, in some respects, it was irrelevant. Both were alcoholics, and the blood tests indicated that neither of them should have been at the wheel.

The children were cared for by grandparents too aged to cope. Four years older than Will, Meg had ended up cooking, cleaning, protecting and directing. She teased out Will's halting French verbs, wrestled with his algebra and, by the time he left home to train as a barrister, had forgotten about herself. 'It was as if there was a vacuum inside me, sucking up the person that was me,' she confided, soon after she moved in with us, 'and I could only fill it one way.'

When she married Rob, another barrister, the drinking had been sly, furtive, but apparently under control. After Sacha was born, and the strains of marriage to a busy man became clear, Meg began to slip. Eventually, Rob said he could no longer live with her. Then he informed her he'd found someone else who would look after him and Sacha properly.

'It was the "properly" that really hurt,' said Meg.

'Meg became my mother,' Will said, when he asked me

if she could come and live with us, 'and my father. She gave up everything to make sure that I was all right.'

After Will had gone, I went upstairs. Our bedroom was still frowsty from the night and I threw open the window. A man wearing a bright orange jacket was walking up the road and the colour imprinted itself, vivid and garish, on my retinas. He did not seem to be in any hurry, and looked neither sad nor happy, just indifferent.

That's how I felt.

I made the bed and pulled my mother's quilt over it. With a forefinger, I traced the tree hung with red cherry blossoms. One of the flower bracts had been unevenly sewn. I often wondered about the creator and why she had made the mistake. Had it been deliberate? A gesture of rage, rebellion or misery?

Will's clothes from the previous week were stacked on the chair and, working automatically from long practice, I set about sorting them – laundry basket, shelf, cupboard. Nowadays his ties were silk, and his shirts were soft and expensive, made in subtle colours with battens inserted into the collar points. Sometimes I remembered to remove them, sometimes not.

A shirt in hand, I sat down on the bed and buried my face in its folds. It smelt of Will, the Will I had always loved.

There was a knock on the door. 'Fanny, are you there?' Without waiting for an answer, Brigitte stuck her head round the door. 'Yes, you are.'

Guiltily, I dropped the shirt. Although she was only a temporary feature of the Savage household, Brigitte had that effect on me and I was so thoroughly in awe of her that I was never sure if I employed her or she me.

Brigitte, who came from deepest Austria, disapproved of the Savage set-up – Meg's oddness, Sacha's coming and going, Chloë's truculence – and she had a way of conveying this that made it matter. As a tactic, I admired it.

She glanced at the photograph on the dressing-table of a family group. Today, it appeared to draw particular disapproval. 'The shopping list, Fanny, I cannot find it.'

'Sure.' I reached for the notebook, which was always beside the bed, tore off the top page and handed it to her. Brigitte scanned it. 'You forgot the polish.' She tapped her nose with a finger. 'I don't forget. Or the bread.'

She gestured with her large, capable hands in a way that expressed her desire to ensure that the Savage ménage remained provisioned. It was a task that appeared to give her authority and purpose. Back home, Brigitte was an ardent, paid-up member of the Green Party and washed her hair in soap, never in *harmful* shampoo. It was a sacrifice worth making, she had explained. Observing the state of her hair, I am sorry to say that I did not agree.

'I'll take the laundry.' She brushed past me, swept up the clothes and marched downstairs. The sound of raised voices informed me that she and Maleeka were agitating for space in my home.

Bearing a tray with a breakfast of mashed banana, toast and tea, I knocked on Meg's bedroom door. There was a muttered 'Come in'.

The room stank of whisky. Meg was lying on her side and I drew back the curtains.

She flung an arm across her eyes. 'I suppose yet another apology is needed.'

'Only if you wish.'

'I don't.' She struggled upright.

I handed her a cup of tea. 'Get that down you.'

Between mouthfuls, she asked, 'Is Sacha OK?'

'He kept watch. He's probably asleep.'

Meg gave a wry smile. 'Sacha says he writes his songs late at night. He says his mind is more receptive and fertile then.'

'Does he?' I knew what Sacha meant. When I was feeding Chloë as a baby, those small hours of the night provided strange, heightened interludes where, the baby at my breast, I was free from busyness, and at liberty to try and grope my way towards clarity and knowledge.

'Why do I do it to him, Fanny?'

It was not the first time Meg had asked the question: nor, if both of us were honest, was it likely to be the last. I followed the uneven progress of the cup to her lips. 'Would you like more help? We can organize it.'

She cut me off. 'Nope. Done it. It's up to me now. Battered, unreliable old me.'

'Please don't, Meg.'

'Don't worry,' she said quickly. 'It won't happen again.'

I sat down at the end of the bed. 'What about Sacha and Will?'

She grimaced.

'Shouldn't be drinking tea on an empty stomach. It doesn't like it.' I cut the toast into squares and handed her one.

Meg edged the cup on to the bedside table. 'So many

people to fuss and worry over, Fanny. It must positively warm your heart.'

'*Stop* it.'

'Sorry, didn't mean it.'

At times like this, Meg took pleasure in driving me, or whoever was coping with her, to the edge, but we both knew the boundaries of our co-existence. Meg wanted love and a place in the family. Like Will with his passion to change the world for the better, I wanted to help, and somehow, muddling along, we had managed to keep a balance.

She looked up and said softly, 'I'm a good cause, the kind you like. The best, because I'm unredeemable. So none of you can blame yourselves when the worst happens.' She dropped the half-eaten toast back on the plate. 'Go away, Fanny. Go and be busy and keep everything in order.'

I removed the tray from her lap. 'Rob rang this morning.'

'So? I talked to him yesterday.'

'He forgot to remind you that it's Sacha's birthday at the weekend. He wanted to know what you were doing about it.'

Meg buried her face in her hands. 'What have I done?'

I bent down, picked up her discarded jumper and trousers and placed them on the chair. 'I'm busy today. I'll see you later.'

'It's all Rob's fault,' she muttered. 'If he'd stayed married to me, I might have got through.'

At my wits' end, I whirled round. 'Meg, you *drove* him to it. He fell in love with Tania out of the exhaustion.'

'I'm sick,' she said flatly. 'He should have tried harder. You shouldn't give up on sick people.'

'Have I ever given up on you?' I asked.

'You've *wanted* to. Be honest.'

We stared at each other. Meg was the first to drop her gaze but only because she knew she was the victor. She knew she had made it impossible for me to walk out of the room.

I drew up a chair, manipulated the banana on to the spoon and handed it to her. 'Eat.'

A smile hovered at the corner of her mouth, but her eyes darted towards the whisky bottle in the wastepaper basket, before she parted her lips.

I used to dream of a big, generous, blowsy household where children rustled and muttered in the bedrooms – two, three, even four. And every night I would go round and count them. 'This is Millie', I would say, smoothing fair tangles away from her face. 'This is Arthur', removing the thumb from his mouth. 'And *this* . . . this one is Jamie, the terror.'

But it had not happened that way. After Chloë there were no more babies. My body pulled and strained to obey my longings, but it could not do what I asked of it. They haunt me, my non-children. Those warm, sleeping, rosy bodies, the children-who-never-were. Sometimes, I listen out for them playing under the eaves of my ugly house.

'I don't mind,' Will said to me once. 'We have Chloë, that's enough. We look after her. I look after you. You look after me, Fanny. *Be content, please.*'

'Don't you mind at all?' I asked.

He touched my cheek. 'I mind for you. I mind anything that hurts you.'

Yet my household was full and we had been happy. First Chloë was born, and I was catapulted into the terror and mystery and exultation of a love that would never die. Then Meg came to live with us; Sacha too, after his sixteenth birthday. The au pairs came and went; the party workers slipped in and out; each leaving a ghostly imprint on the atmosphere, their rustles and murmurs dissolving into the general murmur of our lives.

3

'Is anything wrong Francesca?'

My father was the only person who ever called me by my full name, and very little of what I felt or did escaped his scrutiny which was sometimes critical, but always loving.

'Not really.' I looked up from our scratch lunch of mushroom soup and cheese in the dining room at Ember House. It was only five miles from our house and I wrestled him into the diary at least once a week.

The clock ticked reassuringly on the walnut sideboard and the blurred reflection of the blue and white fruit bowl beside it had the depth and stillness of a painting.

The electric light emphasized the lines on my father's face. New lines? And his tweed jacket seemed looser than I remembered. He had always been bony: all his energy had gone into running his wine business – and into me, his only child. I don't know what he thought about my situation, for there were some things about which he was guarded, but his pride in Battista Fine Wines was immense. It was a highly respected, idiosyncratic operation, catering to a growing number of wine lovers who were prepared to trust my father to select their wines, rather than the supermarket.

I speared a gobbet of dolcelatte on my knife. 'Once Chloë's exams are over, things will settle down.'

How did one admit to the feeling that a crossroads had been reached? How did a girl – *no*, a woman come to terms with the fact that her daughter was about to leave home? How could I argue that the choices I had once made no longer offered me surety and comfort, or gave me validation. I forced a smile. 'I'm fine, Dad. Just a cloud passing over the sun. And talking of which, I think *you* could do with some vitamins.'

'Stop fussing,' he said happily.

A hem of the curtains that Caro, my father's ex-mistress, had chosen so long ago required repair and I added that, along with the vitamins, to my mental list of Things To Do.

My father tapped a finger against a bottle of Le Pin Pomerol – the gentlest, richest of clarets. 'Think about this instead. Raoul put me on to it.'

Raoul Villeneuve was the son of one of my father's closest business contacts – not that 'business' adequately described the perfection with which trade and a lifestyle had been blended. Raoul was a friend. He had also been my first lover – but I don't think about that.

Yes, I do. Sometimes. I strain to catch the exact sensation, recapture the sear of my startled reaction. Not because I want Raoul, but because I had not worked out what went wrong exactly.

'How is Raoul? I haven't spoken to him lately.'

'Expanding the business. Busy with the family. Enjoying his reputation.'

'Ah,' I said. In material terms, Raoul had done better than Will, but he had had an advantage: his family's wine empire had been waiting for him to assume command. It had been different for Will, whose background had been bare of luxuries.

'What does "Ah" mean?' asked my father.

'*Nothing.*'

My father was an Italian refugee, brought to England from the village of Fiertino, north of Rome, by his widowed mother who fled the war and settled in the Midlands. The Villeneuves were wine aristocrats who lived in an historic château. They made contact during the fifties and a close friendship developed despite their differences. That was the way with wine people.

After I had Chloë, and found it difficult to juggle all my commitments, Raoul took my place at my father's side for a while before returning to his family business. We still kept in touch. We still talked on the phone . . . oh, about many things.

We discussed why the French drank their vintages young and hopeful. We discussed oak casks, sandy soil, the amount of sun for that year, the use of technology in Australian and American wine-making. The results? 'Simplistic,' concluded Raoul, the Frenchman. But perhaps that was not a bad thing. Clean, stable, sediment-free wine suited our age better than the muddy, sometimes fractious, yields of the Old World.

We agreed that the finest wine defied categorization. Any reasonably intelligent observer, we said, could point to the best soil, position and climate, the necessity of keeping vigil until the grape trembled at the peak of ripeness and say, yes, that was the formula. But good wine, great and successful wine, like a marriage, was a glorious fusion of nature, substance and will. It was a product of patience, understanding and knowledge, of great passion and love, which could never be quite regulated or predicted. One sniff, one drop balanced on the tongue, is all it takes to exult the mind and flood the senses with the delirium of discovery.

My father poured two glasses of the Pomerol (the creation of an inspired Belgian vintner and the merlot grape) and waited for me to ready my palate.

Rich ruby. Dark garnet. Depth and sweetness. I saw through the glass darkly, held its ravishments on my tongue.

'Describe,' ordered my father.

'Fleshy . . . concentrated. It has a rich inner life.'

My father was amused. 'I hope you do, too, Francesca.'

When I first began to work for him, travelling and learning, talking to clients, wine represented a mysterious combination of provenance, production and perception; I yearned to unlock its secrets and become proficient in its lore. But then I fell in love with it, and learned that wine was life, and for life. It was sun and warmth – it could be bitter, unfair, disappointing, but the possibilities of greatness always remained.

'You must come back to work properly,' said my father, 'now that Chloë is leaving home. I need the help and you must be ready to take on the business.' He looked at me lovingly across the table. 'After all, it is in your blood.'

I felt the answering beat of excitement. I could best describe it as the quiver that accompanied the wakening from long sleep. My father was right. Wine was in my blood.

*

When I was three, my mother, Sally, absconded with Art, an estate agent from Montana, where she still lived and where I had visited her every other summer until I married Will. Unless it was absolutely necessary, my father never mentioned her. 'She went,' he said, 'and that is that.'

Like it or not, and for years I picked over the imperfectly healed scars, my mother took with her far more than the clothes she had stuffed into two suitcases: my belief that things were strong and permanent, I suppose. She left my father (and me) warier, more fragile.

In place of a mother, my father summoned Benedetta from Fiertino (home to generations of Battistas) to help him look after me, and she lived with us until Caro took up residence in Ember House. Benedetta, a third cousin by marriage in a complicated Battista family tree, dark-haired, and not as slender as she would have liked, held my father in check, which few could. It was Benedetta who decreed on my tenth birthday that there should be no more bathtimes with my father. That puzzled me. Perhaps ten was a magic number. Perhaps it was secret, like my mother was a secret. But if I had questions, I had not yet learnt how to ask them. On my tenth birthday then, washed and brushed within an inch of my life, tied into a thick, old-fashioned dressing-gown with a cord belt, I was escorted downstairs by Benedetta to the door of my father's study.

He was at his desk, surrounded by wine books, writing up the day's business. Conscious that 'ten' hung over me, I went to stand beside him. When he patted his knee, I shook my head.

'I was forgetting,' he said sadly. 'You're a big girl now and we must talk about grown-up things.'

I was more interested by the framed photograph on my father's desk. It was of a man and a woman carved in stone, lying together on an ornate couch draped in material. He had a square face and a beard; she had curls falling down her back and dangling earrings. His arm was round her, and she leant back against him.

I swivelled to look at my father. Greatly daring, I asked, 'Is that Mummy?'

There was a short, tense silence. No, it was not, he answered, and, if my question hurt him, he did not betray it by so much as a flicker. No, the picture was of an Etruscan funerary couch. Fifth century BC.

'Was that when I was eight?' I asked, for time had no meaning.

My father laughed. 'The Etruscans were a people who, long, long ago, lived in the Fiertino area where the Battistas come from. They made such a lot of things that people are always digging up bits and pieces and putting them in museums. I like this one particularly because he and she will never be . . . parted.'

Bedtimes were usually reserved for my father's inexhaustible supply of Fiertino stories which, it must be said, were a little different each time he told them. I enjoyed pouncing on the discrepancies. 'But, Dad, you said the oxen were grey, not white.' At which point he would tap my hand and say, 'Don't be too clever, my darling,' and continue.

'Fiertino is only a little town, but a town all the same. It is in a valley north of Rome which was originally lived

34

in by the Etruscans, an ancient people who loved the good things in life. Chestnut trees grow on one slope; on the other, wheat, olives and vines. It has a square with a large church at one end, and a beautiful colonnaded walk around it, which gives very necessary shade from the sun. Our family, the Battistas, lived in the *fattoria*, the farm, just outside the town, and your grandfather was the *fattore*. He supervised the granaries and cellars, the oil presses and the dairy. We had our own vineyard and grew the Sangiovese grape.'

Like the horn of plenty, the stories never appeared to be finished and Fiertino became synonymous for me with drowsiness and sleep. I heard about hot sun and the harvesting of olives, of the huge family house, the *fattoria*, which echoed to the shrieks and exchanges of a large, extended, uninhibited family. I knew that the town had suffered badly in the war. I heard the story of the three-legged goat, the miraculous olive tree, the runaway Battista bride, and of the young wife who was murdered by her much older husband for taking a lover.

'You see, there is the code,' my father said. He spoke in the present tense.

He was clever, my father. He knew how to plant a footprint in a child's mind. Images crept into mine and put down long, tough, fibrous roots – just like the vine.

'It's time I went back to Fiertino,' said my father. 'We have left it too long.'

Curiously, we had not been there together. In fact, my father had returned only once, as a young man. We travelled everywhere else in the world and we did business in the

35

north of Italy but my father had never cared to go south to Fiertino. Partly, I suspect, this was because of Benedetta, who had wanted to marry him. But *that* was another story.

'How many times have you said that?'

He looked a little sheepish. 'I mean it this time.'

I rose to leave. 'How about September when Chloë is in Australia? Then I'll be free.' I corrected myself. 'Or I can negotiate with Will and Mannochie. I'm due time off.'

My father brightened in a way that caught at my heart. 'If you think it is possible, there is nothing I would like more.'

I tried a bit of role reversal. 'On one condition. That you go and see a doctor for a check-up. I'll make the appointment. Then, I promise, we'll go to Fiertino.'

My father looked guilty. 'I've already been. Just a shade of concern about the heart. He's given me pills. Everything is fine, except *anno domini*.'

Driving home, I turned on the radio and music filled the car.

'Quick, Francesca, before Benedetta orders you to bed. Tell me which are the grapes grown in Tuscany?'

I pressed my cupped hand to his ear. 'Sangiovese,' I whispered.

'Good girl. Now, which are the big reds of Piedmont?'

'Dolcetto, Barbera, Nebbiolo . . .'

Wonderful Benedetta. She scolded my father so many times for heating up my poor little brain. '*Santa Patata*, Alfredo, you are a cruel man.' *Santa Patata* was the nearest the devout Benedetta would allow herself to swearing. 'The child is too young.' She need not have worried. My poor little brain was quite capable of sniffing out an opportunity to draw attention to me. Anyway, I was quick to see that I was being invited on to my father's territory. What the French call the *terroir*.

I know that *terroir* really means topsoil, drainage and climate. But, to me, it suggests something more profound and interesting – the territory of the heart.

Back at the Stanwinton house, I parked the car in the drive beside the laurel hedge and let myself in at the front door. It clicked shut behind me.

'Mum,' Chloë greeted me in the kitchen, 'I'm hungry.'

I opened the fridge door and got out a fish stew.

'Not *fish*,' she said.

'Good for the brain. It's fish from now on.'

Chloë bit her lip. 'I wish I didn't have to do these exams.'

'Just one last effort, darling, and then you're free. You'll be off to Australia and fretting about something different.' I put the stew on to warm. 'Do you think Sacha would like some?'

'Probably. He's been helping me revise.' Chloë extracted knives and forks from the drawer. 'I do love him, you know, Mum.'

'Of course,' I said swiftly. 'He's your cousin.'

Chloë positioned a fork on the table with care. 'He's so kind. He just *knows* things.'

I wanted to say to my daughter, 'Please be careful. Don't go into dangerous territory.' Chloë did not lack friends, far from it – they swarmed in and out of the house, demanding coffee, meals, television, a bed for the night – yet it was Sacha to whom she turned. Darling, lovely Sacha, who dressed in leather and wore his beautifully clean hair in a crop that emphasized his bony, but fine, features.

While they ate, I sipped a glass of cranberry juice – my friend Elaine said it was system-cleansing. They discussed exam tactics and Chloë admitted how frightened she was.

'All you need to do,' said Sacha, 'is to have the good idea when you've seen the questions. Don't bother thinking up ideas now, otherwise you'll fit the questions round them and that doesn't work.'

As a principle for life, this seemed sound.

Chloë sent him one of her melting looks, and ate a huge plate of fish stew. I worked away at my internal cleansing and thought how lovely it was just to be sitting there peacefully, listening to them.

Then Meg came into the kitchen. She looked groomed and well pressed, and her fair hair, in shades of light caramel, was twisted on top of her head. 'Darlings,' she said, 'you should have called me down from exile. I would have liked to join you.' She sat down at the table. 'It's been a bit of a lonely day. Everyone was out.'

I was refilling my glass but I knew Meg's gaze rested on me. 'Be quiet,' I wanted to say to her. 'Please be *quiet*.'

'Still, it's productive working away at chores and, no doubt, good for the soul. And we all know that my soul certainly needs some good done to it.' Meg's expression held a touch of complacency and plenty of mischief. When no one made any comment, she added, 'Could I point out, I have been virtuous today?'

Sacha sprang to his feet and the chair screeched across the tiles. 'Why don't I make you a cup of coffee, Mum?'

Meg tapped the table with her exquisitely shaped nails – her hands were quite lovely and she kept them immaculate.

'Coffee is so . . . *brown* . . .' she said. 'But I guess I have to settle for it.' Again she looked in my direction – and a shock of loathing suddenly pulsed through me. 'Joke,' she said.

Hatred is a curious emotion. It can be dulled with weariness, then spring into sharp, destructive life. Or, and this never fails to astonish me, it sometimes turns into what could only be called affection. That's how I found it with Meg.

For some reason, Will's late-night call came through on the business line. 'This is Mrs Savage,' I said, 'and it's far too late to be phoning.'

'You're completely right,' said my husband. 'You shouldn't be talking to strangers at this hour.'

'You'd better put the phone down then.' The words issued tartly from my mouth before I could stop them.

There was a second's silence. 'It's not like you to sound so fed up. What is it? Have I done something?'

'Sorry.'

Will tried again. 'Can I help?'

I resisted the temptation to tell him he sounded as though he was dealing with one of his crankier constituents. 'OK. This is the daily Sit. Rep. There are three photographs of you in the local press. One is not good, the others are fine. There is also a piece about the Hansard report which shows how hard you're fighting for the constituency even though you're a minister.'

He sighed rather wearily, which made me feel churlish. 'What *is* wrong, Fanny,' he asked.

I wanted to say that I wished he were at home more

often. That he *should* be at home more often, before it started not to matter if he was or wasn't.

Instead I stuck to routine exchanges of information. 'Meg is fine. Chloë is seesawing between terror and elation. Sacha is being . . . Sacha.'

This appeared to satisfy Will. 'Busy day tomorrow,' he said, and I wondered if he realized that he said that most days.

'So have I.' I wondered if he noticed that I said that most days.

'Good night, darling. Hope you are feeling more cheerful in the morning.'

'Good night,' I said.

The first words I ever heard Will utter were: 'No more government waste. No more schools that betray their children, or hospitals that kill their patients. Ladies and gentlemen, I see these wrongs, daily, in my work as a barrister. I know how the trusting, the innocent and the deprived can suffer. I know how much they need a champion.'

He stopped, thought for a moment. 'Ladies and gentlemen, I consider politics to be a means of building a bridge between what we feel to be just and right in our private lives and putting them into practice in public life . . .'

It was a bitter January afternoon and I had nipped into Stanwinton town hall to escape the cold, rather than waiting at the station for the train I was due to catch, and stumbled on the meeting. I read the papers, but I had only a vague knowledge of politics and my interests lay elsewhere.

Will was speaking as the adopted candidate for his party. At the very earliest, a general election was not due until the spring, but he was making himself known in what I later learned was a carefully constructed programme.

I remember thinking: does he mean what he says? But as I gazed at a tall figure with hair the colour of corn in high summer, and at features which were lit up by humour and passion, I became convinced that he did, and I was possessed by a sudden, intense hunger to find out who he was. I mean, who he *really* was.

I remember, too, that after the speech, as I made my way rather boldly towards him to introduce myself, I was stopped by a woman in red.

'Can I help? I'm Will Savage's sister.' She looked me up and down. 'You won't bother him?' she asked, anxiously. 'He has so much on his plate, and he gets so tired.' Then she smiled, and her delicate face came alive in the same way as her brother's. 'I'm here to protect him, you see?'

4

Half-way up the drive to Ember House, Will slammed on the brakes. 'Just a minute, Fanny, have I got this wrong?'

We had known each other for six weeks and I was taking him home to meet my father. He was twenty-eight and I was twenty-three, and both of us knew that this was a moment of great importance in our respective lives – more important than taking off our clothes in front of each other for the first time. This meeting, in effect, would cause us to be naked and exposed in quite another manner.

'You didn't tell me you lived like this ... A stately home?' Will wound down the window and gestured at the drive, which was flanked by clumps of snowdrops and crocuses and disappeared round a bend. I remember noting that the drive was at its best, before the pushy, blowsy azaleas took over and drowned it in pinks and reds.

Already I was sensitive to how seriously Will considered his image, his positioning. 'Don't worry, it isn't. The original house must have been, but it was knocked down in the fifties and a new one built. The drive is the only bit left of the grounds. My father bought it at a knock-down price when he set up the business. Nobody wanted it. The house is quite small, in fact, and not at all distinguished.'

Will relaxed. At one of our meetings – snatched between his commitments in chambers and at court, the photo-calls, sponsored walks and chicken lunches, and my clients, negotiations with suppliers, sessions choosing wines for seasonal tastings – Will had explained he was committed to working for a society where people made their way by merit and not by privilege.

'And what do you think you are?' I teased. 'Barristers earn telephone numbers.'

I touched the long, sensitive-looking fingers that rested on the wheel. Everything was miraculous about Will, including his fingers. 'You needn't worry,' I heard myself gabble and fumble with the words, 'we're not rich, not at all. We're practically poor.'

Will smiled at me lovingly. 'Don't be silly.'

I blushed. 'Silly,' I agreed.

Was this me? The girl who helped her father so confidently to run his business, who lived a life so confidently in London? It was and it wasn't. Falling in love with such suddenness and abandon had cut the ground from beneath my feet. It puzzled and – almost – frightened me, this violent, sweet, sharp, desperate emotion.

Will's knuckles whitened. 'I'm a bit nervous,' he confessed.

Now I was in charge. 'Just don't pretend to know about wine, that's all.'

He grinned. 'Political suicide.'

Father was waiting for us in the sitting room with Caro, his mistress of ten years. After she had come into his life, which had been the cue for a thunderous-browed, red-eyed Benedetta to pack her bags and return to Fiertino, the interior of the house took a turn for the better. Caro had given it a more settled touch: a cushion, the repositioning of a chair, a pot of white hyacinths in spring, a lamp that cast a subtler light. They were only minor changes, but so effective.

'I hope you don't mind?' Caro had asked, when she first arrived. I was thirteen, almost feral in my dislike – my terror at how things could change overnight. And I was in mourning for Benedetta. Caro had laughed and flipped back her hair, which had been long and naturally blonde then. She was so sure of her position as the woman likely to marry my father that she was careless of my reply.

Five years or so later, when we had become friends and Caro was no nearer her goal, she turned to me and said bitterly, 'Alfredo never notices what I do.'

I saw myself reflected in her large, pleading eyes and I was angry with my father, sick at the thought that I had made her unhappy in the past. 'You know my feelings on the subject,' he had said, with his guarded look when I tackled him.

'This is Will.' I led him up to my father, who was standing in front of the fire.

'Ah,' he said, in his driest fashion, and my father could be very dry – my heart sank, 'the politician.'

In reply, Will could have said – might well have said, 'Ah, the self-made man,' which would have described my father perfectly, but his polite rejoinder managed to include Caro, who was sitting on the sofa. It was, I had noticed, a trick he had: *bring everyone in.*

At dinner, we drank a sauvignon blanc from Lawson's Dry Hill in New Zealand. Will barely touched his, prompting a slight frown to appear on my father's face. We had coffee in the sitting room. Caro returned to her seat on the sofa and I sat beside her. My father took up his stance by the fire. 'The papers are not very flattering about your party. They consider you a wily lot.'

Will brightened. 'That makes for the best battle,' he said, at home on this territory. 'In the end the voters will see that we have the right policies.'

'Really,' said my father. He looked up at me. 'I never knew you were interested in politics, Francesca.'

'I am now,' I said.

The fire flickered. I heard Caro's cup rattle back into the saucer. I was so proud of Will that I almost wept. Instead I took refuge in the practical: I reached for the coffee-pot and refilled the cups. As I bent over my task, I asked myself why I had been singled out by the gods to be blessed in this way. Why had I, Fanny Battista, been lucky enough to find my other half?

Will came over to stand by me and held out his hand. 'Fanny?'

I took it and sprang to my feet. Will turned to my father. 'We would like to tell you something. Fanny and I have decided to get married.'

My father rocked back on his feet, as if he had been dealt a blow. He looked at me and I knew that I had hurt him by not letting him into my confidence.

'We decided last night,' I explained.

'It's too quick,' said my father. 'You barely know each other.'

Will slid his arm around me. 'Swift, but sure.'

Will sneaked into my bed in the small hours and I spent a wakeful night. It was still early when I decided to get up. I slid out of bed, leaving Will folded on to one side, one hand flung out. Foolishly, lovingly, I bent over and checked his breathing.

On the way down to the kitchen, I had to pass Caro's bedroom, which was opposite my father's. The door was open, the light on, and I put my head in to ask if she wanted some tea.

Clothes were littered over the bed and Caro was packing. We stared at each other. I, rumpled and sated, she beautifully dressed but desolate.

'Why are you packing?' I closed the door behind me.

Caro picked up a green jumper and folded it. 'Fanny, the one good thing in this mess has been our friendship. That has been . . .' She blinked back tears. 'It helped. Otherwise . . .' she shrugged helplessly ' . . . it has been a waste of my time.'

I removed a pile of shirts from the bed and sat down. 'Why now?'

She fiddled with the jumper. 'Put it this way. You're getting married and I'm not. I know it's stupid to worry about a piece of paper, but I do. A lot of people do. That's the trouble with being pretty ordinary.'

I snatched the jumper away from her and pleated it between my fingers. The material was soft and expensive. 'Caro, you've been together for such a long time.'

She raised an anguished gaze to me. 'All good things come to an end.'

'Would you like me to talk to him?'

She shook her head. 'No point.'

'But you've been happy. I know you have.'

'Let's see . . .' she ticked off the points. 'Your father is kind enough to allocate me a very nice bedroom and a place at the table. I can order groceries and ask Jane to hoover the carpets. But that is it, Fanny.' She repossessed the jumper. 'You won't understand yet, but it is not enough to look decorative when your father entertains. I want a real, live, working partnership. So . . .' She got up and packed the green jumper. 'I am drawing a line under the last ten years. I am relying on you to tell him.'

'But *you* must tell him.'

At that, she sparked with anger. 'No, you can give him chapter and verse.' She wrenched one of her suitcases shut. 'What's more, I am giving you your most useful wedding present.'

I had no idea what she meant.

With a foot, she nudged the suitcase towards the door. 'I'm showing you how to leave, Fanny. It's a good lesson.'

On honeymoon in the Loire valley only six months after our first meeting, Will laid his head on my breast and said, 'Your heartbeat is louder than a drum.'

'And how many heartbeats have you listened to this closely?'

'Very few.' He smiled. 'Promise. Apart from my own, of course.'

'That's good,' I heard myself saying. 'I don't want to have shared you with too many.' I luxuriated in the feeling and the smell of him on my skin. 'Do you think our heartbeats match?'

'Of course.' He wrapped his arms tighter around me and said he had known they would as soon as he spotted me. 'Five seconds is all it took. All right, perhaps *ten*.'

'I saw you first.' I kissed the damp, faintly salty hollow of his neck.

'Hussy,' he said and made me lie still, and I looked up into the dark eyes and saw a life ahead filled with possibilities, and thought how lucky I was.

On the third day of our honeymoon, we had lunch in one of those plush, well-manicured but sleepy villages by the Loire. It was hot for early June and the heat shimmered off the stone streets. The big, sleepy, shiny river murmured beneath the clatter of cutlery and chink of glasses.

Will did not eat much. Eventually, he dug into his pocket for his cigarettes. Officially he was a non-smoker, and would never do so in public – except in France, which was 'different'. In fact, he was very fond of white-filtered American cigarettes and it made me smile then that a testament of our intimacy was having smoke blown in my face.

I fussed with the waiter over the wine – I had never rated the Chinon red which colonized most of the list. Will watched me and then said, 'I love seeing you with your wine. You know such a lot, and you know exactly what you want. You're your father's daughter.'

We had agreed that if Will was elected to Parliament then he would give up the law and I would continue to work with Dad at Battista Fine Wines. The finances seemed to work, at least on paper, and I was looking forward to trips to Australia and America with my father.

The waiter poured out the wine – a raspberry red, which looked pretty enough.

'I love you, Mrs Savage.' Each time Will said that to me, and he did so often, it was as if he had only just thought of the idea which made it the most delicious, the most delightful, the most necessary thing in the world for me to hear.

I turned away and gazed at the river. I did not know Will very well yet. Yet I knew beyond any doubt that our marriage was right. This absolute certainty made me feel both old and tremblingly young.

'Will you think about going to the Val del Fiertino with me sometime, to see where my family came from?'

He stubbed out the cigarette. 'I can't think of anything I'd like more.' His expression clouded for a moment. 'I don't have much family, except Meg and Sacha, of course.' He brightened. 'I'm looking forward to adopting yours.'

I caught the echoes of his past distress. 'Do you want to talk about it?'

He lit a second cigarette. 'My grandparents were too old and bewildered by what happened to really get a grip on things. They blamed themselves for letting my mother marry my father, and blamed themselves even more when she began to drink too. I'm glad they never knew about Meg.'

This was delicate territory, and one we had not yet fully explored. 'When did Meg . . .?'

'I don't know. She kept it secret. I never smelt it on her. I never suspected. It probably wasn't a problem until she married Rob. Just a drink at the end of the day. But I was busy with other things, school, exams, the desire to get away. I'm ashamed to say it, but I didn't think much about Meg. She was just there. It was only afterwards that I realized how much she'd done for me; and what it had done to her.'

I remember . . . what exactly? A tiny ripple of unease; the merest suggestion of a shadow, to dull the vivid quality of our companionship. The glasses on the table, the sun on the white stones, river sounds . . . us, together . . . all this happiness, and yet?

'Will,' I said, and the breath caught in my throat, 'we must never turn into Pa and Ma Kettle.'

He grinned. 'Do we look like Pa and Ma Kettle?' His eyes narrowed. 'I've just had a thought.'

'What sort of thought?'

'It involves going back to the hotel . . . now.'

But, when we got there, there was a message waiting for him. Will read it and then he put his arms around me and said excitedly. 'Mrs Savage, we have to pack. The election is on July the fourteenth and there's no time to waste. Not even a day, not a minute. If we drive fast we can be home by midnight.'

In our room, I looked down at a pile of unsent postcards on the table under the window. Virgin postcards of pretty French villages and sleepy French rivers. 'I haven't even written these,' I said.

He snatched them up. 'You can write them in the car.'

I sat down on the bed. I thought I had prepared myself very carefully for a moment like this. I had known that if I married Will I would be called on to make these kind of sacrifices. But disappointment made me temporarily speechless.

He took on board my stricken expression and his own grew anxious. 'Fanny . . . I know the timing couldn't be worse, but this means everything . . . well, not everything exactly. *You* mean everything to me, of course . . . but we have worked for this moment. You do see that?'

He looked so anxious, so determined, so serious, that I could not protest. How could I possibly make a fuss on this most important occasion of Will's life? When all was said and done, what was a honeymoon? Not vital, compared to what Will was setting out to do – which, to put it at its simplest and boldest, was to solve the problems of the nation.

'Fifty-fifty deal,' he said. 'I promise, the first moment we can, we'll have a second honeymoon.'

More than anything, I wanted Will to be happy. I held his hand and agreed: 'Fifty-fifty.'

Before we left the hotel, I sat down and wrote on one of the postcards: 'Dear Fanny, having a wonderful time. Wish you were here. Love, Fanny.' When we checked out, I asked the concierge for a stamp and dropped it into the post box in the lobby.

On the drive north, Will jiggled frantically with the car radio. Once he insisted that we stop at a motorway service station and leapt out to phone Mannochie. I watched him from the car. He placed his free hand on the glass, and leant against it, leaving a cloudy imprint. After a moment or two, he took it away and wrapped his arm across his stomach.

That little display of nerves affected me more than I could say, and I was shaken by just how precious he was to me, and by how important it was that he achieved what he wanted.

5

Meg asked, as a special favour, if she could fetch Chloë from school on the day of her final exam. Chloë burst through the kitchen door. 'Mum – ? They're over. Finished.' She was pale, shaking and elated.

I wrapped my arms round her and held her tight. Then I led her upstairs, made her take a bath and fetched her a mug of tea.

Face turning pink in the steam, she slumped back in the water. 'My nice mummy.' She was silent for a minute. 'I can't do anything. I can't move. I can't think.'

It was cold for the end of June and I put the towel to warm on the rail. 'Shall I wash your hair?'

The shape of her skull was so familiar, so beloved. The shampoo made the strands feel curiously wiry. Very carefully, I rubbed and rinsed, wiped teardrops of foam away from her eyes.

'Now my life begins, Mum,' she said, as I towelled her dry the way I used to when she was tiny, unformed, still all mine. 'How about that?'

When I woke a few days later, I put out my hand. If Will was there, my fingers encountered a warm back, the curve of his shoulder. It was an early-morning memorandum to myself: a reminder to be kind to one another, which I too often neglected.

Today, Will's side of the bed felt particularly empty and cold.

I got up, dressed in jeans and a T-shirt, drew back the curtains and watched as a summer day shook itself damply into life. It was a moment or two before I noticed the two figures walking down the road. They moved slowly, dreamily, seemingly transfixed by each other.

Chloë stopped by the laurel hedge and I could see there was nothing childlike about her any more. Sacha bent over and whispered in her ear. She replied and turned to him, her arms snaking up round his neck. Sacha threw back his head and laughed. I had not seen or heard him laugh for a long time.

Conscious that I was spying, I stepped back from the window.

As I was making coffee Chloë ambled into the kitchen. 'What are you doing up so early, Mum?' She sniffed. 'Coffee. Great. Can I have some?'

'Have you been out all night? Did you have anything to eat?'

Chloë shook her head and her long hair flew around her shoulders. 'You always ask the same questions, Mum.'

'Sure. We were up all night.' Sacha, who had followed her in, fetched the cups from the cupboard. 'No big deal.' He smiled at me teasingly. 'Can't you remember?'

'Dimly,' I replied, with a touch of acid. 'How was the club?'

Chloë and Sacha's eyes met, and a private message was exchanged. 'Brilliant.' Chloë's voice was a note higher than normal.

I hacked at the bread and slotted two slices into the toaster. 'I hope you didn't do anything . . . silly.'

Chloë's eyes flashed me a warning. *Don't go there.*

'Yup . . .' Sacha unzipped his leather bomber jacket and arranged it over the back of the chair. 'The club isn't bad. The boys and I might just do a gig there to help out.'

Sacha tried so hard not to imply that they were desperate for any gig. He would never admit that, two years on from its formation, the group's progress to fame and fortune had hardly lifted off the ground.

Chloë hunched over her coffee. There was faint flush on her cheek and a faint smile on her lips. She looked happy and untroubled.

The toast was stuck in the toaster so I pulled it out – spraying a waterfall of crumbs on to the floor – and put it in front of them. 'Have some Tuscan honey.'

'What's wrong with English honey?' She feathered her impossibly long eyelashes. 'Or anything English, for that matter. It's Italian pasta, Italian ham, Italian this, that and the other.' Again she fluttered her eyelashes and Sacha watched, seemingly enraptured. 'You must go this year, Mum, get it out of your system.'

I fetched the dustpan and swept up the crumbs. 'As it happens, I'm planning to go with your grandfather.'

Chloë raised her eyes to the ceiling. 'So you say.'

While they ate and drank, I sat at the table and puzzled over the agenda for the Stanwinton homeless-persons committee. Afterwards, Sacha got to his feet and lifted his prized jacket off the chair. 'Bedtime,' he said, and disappeared.

'What about you, darling?'

Chloë drained her coffee and hunkered down beside me. 'You mustn't interfere, Mum. Not any longer.'

I slipped my arm round her. There was a smudge of honey at the corner of her mouth, and I nipped it away with my finger. 'He's your first cousin, Chloë.'

Chloë's happy look vanished. 'He's my first everything, Mum. He's my blood and bone. He knows me. I know him.'

'He's your first cousin,' I repeated.

Chloë straightened up. 'Forget it, Mum,' she said, in a flat voice that was new to me. Then she, too, was gone.

I looked up and out of the window where, like black and bruised plums, summer rainclouds were gathering.

Later that morning, Chloë and I sorted through bags of discarded clothing that had been dumped in our garage. 'There's so much, Mum. I don't see why we have to do all this.'

I upended a bag, and a drift of grubby sweaters and trousers spread over the floor. Their smell – musty, used, depressing – made us recoil.

'Ugh,' Chloë said. 'Throw them away.'

I surprised myself by saying heatedly, 'I can't. They might be useful. Someone might need them.'

Chloë inspected a second bag. 'Actually,' she pulled out a pink cardigan that looked suspiciously like cashmere, 'there's quite a nice one here.'

I gathered up an armful of clothes and plodded into the kitchen, where Brigitte was cleaning the sink. 'Could you put these through the machine?'

She took a step back. 'These are not nice.'

'No,' I agreed, 'but they'll be better when they're washed and ironed.'

Brigitte loaded them sulkily into the machine and banged the door shut.

Chloë had followed me in and handed Brigitte the detergent. 'It's a funny old life,' she said. 'Do you think it's OK if I keep this cardigan?'

I gave Meg a lift to the doctor on my way into town. She snapped the seat belt into place. 'Sacha tells me that you've . . . been talking to Chloë about Sacha. I gather you don't approve of him and Chloë being together so much . . .'

I eased the car out of the gateway and into the road. I should no longer have been surprised by the way information circulated in the house. 'Does he discuss everything with you?'

'Mostly. We've always talked. As you know.'

It was unfair, but the remark set my teeth on edge. 'Chloë edits any confidences she grants me.'

'Tell me,' Meg searched in her bag, 'is it my son you object to, or my genes?'

'I love Sacha, and Chloë shares your genes.'

Meg flipped down the passenger sunshade and used the mirror to apply bright red lipstick, while I wrestled with a gyratory system which had been expressly designed to send drivers mad. 'You know, Fanny,' she said, 'we were once better friends.'

I felt her stare burn into my cheek. 'Meg,' I said, rashly. 'I've been thinking that it's time to make a few changes.'

As ever, she was as sharp as a knife. 'You want to chuck me out?' Then she gave one of her laughs. 'I would if it was me.' She pushed her hair behind her ears; an uncharacteristically nervous gesture. 'Does Will know what's on your mind?'

'I haven't discussed it at length. But Chloë will be leaving home fairly soon, and I thought maybe . . . maybe it's time for a smaller house.'

'Will wouldn't like that. He'd never chuck Sacha and me out.' She shot me a wary look. 'And you wouldn't either, would you, Fanny?'

'Won't Sacha be leaving home too?'

Meg flung the lipstick into her bag. 'Yes.'

Rather as my mother had departed from Ember House virtually empty-handed, Meg had arrived in Stanwinton with almost nothing, just a suitcase and a small bag of Sacha's clothes for his weekend visits. 'I couldn't cope with choosing,' she'd said.

Years later, when I talked to Rob at Sacha's eighteenth birthday party, he told me he had begged Meg to take it all – furniture, clothes, china – but she'd resolutely refused, telling him she wanted space for her grief. Rob had been puzzled by this, but, in a curious way, I felt it made sense.

Meg raised her hands in front of her. 'Look, only a little tremble. I'm improving. The other night was just a lapse. I am going to try for another job, you know.'

'Sure.' I drove into the surgery car park and dropped her by the entrance.

Meg gripped the door handle. 'But I'm not quite sure enough to cope on my own.'

I leant over to close the door. 'Meg,' I called after her. 'I didn't mean it.'

*

After the committee meeting, I drove up to London. It was raining again. I peered through the windscreen. My father made a big thing of the Italian summer and, not for the first time, I realized why. Oh, to be there where it was so hot in the valley that if I sat under an olive tree, and looked up, the leaves would resemble flickering tongues of fire.

Will had left a note on the hall floor of our London flat where I would be sure to tread on it: 'See you at the embassy. Don't forget Pasquale. Plse don't be late.'

Of course I was. I made the mistake of taking a bath and, as I soaked, the phone rang twice. The first was a journalist from a broadsheet saying they were planning a piece on possible future senior figures in the party and could they interview my husband? I told him to contact Will's office. The second was Will's private secretary, warning me that if I spoke to anyone from the Italian delegation I should steer clear of anything remotely political. The word had been passed round all the wives. What do I steer on to? I wanted to know.

'There has been a recent find of Etruscan bronzes that are considered very fine,' he replied.

I traced a pattern of hearts on the steamed-up mirror in the bathroom. 'Talk me through the bronzes.'

'Unfortunately, Mrs Savage, they're well . . . rather erotic. But you can keep off the detail. And . . . Mrs Savage . . . if you could avoid the words "car" and "tax" . . . the negotiations are at a rather tricky stage.'

Hobbled conversationally, and late setting out, I took a taxi to where Will was waiting for me. He smiled and kissed my cheek, but his grip on my arm was almost painful. 'You're late.'

'Traffic.' I laced my fingers through his and made sure I got in with my list of topics to discuss. 'We must talk about Chloë.'

He squeezed my fingers and then dropped them. 'What about her?'

'Her and Sacha. I'm a bit concerned.'

'Meg says that's nonsense. They're just very close, as cousins sometimes are.'

'You've talked to Meg? I've been trying to ring you all week, but you were always busy . . .'

'Hallo, Ted.' Will transferred his attention smoothly to one of his fellow ministers.

A good champagne was served in a long, narrow reception room. Obedient to my briefing, I talked about weather and flora to an ambassador who was dressed in a multi-coloured tie, and about wines to a junior consul, who informed me he had been brought up on beer. I took Antonio Pasquale aside and astounded him with my grasp of Italian and Italian wine. When we said goodbye he kissed my hand and I knew I had done a good job.

Back in the flat, Will made straight for the drinks tray, which was unusual, and poured himself a glass of whisky. 'I'm whacked. Pasquale's wife was a nightmare.'

'We ought to eat something.'

'Too tired.'

'So am I.' I kicked off my shoes and curled up on the sofa. 'Tell me what's happening.'

Will sighed. 'Haven't the energy.'

'Oh.' I studied my feet, encased in their light, evening tights.

'I'm sorry, darling.'

I reached for the cushion and hugged it. 'How would you feel if Dad and I went on a trip to Italy?'

Will snapped to attention. 'When?'

'While Chloë's away. September probably. We haven't settled on anything yet.'

'Without me?'

'Yes.'

Will put down his glass and came and sat down beside me. 'Of course you must go. I know what it would mean to you.' He paused. 'But do you have to go this year? There is so much on . . .' He took away the cushion and put his arm around me. 'I need you on board.' I sensed the energy flowing back into him as he concentrated on bringing me back into the fold. 'Just at the moment, I'm not sure I could manage without you.' He took another gulp of the whisky. 'Perhaps I'm being selfish.' When I did not reply, he said sharply, 'Fanny, are you listening?'

I raised my eyes and saw my old Will: the clever, funny, passionate, committed man with whom I had fallen in love, and I wondered what he could see in me, and whether or not he was looking.

'Ours is becoming a curious marriage,' I heard myself say. 'I've been trying all week to talk to you about your daughter . . . where do I come in the queue?'

'Don't be silly.' This was said with a flash of irritation.

'It's true.'

He caught my chin. 'Is this because I talked to

Meg? She just happened to phone at the right time, you idiot.'

'Partly.' I shook his hand away and started to pick at the braid on the discarded cushion. 'I mind about that.'

He sighed. 'I honestly don't think there's any need to worry about Chloë.'

'But I do worry about her. And I worry that I have to worry about her on my own.'

'When she goes to Australia, she'll forget Sacha; she'll meet other people. It's not so odd at her age to have a passion – if she does – for someone unsuitable.'

He was probably right, but I'd had enough politician's answers for one evening. I heaved myself to my feet and went over to the window and looked out at the dull summer night. 'I would like to go away with my father, Will. I don't think he is all that well, and I'd like to spend some time with him.'

'Rather than with me . . .'

I turned round and glared at him. 'I'm going to forget you said that.'

Will set his glass down on the table with a snap. 'Did you really suggest to Meg that she move out?'

'Not exactly,' I replied. 'The idea was proposed, but not voted upon.'

'Don't you think you should have discussed it with me first? She's upset and unsettled, and it can't be good for her.'

'Discuss things with you? What an excellent idea. I've being trying all week. Shall I see if Mannochie can squeeze me into your schedule at some point? Perhaps during one of your surgeries – between erroneous gas bills and the violent neighbours . . .' I made for the door. 'But right now I'm going to bed.'

As I walked down the corridor, he called after me, 'I can't hurt her, Fanny. I can't abandon her.'

6

Will and I arrived back at Ember House from our curtailed French honeymoon in the small hours, smelling of the melons I had insisted we buy, which had filled the car with their sweet, ripe aroma.

Early next morning, we stumbled out of bed, hoicked clean clothes out of the unpacked suitcases, and drove into Stanwinton. Mannochie met us at the party headquarters on the high street.

Will was immediately claimed by a party apparatchik and Mannochie materialized at my elbow. 'You must meet the chairman of the association and you must get on with her.'

'Will I be put in the stocks if I don't?' I asked, and realizing that it did not sound very amusing, wished I hadn't.

The headquarters seethed with people, and was stuffed with chairs, photocopiers and baskets overflowing with brown envelopes. The persistent sound of telephones piped above the movement and activity. Mannochie piloted me towards a table where a woman was directing an elderly couple on the sorting of pamphlets. 'No slacking,' she addressed them collectively. 'No mistakes.'

'Pearl, this is Fanny.'

A heavy woman, she pulled herself to her feet. 'About time.'

Did she always speak in such staccato sentences? A gust

of nervous hilarity threatened but I said, 'Will and I got here as fast as possible. We drove through the night.'

Pearl Veriker should have met me before – *wives have to be vetted* – but at the time she had been in hospital. Tall and long-nosed, she did not trouble with fashion. Her cotton shirt clashed with her skirt and she wore flesh-coloured tights with white fretworked leather lace-ups. Her scrutiny, however, was clever and merciless. Eventually, she held out her hand. 'I'll call you Fanny since we'll have a lot to do with each other.'

If I had hoped for consolation over my ruined honeymoon, I was wrong. 'As you can imagine, it's battle stations here. I hope you're wearing comfortable shoes.' She glanced down at my bare legs under a short denim skirt. 'I'm sorry, but it would be better if you wore tights and a longer skirt. The more far-reaching and revolutionary our ideas, the more non-threatening and respectable our appearance should be. You should have been told that.'

She meant: You should have known. I flushed at my ignorance.

A young woman carrying a pile of envelopes pushed her way past us. Pearl Veriker's hand shot out and barricaded her passage. Where was Marcia taking these, she wanted to know. A brisk exchange ensued and the captive Marcia was released. 'My job is to keep tabs. Keep an eye on everyone.' Without a pause, she said, 'I hope you're healthy, it's going to be a hard few weeks.'

'I'm sure Will will brief me.'

'Your husband, Fanny, is new to the game. Have you sorted out where you plan to live in the constituency if we triumph?'

'When we come down we'll stay with my father at Ember House.'

Pearl shook her head. 'Won't do. You need a quiet, modest, cheap house. It's important that you have roots here.'

'Apparently, we need a quiet, modest cheap house in the constituency,' I informed Will in the privacy of the bedroom at Ember House.

One sock off, one sock on, he swung round. 'We will live here. Of course. If we win. You knew that.'

'No, I didn't.'

Will peeled off the other sock and dropped it on to the floor. 'I did explain.'

'You said it was possible. I don't want to live here. The bulk of my Battista business is in London. You forget, I've lived here most of my life and I know what it's like. We want to be in London.'

'Fanny . . .' Will came over and sat on the bed. 'Darling . . . look at me. This is important. We're going to have to make sacrifices. Remember what we believe in. All the things we've agreed.' He slipped down on to his knees beside the bed. 'No one said it would be easy.'

I heard him utter the words, witnessed the conviction and belief that lit up his face. 'Will, we don't have to live here. We can come down, lots.'

'There can't be any half-measures. This is a war of sorts. I see it so clearly now.'

I gazed into the dark eyes that so delighted me. 'Will, could I point out that *truth* is the first casualty of war.'

'Mrs Savage, that is not being helpful.'

*

I gave my all. True, I was not an expert but Mannochie did his best to ensure that I became one. Constantly at my side, he murmured instructions, dropped information, prompted my replies. He told me about those who ran the town, owned the building businesses, set the local taxes, which housing estate was likely to vote for Will. He drip-fed me facts, statistics, advice, and taught me the rules of this strange campaign. *Take no prisoners.*

'Mercy isn't part of the deal, then,' I teased.

He turned very serious. 'No. And don't let anyone persuade you otherwise, Fanny.'

By then we were on 'Fanny' terms but he was never called anything but Mannochie. His Christian name, he said, was not for public consumption.

If I gained Mannochie, I lost Will – or, rather, my private Will. The public Will was surrounded by aides with clipboards, potential voters, voters who hated him. He was admired and spat at in equal measure. But one thing was constant: wherever he went, Will was noticed.

'Don't say anything,' Pearl Veriker ordered. 'Ever. That's not your role.'

So, silently, I climbed on to the battle bus and went the rounds with my instructions ringing in my ears. Sitting well back on the platform, I attended meetings and came forward to stand (silently) beside Will to take the applause. Suitably dressed, I attended photocalls with my arm linked in Will's, and the results were not bad.

'It's so lucky you're good-looking,' said Pearl. 'Your husband obeyed orders.'

I stared at her and she patted my shoulder. 'A little pleasantry, Fanny.'

66

If Pearl was cracking jokes, I could only suppose that she and I were making progress.

Obediently, I trudged the streets for hours at a time and knocked on doors. More often than not a woman answered, and I caught glimpses of interiors where baskets of wet laundry waited to be hung out, children's bicycles and pushchairs cluttered the hall and school satchels spilled their contents. Sometimes their men appeared. If they did not like me they told me so, and if they were menacing, Mannochie pulled me away.

My feet swelled and my shoulders ached from the weight of pamphlets. It *was* a war of sorts, even if it had to be fought on the domestic front. On our lists, we ticked off blocks of flats where the walkways reeked of urine, and quiet, net-curtained homes in neat tree-lined streets. We trudged up gravel drives to capacious, well-maintained villas, which had been built by the industrial barons at the turn of the century. Their occupants were the worst for they couched any hostility in a more polite and deadly form. 'Don't think any of you lot do much except tax us,' said one heavily jewelled and made-up woman. 'Can't think what you get up to all day.' She made to shut the front door in our faces. '*Who* did you say you were?'

Mannochie cornered me one evening. He looked embarrassed. 'Fanny, could you keep your thoughts on local transport to yourself?'

I was startled. 'Do I have any?'

'Apparently you do, and you were overheard talking about them at the Guides' coffee morning.'

'I said I thought there should be more buses.'

Mannochie looked concerned. 'Precisely. You are playing into a lobby.'

On the evening before polling day, I planned that Will and I would eat together quietly in a local Chinese restaurant. But he was caught up with a last-minute conference at the headquarters and we made do with a snatched sandwich that Mannochie had conjured. Will barely touched his but drank two glasses of a dreadful wine.

At the other end of the room, the television beamed last-minute predictions and figures. I eased my aching shoulders. Only a few more hours . . . Then Will and I would have some privacy and we could return to the business of making our lives together.

Mannochie came up. 'Figures are looking quite good.' The two men conferred and I ate my chicken sandwich. I listened and I did not listen but, at that moment, it flashed across my mind that in marrying Will I had launched my boat on to a sea that was stormier than I had supposed. Eventually Mannochie moved off and Will grabbed my hand.

'Do you hear? The figures. We might be in with a chance.' He squeezed my fingers painfully. 'Do you think we might just do it?'

My heart filled with love and hope for him, I cherished his hand in mine. 'Yes. Yes, I do.'

At midnight we arrived in the town hall. The last two ballot boxes had just been brought in and the final count was on. The tellers bent over the trestle tables, forefingers and thumbs encased in rubber guards. The piles mounted, shifted; a couple were re-counted, the tally noted.

Will and the other candidates strode up and down between the trestles, but kept a wide berth of each other. The returning officer hovered by the microphone on the stage.

Someone touched my arm and I turned. 'Hallo,' said Meg. 'Sorry I didn't get here earlier.' She was flushed and bright-eyed, impeccable in a red linen dress and pretty shoes. 'I couldn't miss little brother's big day.'

At one thirty, Pearl Veriker chivvied me into a side room. 'Looking good,' she said. 'Let's check you out.'

Skirt long enough? Tights? Make-up?

'Where's your wedding ring?' Her eyes were fixed on my naked left hand.

I fished it out of my pocket. 'It's given me a rash. I'm not used to it yet.'

'Wear it, Fanny.'

I pushed it over my red, swollen finger and endured the itch and burn. To my astonishment, the itch and burn of my rebellion was no less urgent. As surely as an ox, I was being yoked and, if I had not bargained on it, it was far too late to do anything about it.

I pulled myself together and went over to talk to our party workers, whose average age was well above mine but there were one or two younger ones. 'Isn't it funny how the other side always seems so much uglier than your own?' a sharp youth breathed to me.

I was pouring orange juice into plastic cups when I happened to look up and caught Will's gaze. Our eyes met for a long moment and his mouth moved in a faint smile. He was asking me to keep faith. Short-lived and unfocused, my rebellion died.

At three o'clock in the morning, I stood beside Will on the platform as the returning officer read out the votes and Will was declared the new Member for the constituency of Stanwinton. We stood side by side, both of us light-headed and almost incoherent. There was pleasure and pride – and an explosion of joy in my chest. The future seemed as if it could be tackled.

Down below, the indomitable Pearl sat down suddenly and pressed a handkerchief to her mouth. Mannochie was clapping, and a couple of the party workers danced.

Will slid his arm round my shoulders and kissed me, and I promised silently to give him what I had and more. I promised to do my best for him.

'Will . . .' Meg pushed her way up to the platform, her red dress a bright blur, and linked her arm through his. 'Darling Will . . .'

The photographers flashed away, someone else cheered, Mannochie continued to clap.

Later that day the official photograph was published in the *Stanwinton Echo*. It had that grainy, blurred look that local papers sometimes have and it was hard to make out some of the figures crowded on to the platform. A smiling Will stood tall and straight. He looked young, happy and full of promise. Beside him was a slender, fair-haired figure, wreathed in smiles. It was not me. It was Meg.

I set about my first task as Mrs MP of sorting out Will's

tiny one-bedroom London flat. This involved wresting an extra inch in Will's cupboard to hang up my clothes, winnowing out boxes and papers, and rearranging the sitting room to accommodate my antique chair. I gritted my teeth and searched for a space to stack my business files.

I made the bed and my foot nudged one of Will's abandoned shoes. I picked it up and my heart melted. It was part of Will, the man I loved. I slipped my hand inside. Burnt into the inner sole, was the private imprint of a person. My shoes held one too. Will's second toe was longer than the first and I rubbed my finger over the indentation in the leather. It was my secret, and my secret knowledge.

The phone rang. 'Fanny Savage? My name is Amy Greene.' She went on to explain that her husband was a backbencher and she was organizing a get-together in Westminster for the new wives. 'We oldies like to take care of you infants.'

For all the briskness, an underlying note of depression was detectable. I asked her politely how long her husband had been in Parliament. 'How long as an MP as opposed to a sod? Twenty-five years, three months and two days.'

'Oh.'

She gave a smoker's cough. 'You might as well know that Parliament hates women. *Hates* them. Be warned.'

Will made his maiden speech in October when Parliament reassembled after the long vacation. The night before, we argued over which colour suit he should wear. I opted for the grey. He preferred the blue. Did it matter? Apparently. Colours (or so the apparatchiks had suggested) conveyed subtle meanings. This was, I felt, a little puzzling for I had assumed it was the message that was the important thing.

'I know it's nonsense,' he maintained stoutly, 'but just this once, I think I ought to listen to what the advisers advise.'

I rubbed his shoulders which felt like tensed steel. 'Hey, take a few deep breaths. Loosen those muscles.'

I did not tell him that my own nerves were conducting a nauseous dance in the pit of my stomach. All I had to do was to watch Will get to his feet and talk about the social benefits of cheaper housing, and impress his peers. But this first showing would affect his future – and mine.

'I must not muck this up, Fanny,' Will said.

'Spare a thought for your sister and me,' I pointed out. 'We get to look down at all the bald spots where we sit in the strangers' gallery.'

He gave a muffled snort.

Will's speech went off well.

At least, I think it did for, when he got to his feet, cleared his throat and began to speak easily and fluently, my attention veered off into another sphere.

It was nerves, I know, but I found myself thinking about trees. Tall ones, like the sycamore, whose stout uncompromising leader branches emphasize its winter nudity. I thought of poplars swaying in the summer breeze, and feathery acacias and the astonishing reds of the maple. But the trees that speak to me most particularly have always been the cypress, the *Cupressus sempervirens*, the dark exclamations dotted over medieval and Renaissance Italian paintings. And the box, which is not strictly a tree. Box was probably introduced to this country by the Romans and its stems and roots are so heavy that they sink in water.

Meg caught my eye, and I coloured up guiltily. I had promised to hang on Will's every word, in order to assemble a useful Situation Report.

You spoke too quickly. Your hands were too busy, they distracted the listener. Don't look at your feet.

Etc.

'To the manner born,' whispered Meg.

Meg misinterpreted my lack of response as lack of control. Furthermore she would be thinking of Will: indeed, I suspected, that she thought of little else. Her Situation Report would be immaculate and very helpful.

She laid one small hand with its exquisitely shaped nails on my arm. Today, they were painted pink to match her lipstick. 'You have to learn to lighten up, Fanny,' she advised in a low, concerned voice. 'Develop a sense of humour. Then you will cope better.'

I gritted my teeth. Quite apart from the insult to my perfectly operational sense of humour, did she consider I was *that* lacking in the requisite qualifications? Was my ignorance and inexperience obvious? 'I will bear it in mind,' I muttered.

Meg pressed on. 'Please don't be offended,' she said. 'You are so nice, Fanny, and I am only trying to help.' She smiled understandingly. 'I've been at it a bit longer than you.'

Outside the House of Commons, a photographer was on the prowl for a national newspaper and he inveigled Will and I to pose for him and we were snapped, hand in hand, framed in the doorway.

'Parliament's newest Golden Couple,' ran the caption

in a weekend paper. The camera had caught Will looking grave but irresistible. I less so, I concluded, after glancing briefly at the photo, for I had a wary look on my face, startled almost.

At any rate, Mannochie, who had bedded down overnight on the sofa in the flat, pronounced himself pleased. 'This will go down well in the constituency.'

Will studied the photograph for longer, it seemed to me, than was decent. 'Better of me than you,' he pronounced.

'That's what I think.' I concentrated on frying up the bacon. 'But I'll pass.'

'Certainly you do,' said Mannochie.

Will still had his teeth into the subject. 'I can't afford to photograph badly. Ever. Back me up, Mannochie. One bad showing and it takes years to eradicate.'

We perched on the sofa and chair in the sitting room, ate bacon, egg and toast, drank coffee, and rifled through the morning papers. Will and Mannochie discussed tactics and, at great length, diary commitments.

I looked up from the paper and tossed a fact into the date discussion. 'I shall be in Australia in December.'

As one, both men turned in my direction.

Will said: 'You didn't mention it to me, Fanny.'

'Yes, I did. You've forgotten.'

Mannochie brushed the crumbs surrounding his plate into a tidy little heap. 'Stanwinton is big on Christmas. It's part of the civic pride. There's a frenzy of fund raising which the sitting MP always supports. Then there are parties for the local children's homes, the evergreens and the disabled.' He smiled apologetically. 'Attendance really is compulsory.'

I addressed Will. 'Fine. You will be there.'

Will fumbled for a second piece of toast and buttered it. 'Fanny. I am not sure how to put this, but I need you with me.' He looked especially desirable: slightly rumpled, boyish and pleading. It made me want him very badly.

I shook my head. 'Dad and I have set up a lot of business. We're due at the Hunter Valley, we are guests of honour at a dinner in Adelaide and Bob and Ken are coming over from the Yarra.'

These names meant nothing to either of the men. They were part and parcel of my and my father's territory and we had done business with them for years. 'You want me to smile sweetly, kiss cheeks, sing carols, pat sticky hands?'

'That was the deal.' Will's gaze shifted from Mannochie to me.

Will and I had discussed the theory of our division of work plenty of times, and I assumed that I would be at liberty to choose when to go on duty – when to be a good wife. 'This is business, Will. These are long-term commitments.'

Mannochie picked up his egg-stained plate and edged towards the door. 'Will, Fanny, I am sure you need to talk things over . . . Fanny, perhaps it would be a good idea if we went through the diary for the year. That way, we will avoid future clashes.'

This was the cue for our first quarrel . . . which went along the lines of: why didn't you say something earlier? And me saying tartly back at him: you don't listen to what I say. Then Will demanded how could I have made him look a fool in front of Mannochie?

'Very easy,' I said, quick as a flash.

75

That made Will grin. After that, the atmosphere calmed down and we began to talk properly. It was clear we had not agreed demarcation lines and we needed to sort this out.

It was not as if Will demanded that I give up my work for his. 'No, not at all,' he said. He scratched his head with the Biro. 'Your work is important, and it has to be slotted in. It's just, I would have liked you to have been there for the Christmas run-up. Just this first year.'

This caused me to lie awake for most of the night, sifting over the pros and cons of the respective demands on our time.

The subject suddenly appeared so vexing that I ended up making myself tea at four o'clock in the morning. While the kettle boiled, I ran my fingers over the glass jars with red screw tops that I had bought soon after we married.

Kitchens should be larger than this. They shouldn't be mean proportioned and stingy with storage.

Not like the big house in Fiertino, if my father was to believed, where a larder led off the main kitchen. This was used to store pâtés and dried meats, and tins. 'There were rows of bottles in there, in wonderful colours,' he told me. 'Fruit and pickles and walnuts . . . if you could bottle summer, it was in those bottles. My mother checked the larder every day. It was a habit, and it was unthinkable to her she did not make that daily check. "It is important for the family," she always said. "I have to make sure there is food otherwise I can't sleep nights."'

Meanwhile, I was going to make do with two small shelves in the kitchen and fill my glass jars with rice, nuts, pasta and lentils. I had already arranged my wine manuals on the spare bit of worktop by the toaster.

The kettle boiled.

Next door, a bedspring creaked and feet hit the floor. Will appeared at the door. 'Fanny . . . you must be freezing.' He squeezed into the kitchen and slipped his arms around my waist. 'You *are* freezing. Here, let me make the tea.'

We took it back to bed and drank it, with my cold feet resting on Will's legs to warm them up. 'My fault,' he said.

'It's my fault, too.'

Then, he took away my cup of tea and put it down on the bedside table. He stroked my hair and I had a minor revelation as to why arguments were so necessary, for making up was extremely sweet.

'Mannochie and I will manage,' he said cheerfully.

'Are you sure?'

'Almost.'

That made me laugh. I slipped my hand under his T-shirt and rested it on his exciting bare flesh.

During what remained of the night, Chloë was conceived. I had no inkling of this when, at the first opportunity, I bought a large, looseleaf, leatherbound diary and gave it to Will. 'It will last us,' I said, 'for years and years.'

7

Looking back, there was a peculiar intensity about living in virtually one room. We touched constantly: if I went into the kitchen, I brushed against Will; if he sat down on the bed to lace up his shoes, he dislodged me; if we passed each other, our shoulders met.

After we moved, and there were rooms in which to expand, it was different. But, then, we had a new life, and different things to occupy us.

At the very last minute, Will was ordered to join a fact-finding tour of Europe for the car-tax scheme which put paid to his plan to spend a couple of days at home with Chloë before she left on her travels. He broke the news to her over a Sunday lunch. 'Sorry, darling. I hope you understand.'

Chloë continued to eat. 'It's OK,' she said.

I couldn't bear the disappointment on her face. 'Will, couldn't you just manage an afternoon?'

'It's OK.' Chloë did her best to look as if she did not care.

Will shot me a look and I mouthed at him, 'She's upset.'

'Chloë,' he said, 'I feel miserable about it.'

She stood up, and I saw the much older Chloë in her expression. 'But not quite miserable enough, Dad,' she said. 'So let's leave it, shall we?'

She left the room, closing the door with a distinct bang. I looked at Will. 'She's been planning this for ages . . .'

Will looked really distressed. 'I wish I didn't have to go.'

'Oh, well.' I began to clear up the plates. 'It's done now.'

He winced, and studied his shoe laces. 'Fanny,' he said at length, without looking up, 'I have a favour to ask . . .'

'Don't tell me,' I said. 'Let me guess.'

Surgeries took place in one of the smaller rooms of the town hall. Its window was stuck shut, trapping in the odours of stewed coffee and stale air.

Tina, the constituency secretary, bustled in with two shopping-bags and dumped them on the floor. 'The whole bloody lot is bound to thaw,' she said, 'chicken korma, peas, but if the old man demands his dinner pronto, who am I . . .?'

Tina was a compact, motherly woman who had a habit of clicking her tongue in protest as she listened in to some of the worst cases. Her husband was out of work, and to make ends meet she sold make-up from door to door. Today she was wearing turquoise trousers and a shell-pink lipstick, which, if it had been the last lipstick on earth, should have been burned in an *auto da fé*. But she wore it with defiance and an air of 'never surrender'. She shoved the chicken korma under the table. 'My old man thinks we should have a bodyguard. There are madmen out there.'

'Mannochie will do, won't you, Mannochie?'

'To the death,' he said, in his dry way.

First in was Mrs Scott. She was a regular at the Saturday surgeries. Over the years Will had struggled to sort out her damp flat and the family next door who terrorized her. She was tiny, twisted with osteoporosis and, long ago, had lost any remaining family of her own.

'Oh, it's you,' she said. 'The minister busy? Something important?' Touchingly, Mrs Scott considered Will's seniority a personal plus. I explained I was not exactly taking the surgery but sitting in for him. Today she had an arm in a sling. 'Tripped on the stairs, didn't I? The council said they'd come and see to them so I want you to sue them for me.'

We discussed what we could do for her and the continuing and losing battle against her neighbours' regime of terror. Mrs Scott's mouth was drawn tight with pain and stress. 'Should we get the doctor to come and check you over?' I asked.

The remnants of her old spirit revived. 'The last time a doctor set foot in the place, Queen Victoria was on the throne.' She delved into her bag. 'I've brought you something. I was going to give it to the minister to give to you.'

She passed over a soft piece of netting edged with beads. 'It's for your milk jug,' she said. 'I made it.'

I spread it out on the desk. The beads were lapis-lazuli blue with gold flecks and very pretty. A lump came into my throat.

She watched me with shrewd eyes. 'Not all a waste of time, eh?'

No, it was not. 'That must be your best one, Mrs Scott.'

'I wanted you to have it now. I might not be around for too long,' she said.

With an effort, she pulled herself to her feet and shook

her head as if she were trying to release stored information. 'It's gone in a flash,' she said. 'Life. And I wouldn't mind if it hadn't been so bloody rotten.'

At her desk, Tina clicked her tongue and typed away while Mannochie patrolled the entrance to keep the madmen at bay.

Surgery over, he and I sorted out the urgent from the non-urgent tasks and talked over any problems. If I required proof – which I did not – that politics existed on mysterious levels, the surgery provided it. At Westminster there was plenty of talk and gesture but it was here, on the ground, that the cogs turned.

I drove into town to meet Chloë.

My father and I had friends throughout the Australian wine areas and any one of them would have taken in Chloë. But, no: Chloë was being Miss Independent. So far, her itinerary for Australia included a week's stay in Adelaide, and a trip to the Hunter Valley. But that was all she would permit us to arrange.

We met in the backpacker shop: I was clutching a wad of cash and she the list she had promised to make. On inspection, it was pitifully short. Mini-karabiners. Walking sandals. Walking boots. Insect repellent. Padlock for the backpack. 'There *must* be more,' I said. 'You can't take off to the other side of the world without proper equipment. It's not safe.'

'Honestly, Mum, you should listen to yourself. I'll be fine.'

I longed to reach inside my daughter and tease out exactly what she was thinking. To be allowed to smooth out any ruffles of apprehension. To do a mother's work of being infinitely more wise and calm. 'I'm allowed to make a few suggestions,' I said defensively, 'surely?'

She picked up a travelling wallet, designed to strap on under the arm. 'Do you think I should take this?'

'Yes,' I said quickly. 'And sun stuff. Masses of it for when it gets hot.'

'Mother. They *sell* sun cream in Australia.'

Chloë was quiet as I paid. She sat back in the car, and I reckoned the silence was suggestive. Sure enough . . . She picked at her mistreated cuticles. 'Sacha says Aunt Meg told him you're thinking of moving house. You wouldn't do that without me, would you? Not until I come home?'

'Meg shouldn't have said anything.'

'But if it's *true*?'

'It was just an idea.' I drove on a bit further then added, 'I wouldn't mind a change. You'll be leaving home – '

'I *hate* it when grown-ups say things like that.'

I reached over and touched her cheek. 'Where's the girl who couldn't wait to grow up? The one who always said, "I forbid you to treat me like a child"?'

Chloë looked thoughtful. 'Mum . . . That was then. Can't you tell?' She hunched her shoulders and gazed out of the window at the speeding landscape. 'Are you and Dad getting on all right?'

I negotiated a bend with extra care. 'What makes you ask?'

'Just asking.'

'We're fine.'

'It doesn't sound like it when you talk to him on the phone.'

I considered my answer. 'My phone conversations are supposed to be private.'

Chloë looked both pitying and superior. 'Get real, Mum, this is a family.'

I laughed but with genuine pleasure. 'That's good.'

Back at the house, we unloaded the packages and Chloë disappeared upstairs to phone her travelling companions. A stream of excited chatter filtered down from her room.

I went downstairs to the kitchen. My father was coming to supper that evening. I removed my wedding ring and hung it on the hook on the noticeboard. From time to time, it still made my finger swell – perhaps it was something to do with my hormones, my mood, the time of the year – and it bothered me when I was doing the chores.

Brigitte poked her head round the door. 'I'm out,' she said. 'OK.' It was a statement, not a question. The back door banged with a decided emphasis.

'I don't think she's a happy bunny,' commented Meg, who had come into the kitchen. 'She's been on the phone a lot. She wasn't very nice about you either.'

I knew perfectly well that the au pairs ran an information service about their employers. I had never quite got over meeting comparative strangers who knew exactly the state of my underwear – not least because I possessed detailed information on theirs.

I began to chop up stewing steak and an onion which made my eyes water.

'You've turned into a good cook, Fanny,' Meg observed. 'Who would have thought it?'

Silence.

She watched me lay the table with cutlery and water glasses. 'You've laid too many places.'

'Dad's coming.'

She nodded. 'Good.' Another silence. 'You seem cross.'

'I am.' I put the final glass in its place. 'I can't trust you, Meg, ever, not to repeat things. You shouldn't have told Sacha, which means Chloë, about the idea of moving house.'

Meg looked defiant. 'Doesn't she have a right to know?'

'You've upset her.'

'Fanny,' she pointed out, gently, 'Chloë is a big girl now.'

That Meg was right made me even crosser. 'Will and I would prefer to be the ones to choose when we discuss something important with her.'

'If you say so.' Meg filled the water jug and placed it in the exact centre of the table where it overshadowed the little vase of pink and white roses I had put there earlier.

Half-way through the meal, I looked up from my plate. Meg was flirting with my father, which he always enjoyed. 'Meg is a smart woman,' he had said once. Sacha and Chloë were deep in conversation. The candles on the table threw a dreamy light over the roses and the water jug. Will's chair was empty, of course, and I thought, he must miss this.

Chloë laughed and, in the candlelight, she glowed with the kind of beauty that you can only possess when the most interesting part of your life lies ahead of you. My father turned his head towards me and raised his glass in my direction. It was a little habit of his. It told me that he loved me, and always would.

I raised mine back.

I had phoned my father first with the news. 'I'm going to have a baby.'

'But that's wonderful, Francesca. *Wonderful* news. Clever girl.' There was a pause. 'You're pleased?'

'Bit taken aback, Dad. Bit of a mad mistake. But, yes, of course.'

'Ah.' Another pause. 'Francesca, we must talk about what this means for the business.'

'I know.' I bit my lip. Suddenly I felt as if I had boarded the wrong plane and arrived at the wrong destination. 'We'll have to make do and mend for a few months after the baby, but everything will go back to normal afterwards.'

Only then did I phone Will, who ducked out of a debate on trade tariffs and rushed home. 'This is brilliant. Wonderful. I'll ring Meg, you ring your father.'

'Dad knows.'

'I see,' he said, and disengaged himself. I could have bitten off my tongue. 'Oh, well, that puts me in my place.'

A couple of weeks later he arrived home with three books on pregnancy and childbirth. 'Must do things properly.'

'Be nice and let me down gently.' I whisked into the kitchen where I peeled garlic and crushed it into butter and spread it over a couple of steaks.

'Fanny, you might like to know you have a broad bean inside you,' Will called.

The look of the steaks encouraged my stomach to perform a tribal dance. 'For a broad bean it's very uppity.'

Will stood in the doorway and waved the book at me. 'Wait until it's the size of an ammonite.'

'I can't wait.'

'Nor can I.' Will chucked aside the manual, switched off the grill and dragged me to the bed. There, with the heightened sensual pleasure of a changing body, I felt my nerve endings double, triple.

Afterwards we lay and talked over the future in lazy, luxurious detail. We would have to find a house quickly, the birth would be in London – or should it be in the constituency? – possible names.

I had saved one piece of information until now. 'Will, I won't be going to Australia after all. The doctor says that if I pick up a bug on the aircraft, or something, I can't have anything to help. It's best not to risk it. Dad says he can cope on his own.'

I was lying on his arm. Slowly, his hand curved round my shoulder and rested there. 'OK.' His voice was purged of any triumph. 'OK.'

The Christmas party at the House of Commons was held in the terrace room overlooking the river. It was full, noisy and hot. We threaded through the crowd, and although I was quite at home in my world this was different. My stomach rippled with pregnancy, nerves and . . . shyness.

Amy Greene came to my rescue. 'There you are. Come along.' She put a hand at the small of my back and pushed me towards the huge window that overlooked the river.

'This is Elaine Miller. Husband belongs to the Other Party, but we like her.' A tall, thin redhead extended her hand. 'And this,' said Amy, 'is Betsey Thwaite. Her husband is One of Us and on the fast track. Like yours.'

Betsey Thwaite was a small blonde whose smile did not extend to her eyes. 'David has just been made a junior whip.'

'So,' said Elaine, 'by being nosy and an official bully you get to be a junior minister.' Betsey looked poisonous. 'What a darling blouse,' Elaine went on. 'Where did you get it?'

To my surprise, they knew I was pregnant. 'Don't worry,' said Elaine. 'The jungle tom-toms beat night and day in this world. They even know the wives' bra sizes. Where are you going to have it?'

I grabbed an orange juice from the waiter. 'At the local hospital.'

Elaine looked thoughtful. 'Just as long as you don't have it when there's a vote going on.'

'*Elaine* . . .' Betsey Thwaite intervened. 'Don't let Fanny down too quickly.'

Amy gave a short, bitter laugh.

Elaine turned to me. 'Betsey's such a trouper, but you mustn't be bullied, Fanny, like so many of us.'

'Come on, Elaine,' said Betsey. 'You're a trouper too. Don't deny it.'

Elaine softened. 'When I married Neil, I disagreed with everything he believed in. But what the hell? I loved him and I fell in behind. So I suppose Betsey's right. I am a trouper.'

Elaine had three children – 'I might as well be a single

parent,' she confessed – and was planning to start up a knitwear business. 'But the goalposts keep moving. Still, with a bit of luck, Neil's party will stay out of power for years.' She gave me an honest smile. 'Welcome to the club, Fanny.'

When I was ready to go home, I went on the hunt for Will and ran him to earth talking to a group of men of about his age, surrounded by a larger ring of admiring women. I touched his arm. For a second or two, it was clear that he had not registered who I was. Then it clicked. 'Darling.' He was elated and his eyes were sparkling. 'You must be exhausted. Look, why don't I get you a taxi? I've got to sort out a few things with Neil over a spot of dinner.'

There were many such evenings.

If Will got back late, he crept in beside me. He offered to sleep on the sofa, but I wouldn't have it. 'You belong with me,' I said, and I didn't mind if he woke me up with his blundering about in the dark.

Word was spreading about Will that, of his intake, he was a man to watch. 'The Honourable Member for Stanwinton,' wrote one political commentator, 'has a whiff of the razzle-dazzle about him.'

After she had read the piece, Elaine rang me: 'I can hear the knives sharpening. Be warned. Grow a tough skin.'

I cut the article out of the paper and stuck it on to the mirror by the front door. When Will came home, I was in the kitchen, battling with a wave of nausea. *One. Two.* I leant over the unit. *Breathe in. Breathe out.*

There was a silence. No 'Hallo, darling.' Curious, I poked

my head round the kitchen door and caught Will staring into the mirror. Unaware of me, he patted his chin and fussed with his hair. He dug his hands into his pockets, squared his shoulders and took a step back.

'What on earth . . .?' I asked.

He swung round. 'Just looking,' he admitted, sheepish yet defiant.

'Practising,' I said.

He went bright red. 'Catching up with myself.'

I slid my arm round his waist. 'Own up. You were practising for the despatch box.'

Pearl Veriker had sent over the particulars of a house a couple of miles outside the town. 'This one would do,' she wrote, in her determined-looking hand, the 'do' heavily underlined. That weekend, while Will did his surgery, my father and I went to see it. We drove down a narrow lane, flanked by two big fields under plough, and turned into the driveway of a harsh red-brick house built in late Victorian Gothic style, with a couple of outhouses tacked on to the kitchen.

It was already empty. As I stepped through the front door, I sensed I was entering a place that had been denied fresh air for a long time.

'Look at it this way,' said my father, 'it's a roof over your head.'

Upstairs, the rooms were better-proportioned and the winter sun was reflected in the large windows. The main bedroom overlooked the ploughed fields in the front. The dun and grey of the soil filled my eyes. Notices had been placed around the perimeters, 'No walkers', and at the north end of the field a rookery clotted the branches of the beeches.

My father tugged open a window and prodded at the sill. Sharp and winter-scented, a stream of air invaded the stuffy chill. 'Fanny . . .' he said.

I sensed what was coming. I inspected my hands. They had swollen slightly. So had my waistband and my trousers felt tight around my thighs. Even my shoulders felt bigger. Pregnancy did not agree with me: my body refused to obey orders, which was both puzzling and enraging. The broad-bean-cum-ammonite was neither well behaved nor polite in its colonization of my body.

'I know what you're going to say. You need someone for the business who'll be more on board. I haven't been doing so well lately.'

'You can come back,' he said quickly, 'after the baby's born.'

I stared at the depressing fields. 'Funny how things change, Dad.' For the sake of a broad bean that was turning into an ammonite.

My father was observing me closely. 'It makes sense. Having a baby isn't like going to the dentist – half an hour's unpleasantness and it's all over.'

'I will come back,' I said. 'I promise. It'll be fine. I'll cope.' My father looked sceptical. 'Dad, there's no question of me giving up work permanently. Will wouldn't expect it either.'

'Yes,' he said, and I read into his inflection a new precariousness, a new treachery even, in my position.

Later, that afternoon, I took Will to see the house. The twilight was kinder on it, dimming its strident colour, and the rooms downstairs were less gloomy in the electric light.

Will was delighted with the house. He pointed out the proportions of the bedrooms and the view over the fields. Downstairs required a lot of work but he was excited by the challenge. 'I can build shelves,' he said. 'And lay floors. I like DIY.'

His energy and enthusiasm were infectious and it was a relief to know we could afford the house and make plans. I stood in the place where he reckoned we should put the kitchen, and looked out at the rookery in the clump of beeches beyond the rather ridiculous Gothic window. Black shapes wheeled in and out of the branches. I told myself that the country was a much better place to bring up a baby and was surprisingly content.

We finished supper early and I was ordered to sit still while Meg, Chloë and my father did the washing-up.

The phone rang. It was Raoul. 'Fanny, I haven't heard from you for a long time,' he said.

'I was just thinking the same. How's business? How are Thérèse and the children?'

'Business could always be better. The French market isn't flourishing.'

I knew perfectly well from my father's records that the French suppliers were more than holding their own. 'How can that be?' I teased.

'People are drinking more and more New World wines . . . I will have to get another job.'

Whichever way you looked at it, the Villeneuves were well cushioned and Raoul would never give up. Cut Raoul and he would bleed Pétrus or Château Longueville.

We talked for half an hour or so: a happy, meandering conversation which flowed neatly past any spectre of an unfinished past.

Eventually, Raoul said, 'Alfredo tells me that now Chloë is off, you are considering coming back properly into the business. Really, Fanny, this is exceptionally good news.'

'I'm thinking about it. It all rather depends on what Will's up to. He's . . . um . . . hoping for big things.'

'It would make you very happy,' he said simply. 'I know it would.'

I allowed myself the merest moment of reprise, of what-might-have-been-possible. 'Dad tells me that Château d'Yseult has been bought by the Americans. Has that caused a stir?'

'I think we will get used to it,' Raoul said. 'Or, rather, I think we French have to get used to it.'

Chloë's flight was on the thirteenth of July and I struggled against feeling superstitious.

The day before, we drove over to Ember House to say goodbye to my father. Before lunch, we walked around the garden and came to a halt under the beech in which, many years before, my father had built me a tree-house.

'Don't look down,' I called up to Chloë, who had decided to climb it.

Don't look down. My father had taught me that – advice that is perfectly obvious once you have received it, but not before.

'Don't worry,' said my father. 'Let her be.'

'Stop fussing, Mum.' Chloë swung herself up into the first fork and straddled the branch. 'Look at me.'

'She's just like you,' remarked my father fondly.

'Was I as pig-headed?'

'Probably. I can't remember.'

I bent down to tip a stone out of my shoe. Tucked into the tree roots were green, vivid moss and the remnants of the miniature cyclamen I had planted over the years. Cyclamen should never be in pots. They belonged outside in the cool, drenched damp of an English spring. 'I wish she wasn't going, Dad, but I know she must. It seems a sort of . . . end.'

'It isn't an end, believe me,' he said, and tucked my hand into his arm. 'Hang on to that.'

Chloë scrambled up to the second fork in the trunk where, I knew, the bark was smooth and flecked with lichen, and the branches were wide and generous. Perfect for the lonely, perennially grubby girl who had made it her den all those years ago. Chloë hooked her leg over the branch and settled back. 'I'm probably looking at what you looked at.'

'Probably.'

She squinted across at the remains of the platform. 'All the planks look rotten.'

'Be careful.' A breeze rippled the leaves. I knew that sound so well. In the end, I had known the pathway up that tree better than the stairs in the house.

'I drank my first bottle of cider up there,' I said, to my father, 'and practised swearing.'

'I know,' he said. 'I used to prowl underneath, just to make sure you were all right.'

'Really, Dad? I never saw you. I always thought I was the clever one.'

'And so you were, Francesca.' He looked pleased with himself. 'But I wasn't a complete fool.'

I looked at him. However much I tried to ignore it, my father was growing older. Fright drove a stiletto into me. 'Why don't I take some work back with me, if I'm to come back to work properly, why don't you give me some stuff today?'

He paused and laid his hand on my arm. His touch was a brittle leaf. 'Why don't I?'

'Guys, I'm coming down.' A moment later Chloë landed beside us. 'Got moss all over my jeans, Mum. And this is my *travelling* pair.'

It was not really necessary for me to brush and pat Chloë clean but, since I would not have her for much longer, I allowed myself to fuss. It gave me an excuse to smooth back her hair and run my hands over her shoulders to check they were not too thin. Close your eyes, I told myself. Savour and memorize: imprint the *feel* of her.

Will – of course – could not come to see Chloë off. 'Send my dearest love . . . and, Fanny, give her some extra money. From me. I'll pay you back.' Nor did Sacha. 'At a gig.' So I drove her and her rucksack to the airport, where we met Jenny and Fabia, her travelling companions.

The three girls listened in silence to the three mothers while the final lecture – *stick together, spiked drinks, drugs, lecherous men* – was delivered in staccato bursts of anxiety.

I drew Chloë aside. 'I'm sorry Sacha isn't here.'

Chloë averted her eyes with their long, long lashes, but not before I had caught a glimpse of panic and hurt. 'Sacha doesn't think goodbyes are important. But I think they are, don't you, Mum?'

'Yes.'

She fingered her daysack, which contained her money, ticket and passport. 'He couldn't come, could he?'

'You did pack all the medicines?' I begged her.

'Yes, Mum.'

'You've got your money-belt on?'

'You've asked me that twice, Mum.'

Her role was to be composed and determined. Mine was to fuss, fear and, finally, to raise my hand in farewell and push my daughter gently into her future.

8

Hoping to catch a final glimpse of Chloë – just a flicker of her head, the suggestion of her shoulder – I hovered outside Departures and watched, without seeing, the progression of passengers file through. Some were girls like Chloë, Jenny and Fabia, young, hopeful, anxious to be tested and tempered by what the world had to offer.

Five minutes sifted by, then ten. I shifted my bag from one shoulder to the other. I dug my hand into my jacket pocket and felt the car-park ticket slide under my nail. I was preparing myself. A tooth after Novocaine is numb, but the pain is not absent.

An official on the gate sent me a look of mixed suspicion and boredom. He'd seen it all before. My mobile phone didn't take international calls and I ducked into a telephone booth, rang Will, and fed more coins into the telephone and waited.

'What's up?' he asked.

'I forgot to check Chloë had her fleece. It's winter in Australia now and she'll be cold.'

'Is that why you've got me out of the meeting?'

'I just wanted to tell you that she's gone.'

His voice sounded tender – but also a little exasperated. 'I'm glad you did. Listen, you idiot, she can buy something out there. They do have shops.'

'I know,' I said, miserably. 'I know I shouldn't have rung you. I'm being stupid, that's all.'

'Well, I'm glad you did,' he repeated, and did not terminate the conversation with the usual 'must go' until he had talked me through Chloë's potential goose bumps and checked that I had enough money to pay for the car park.

I cried all the way to Elaine's. The tears dripped off my chin and on to the car seat.

She was making chocolate cup cakes for the Red Cross charity fête when I walked into the kitchen. There was a deafening noise coming from upstairs.

'That's Jake,' she said as she kissed me. 'Practising the drums.'

'Home from home,' I said.

She grabbed me by the shoulders and searched my face. 'Very down in the dumps?'

'A bit.' I bit my lip. 'Actually, very. I don't know what I'm going to do without Chloë.'

'Right. Let's make a plan,' she said briskly. 'First of all you will help me make these wretched cakes and then you will ring home and tell them you are staying the night, and blow everyone else.' She thrust a wooden spoon at me. 'Get going. Earn your keep.'

Upstairs, the drum beats rolled and crashed. Elaine sighed and brushed back her hair with a hand that trembled. I asked a little anxiously, 'Are *you* all right?'

'Sure.'

But, over a supper of spaghetti Bolognese and a bottle of wine, Elaine confessed, 'I've had enough of this life.'

This was not like her. 'What's happened?'

97

There was a long pause and she dropped her head into her hands. 'I think Neil may be having a serious affair this time.' Her voice was muffled. 'All the signs are there. One of the secretaries in the House. I've been trying not to face it, but I must.'

'Oh, Elaine.'

Elaine raised her head. 'I didn't mean to say anything, Fanny. Not while you're feeling so bereft.'

That was so like Elaine and I cast around as to how I could possibly help and comfort. 'Tell me about it,' I said, 'and then we can work out what's best.'

We spent half the night talking and went to bed not much the wiser and with nothing resolved. We could think of any amount of practical things to do – including Elaine packing her bags – but none of them were a panacea for anguish. Stupid with fatigue, I arrived home mid-morning to find my house in uproar. Overnight, Brigitte had done a bunk. At some point the previous evening, she had packed her bags, dropped the keys on to the kitchen table and abandoned ship.

'Without a word,' said Meg, avoiding my eyes. 'I didn't hear a taxi or anything.'

'She izt horrible womans,' Maleeka said.

Brigitte had not appeared to me to be 'horrible womans'. Irritating, perhaps, but not horrible. Yet when I discovered that her parting shot had been to let herself into our bathroom and help herself to shampoo and bath oil, her malice felt like sandpaper against sunburnt skin.

On Friday night, Will arrived home unexpectedly early.

I was sitting at the kitchen table. Having worked my

98

way through a pile of my father's invoices and shipping orders, I was reading a couple of files I'd scooped up at Ember House. 'Ambitious', he had written of one vineyard, 'but too impatient.' Of another, 'Soil unlikely to yield'. Of a third, 'Terroir limited and undefined.' They were so like him, these precise, careful assessments.

'Where am I?' Elaine had cried. '*Who* am I? Where do I go from here?' Her distress had affected me deeply – for all sorts of reasons that were not only to do with my affection for her.

I sorted the papers into 'Done' and 'Must Do', and surveyed the pile. Come to that, who was I? Certainly, I was not Fanny Savage, wife, mother, wine expert and business woman which, once, had been my ambition.

But that had been my choice.

'Hallo, darling,' said Will.

I looked up, surprised, and did not register for a second who he was. He was in his best grey suit and sported a light tan. 'I wasn't expecting you yet.'

'I managed to get an earlier flight. I thought I'd try and come home early to see how you were.' He smiled rather sadly. 'I knew you'd be missing Chloë.'

I held up my hand and he took it. 'That was nice of you. You look well. You found a second or two to sit by the pool.'

'Yup.' He dropped a kiss on my head. 'What are you up to?'

'The usual Battista stuff. I've been talking to Dad about taking on a bit more; I really think he needs the help. What do you think?'

99

He frowned slightly and flopped down into a chair. 'Any chance of supper? Where are the others?'

'I'll see what I can rustle up. Meg decided to go to an AA meeting and Sacha's in London.' Something in his pose alerted me to trouble. 'Has something gone wrong?'

'Trouble . . . of course.' He sighed. 'The car lobby is getting pretty vicious over the second-car tax. It's got a lot of money at its disposal and a couple of the tabloids have come out in its favour, banging on about personal freedom.' He sounded unusually despondent, and very tired.

I got up and laid a hand on his shoulder. The material of his suit jacket felt smooth, expensive, sophisticated. 'Not so very terrible. And there is always trouble somewhere along the line.'

'It's pretty bad,' he said. 'If this goes wrong, I'll look a fool, and it will mark me out as a loser.'

He twisted round to look at me, and I knew he was still aching for the Chancellorship. I opened the fridge and surveyed its contents. 'How about fishcakes and tomato salad?'

'Fine.'

'By the way, Brigitte's packed her bags and done a bunk. Last night, without any warning.'

Will was not listening. 'Do you care at all about the second-car tax, Fanny? I'd rather you told me now if you didn't.'

I took a deep breath. 'Not as much as I should.' I put the fishcakes into a frying pan and chopped up the tomatoes. They were small, cold and tough and I cheered them up with a sprinkling of chives. What was the point in not telling the truth? 'You know I've had doubts about the idea.'

He was clearly hurt and a little bewildered, and it cut me to the quick. The ingrained habits of love and loyalty resurfaced and I put my arms around him. 'Sorry, Will. But I can't summon the enthusiasm for it.' He leant against me and I stroked his hair, relishing its thickness.

'I get a little tired, too,' I continued, 'of waiting and organizing, and of being on show all the time.'

'Not much of a deal, is it?' he confessed. 'For you, I mean. But I honestly don't know what I can do about it.'

A cool little voice in my head said to me that Will was right and there was no point in pursuing the discussion. There wasn't anything to be done – except to live with it. Or was there? The cool little voice unsettled me even further when it added, sympathetically and most seductively: *Fanny, I think you need a holiday from being married.*

The idea made my knees shake. *Only a holiday?*

Will was searching my face for clues as to what I might be thinking and, unnerved by my own subversion, I thought it best to return to the subject of the second-car tax. 'I still think people don't want to be told what's good for them, Will.'

'Listen to me,' he urged and, once again, outlined the arguments for the scheme. I replied, reiterating mine. We found we agreed on one point, disagreed on another. We laughed about a third. Suddenly, our intimacy was back.

'Come upstairs with me, Fanny.'

'Yes,' I said.

'What a touching scene.' Neither of us had heard Meg appear in the doorway.

Will released me and she glided up and gave him a hug. 'Good meeting?' he asked.

She looked calm and collected. 'Winning the battle. I hope. No more scenes.' She looked straight at me. 'I am sorry about that, Fanny. I hope you have forgiven me?'

'Short meeting,' I said.

She raised a quizzical eyebrow at my lack of response and unwound a pink scarf from her neck. 'It's very simple and it can be said in two words. "Don't drink." Even the stupidest can get that message, and I'm not stupid.'

Will regarded her fondly. 'No, you're not.'

'So what were you two talking about?'

I went to check on the fishcakes. 'Second-car tax, what else? But I was rather hoping to discuss the revival of my career.'

She tucked her arm into Will's. 'I'm not up to speed,' she said. 'Tell me all about it.'

I found myself chopping the last tomato with unnecessary vigour.

In keeping with the summer so far, the week of the twenty-first dawned scratchy and unsettled. To prepare for the dinner, I had got myself to the hairdresser and spent three hours reading up the briefing notes supplied by Will's office. Transport Tariffs. Aids. Agricultural initiatives. So far so predictable.

As Will handed me into the car, he surprised me by saying, 'You look lovely.'

'Thank you.'

In a full, black silk skirt and tiny matching jacket, my

hair highlighted and swept back from my forehead, I sat between Antonio Pasquale – we greeted each other warmly – and the charming Italian ambassador. During the first two courses, I was occupied by Antonio and we discussed rubies. He had noted my ring. 'Is there not a passage in the Bible that refers to a good woman being above the price of rubies?' He smiled into my eyes. 'Your husband should have bought you a bigger one.' Conversationally, both of us did well and, as dessert was served and I turned to my right, I was sure he winked at me.

The Italian ambassador was formidably well educated and good-looking. 'Is something amusing you, Mrs Savage?'

'I think your finance minister just winked at me.'

'Can I wink at you too?'

'If you like.'

'Your husband has been energetic lately. He is a notable politician.' He leant towards me. His breath was scented with raspberries and vanilla. 'We just need a little more time to think out his scheme. You know that we've stuck on one or two points.'

Out of the corner of my eye, I saw Will fix his gaze on me. *Don't let me down.*

Teamwork. The spoon in my hand was cool and hard and the raspberries tanged sweetly on my tongue. Once a team, always a team.

'Why don't you talk to him after dinner?'

'Maybe the Prime Minister ... We're not sure how supportive the Prime Minister is ...'

I smiled. 'The Prime Minister is not a personal friend.'

'But perhaps you will remind your husband to consider everyone's interests.'

I put down my spoon. 'You must talk to him yourself.'

The women retired for coffee, leaving the men in the dining room. 'Terrible,' hissed our hostess, in my ear, 'but they like it that way.'

I accepted a cup of coffee. 'Do you ever get tired of it all?'

She looked startled. 'I don't think so. It has its drawbacks but it's an interesting life. Of course, when the children are young . . .'

We went over to join the rest of the wives, who were huddled in a gorgeous group of reds, blues and gold. They were a jolly group, keen to sample the delights of a capital city, and we settled down to discuss facials, shopping and theatre.

I reported the conversation about the Prime Minister to Will when we got back to the flat. 'Point taken,' he said, climbed into bed and reached for the red box.

Lines of fatigue stood out harshly under his eyes. 'Will, would you ever consider doing something different?'

'Not really. Though there are times . . . it used to seem so straightforward. Get elected and start improving the world . . . It isn't that simple, is it? But I don't see myself getting off the treadmill quite yet.'

I turned away and pulled the pillow under my head. The box hit the floor and Will put his arms around me. 'Fanny . . .'

But the distance had opened up between us again, and I struggled with my feelings of indifference . . . and remoteness. Will had almost – but not quite – become a stranger, a troubling kind of stranger: someone I had once known inside out, but who had slipped into acquaintanceship.

'Oh Fanny,' he said at last. He pulled back my arms and caught me by my wrists. 'I miss you . . .'

I made an effort and put my arms around his neck. It was a matter of faith, I think, and effort of will. I had to believe that the passionate feelings we once shared were not completely dead.

It worked.

Afterwards, he said. 'Fanny, that was so nice.'

I smiled and touched his thigh. 'It was.'

I lay awake, listening to the sounds of the city.

I would have given almost anything to be walking on a hot hillside where my father told me that the vines plunged deep through clay and sand. I wanted to squint through the sunlight at a horizon where *Cupressus sempervirens* pointed to the sky, and to see olive trees, fat tomatoes on skinny stakes, the bright green of basil.

I ached, too, for Chloë and wondered where she was. Did her feet hurt, or her back ache? Was she fed and were her clothes clean? Would she cope with . . . the experiences that lay before her?

From the branches of my beech tree at Ember House, I had spied on cars as they negotiated the bend in the road that skirted the garden. If I angled my (plastic, shocking pink) telescope correctly, I got a good view of the occupants. Often, when a car slowed, the women passengers flipped down the sunshade to check their lipstick in the mirror. Occasionally, the driver wound down the window and chucked out rubbish. This behaviour made me conclude that people were very peculiar.

It was on my eighteenth birthday that I took Raoul up to my eyrie; we clawed and cursed our way up in the dark. For once, Raoul had drunk too much wine, and I was wearing delicate, strappy sandals. The platform groaned under the weight of our bodies, and we embraced clumsily. My thin cotton dress split at the seam when Raoul tugged too hard and he pounced on the tongue of flesh which appeared. 'So brown,' he murmured, and wrenched off his shirt.

Inexperience and ignorance made me shrink and Raoul was unnecessarily rough. We had no saving grace of humour, only a grim determination to get the deed done.

'I'm sorry, I'm sorry,' Raoul murmured at last. He lifted a face sheened with sweat. 'I love you.'

But I pushed him away.

That was unfair of me.

A tree-house is no place for seduction. It belongs to childhood . . . to a different place. Now, it was spoilt.

That night, I quit my tree-house in more ways than one.

I turned over in bed and considered the aspects of my life. The rubies and crimsons, the frail gold and amber of wine. My father. Will. Meg. Sacha.

Pushing my daughter towards Departure . . .

9

. . . as I had pushed her into life.

The first contraction took me by surprise when I was eating an early supper in Will's flat. Alone.

I was thirty-nine weeks pregnant and, when I reflected on the rapidity of the changes in my life, it seemed to me that I had barely known Will for much longer.

The six o'clock news flashed up on the television screen and, in perfect synchronicity, Will rang to say that he would be in a meeting for most of the evening and not to keep supper for him. I felt soggy, pregnant and apprehensive, and it flashed across my mind that Will loved his work more than he loved me. Worse, he understood it better than he did me, and *preferred* to be doing it rather than having supper with his wife.

'Fine,' I said. 'Dinner in dog.'

'Miss me?'

I bit my lip. 'No.'

'I take that to be yes. Do *both* of you miss me?'

At my end, a smile forced its way to my lips. 'No . . . Yes.'

Like an animal, I had gone underground. I had become blind and subterranean, blundering through the days. On one level I craved Will's presence and attention but almost . . . almost he had become superfluous, for I was wrapped up in the female parcel, an enormous, bulky object with embarrassing aches and pains. The books had informed me about backache, varicose veins and a host of other ailments, and explained the body invasion with diagrams. None, however, owned up as to how thoroughly one's mind was invaded. How the broad-bean-cum-ammonite sucked dry the rivers of wit, energy, calculation and inventiveness until there was nothing left except a vague, dreamy nothingness.

With Will frequently not around, and without the energy to visit friends, there was no one in whom I could confide my feelings, and I had fallen into the habit of talking aloud to myself. 'I feel like softened butter, underdone jam, a melting snowman,' I informed the grill pan as I cleaned it, a task that, these days, represented the level of my achievements.

So be it.

Shortly after Will, my father rang to check my progress. He sounded startled. 'You're alone? This is wrong. Someone should be there. What if something went wrong?'

'Don't panic, Dad. It's fine.'

He sounded angry. 'Is there anyone who could come over?'

'Dad, it's only six thirty and Will promised to be back later.'

'Even so . . .' In the background, his second phone shrilled. 'Got to go,' he said. 'I'll keep in touch.'

The first contraction made me shift in my seat in an effort to ease the ache. Fifteen minutes later, a second was intrusive enough to make me shove aside my plate of salad and heave myself to my feet.

I pressed my hand into the small of my back and walked

the five paces or so that measured the length of the room. Then I turned and went back, feeling the weight bear down on my knees. One step too many and they'd snap, I thought. Down I would fall.

More contractions sent shocks through my body.

I would have given much to be sitting up in my tree with a bottle of bright fizzy drink, surveying my domain and practising swearing.

What if I rang up Will and said, 'I'm handing over to you. *You* do this, not me?'

A phone call to the House elicited the information that Will had left half an hour previously and had not left a contact number. I tried his bleeper but it was switched off.

I rang Elaine, who came straight to the point: 'Husbands do this. Mine's probably with yours. Would you like me to come to the hospital?'

I thought this over. Friendship was sweet but no substitute for Will. I thanked her and asked, 'Could you ring my father? Tell him I'm on my way to hospital.'

From then on I don't remember the fine detail, only the general picture, for which I am grateful. The midwife said that was because it happened so fast, which was unusual for a first baby. I do have one fixed image in my memory, of hovering above a large, thrashing, sweating figure, who, with a shock, I recognized as myself. The room was licked by shadows, lit only by a dim light. A midwife merged in and out of it. Sometimes she spoke to me. Sometimes I answered.

Soon I changed my mind about wishing to be alone. I wanted someone to hold my hand and pull me back from the person on the delivery bed. I craved the touch of someone who loved me, and wept for my pain and Will's absence.

'Look who's here . . .' The midwife appeared by the bedside and, wild-eyed, I reared up expecting to see the tall, fair-haired figure of my husband.

'Hey,' said Meg. 'Your father rang.' She was wrapped in a black jumper that was too big for her and, despite the heat in the room, shivering. Traces of whisky hung on her breath.

I fought the impulse to turn away my face. 'Isn't Will coming?'

'He's on his way,' she said, and picked up my hand. 'I think.' Her cold touch was like a burn, and I wished her anywhere but there.

Then things began to happen. Meg stood beside the bed, wiped my face and informed me I was doing fine, and it was Meg who, other than the midwife, was the first person to see Chloë.

She was born at twenty-five to twelve, without the aid of drugs. 'What a good girl,' said the midwife. 'What a brave, *good* girl. So much better for Baby if Mummy does it all herself.'

She placed Chloë on my stomach, a still pale and muted ammonite. Until that moment, I had been preoccupied with the heroic and peculiar physical achievements of my body. Now there was a moment of hush, of expectation. I looked down. How extraordinary, I thought. This is what a forced nine-month occupation of my body and an undignified battle on a delivery bed results in. Then Chloë turned her face in my direction and screwed up her eyes.

Her hand reached into the air as if she was grasping for

her life. That tiny hand unleashed an invisible silken cord, looped it into a cunning lasso, aimed it towards my heart and, with one flex of those shrimpy pink fingers, secured it.

'She's perfect,' Meg leant over to inspect her, and there was a yearning note in her voice. 'I think I should be godmother, don't you?'

She left when Will burst into the room a short while later. 'I'm so sorry, so very sorry.' Unsure of whether or not to touch me, he hovered by the bed. 'I'll never ever do that again. I'll never not check.'

'Your daughter's over there, Will.'

He took a chance and slid his arm round my shoulders and kissed me. He was very, very disappointed and furious with himself. 'It was a late sitting. Regulations about child labour in East and British manufacturers. I don't blame you if you are angry.'

'Not angry . . . empty.'

'I switched off the bleeper, forgot, and went off for a quick supper at Brazzi's. I've missed out, haven't I?'

His guilt was almost comic, but it was sad too. For he *had* missed out – on that special, perfect moment when Chloë tumbled into the world.

The backwash of exhaustion, discomfort and spent hormones was draining my strength. 'Go and look at your beautiful daughter. Then please ring Dad . . . and my mother. I promised her that you would.'

'I hope you forgive me?'

Of course I did. Chloë was here, well and safe and, set against that, there was nothing to forgive.

*

We moved into the new house in Stanwinton when Chloë was two weeks old. I had been reluctant to stir from the safety of the flat but Will had insisted we observe the agreed timetable. 'We can manage,' he said, when I produced excuses about feeding and crying and nappy-changing, all of which still appeared in the light of a complex mathematical theory. 'It is the right thing to do to take our new daughter to our new house.'

Still sore and battered, I struggled to do my best and Will, still repentant for his non-showing at her birth, tried to make up for it by packing, ferrying and driving. I was not to do *anything*. This seemed reasonable for I did not *wish* to do anything.

'I don't want to get up, cook, wash clothes, even think.' Since the birth, my voice had sounded different even to me. I put it down to hoarseness from my cries but I almost believed it was because I was changing so profoundly.

Will took this type of comment touchingly seriously. 'It's normal to feel down after a baby.'

'How do you know?'

'I read about it in the books.' I did not bother to respond to that, and he pressed on: 'You'll feel better once you're settled in the house. I'll be back every Friday.'

I almost felt sorry for him, so desperate was he to make things right.

The fields were bristling with stubble as our heavily laden car nosed between them, and the leaves on the beeches swayed in the breeze. From the back of the car where I sat with Chloë, I looked out on the fields. Like them or not, they were going to be companion presences.

Mannochie was waiting at the front door. The professional smile deepened into the genuine article as he helped me out of the car. 'Welcome to you all,' he said, in a quaintly formal way. On cue, Chloë woke up and began to cry. 'May I?' asked Mannochie, and picked her up. Would you know? Chloë stopped crying.

'I didn't know you were good with babies, Mannochie.'

'She's lovely.' Mannochie was rocking Chloë in a way she liked.

Will peered over his shoulder. 'She is, isn't she?'

I left them to it and stepped over the threshold. The men had been hard at work on the house for the last few weeks, and it had been decorated, with cheap job lots from a DIY store, and carpets had been laid.

The freshly varnished banisters felt a little sticky under my hand as I went upstairs and the virgin carpet was slippery underfoot. The first thing I did in our bedroom was tug open the window and allow the fresh air to dilute the fug of fresh paint.

My body ached and my mind was as dull and spongy as batter that had been allowed to stand overlong. Except when I looked at Chloë, I felt cold and distanced, without life and energy.

Somewhere, far away, a baby was crying. Resentment flickered: I had lost what I now saw as the privilege of being alone.

Mannochie padded upstairs. 'Chloë's crying.'

I did not move. 'I know.'

He tried again. 'She seems hungry.'

I knew I should close the window and go downstairs. But I wanted to remain at my vantage-point, observe the rooks wheeling above their eyries and the gun-metal sky.

Mannochie touched my arm. A non-threatening, polite gesture. 'Fanny, have you seen the doctor lately?'

Tears ran down beside my mouth. I had lost something. My tree-house and the freedom I had known up in the branches were in another country, far, far away. Without a doubt, I would grow older – and old – and never again go there.

My tears were also fearful: I was frightened I would be unable to perform in my roles, that I could not *cope*, let alone soar to the heights of managing house and baby brilliantly.

I put out my tongue and tasted salt. 'Why would I need a doctor?'

'*Fanny*!' Will appeared in the doorway with a screaming Chloë.

Reluctantly, I turned. 'Give her to me.'

He thrust her into my arms and peered at me. 'Are you OK?'

'Fine,' I said.

The men returned downstairs, and while they brought in the luggage I sat down with Chloë and fed her. Enchanted, enraptured and angry, I watched the busy little button mouth, the little veins in the almost transparent eyelids. 'You're a greedy minx,' I informed her.

Chloë took no notice. After she had finished, her head fell back and she slept. Gradually, the jangle of feelings inside me subsided.

Will came up with a cup of tea and watched us fondly. His presence was calming and, suddenly, I felt almost peaceful and happy.

'Here,' he said, and settled me against his shoulder, and took Chloë on to his lap. 'Just sit for a while. There's no hurry.

'I love you both very much,' he added.

'OK, ready,' called the photographer from the *Stanwinton Echo*. The camera flashed. 'Again,' he commanded.

I tried to hide my still bulky stomach behind Will.

'Smile and look to the left.'

The experience was not as bad as I had feared. It fact it was fun to be the focus of attention and, at any other time, I might have taken to it.

'Could we have the baby now, please?'

The one thing that Will and I agreed on absolutely was to stick to the principle of keeping Chloë out of photographs and publicity. Yet, here we were, with Chloë only a month old, in the town hall at a press conference. It was, we agreed, a minor emergency.

A more senior MP had been taken ill, and Will had been press-ganged into a TV discussion panel on transport. In the heat of the moment, he fumbled over a phrase, which made it sound as if he was taking the opposite view to party policy, which was a big, black mark against him.

After the programme, he had driven home to Stan-winton and, during the night, had been very sick. I held his head and mopped up and made him tea.

He drank it gratefully and muttered, 'I do this sometimes when things go wrong. Silly, isn't it?'

His confession touched me deeply and I sat up with him into the small hours while we tried to work out the best damage limitation plan.

The morning papers reported on the programme and picked out Will for special mention. 'Fluency with integrity,' wrote one (upmarket) critic. 'A Prince Charming delivers,' wrote another (downmarket). Mannochie got on the phone and they agreed some well-focused local publicity would go a long way to propping up his image in the constituency.

One of the reporters asked, 'How do you feel about being the most glamorous couple in Parliament?'

A girl in leather trousers stuck up a finger. 'Are you feeding the baby yourself, Mrs Savage?'

Mannochie intervened. 'If you wish to question Will on policy, now is the moment.'

The girl made a face. *Policy? Get real!*

Relaxed and smiling, Will allowed the photographers to take as many shots as they wished and answered all their questions. Then I spotted the expression in his eyes that was neither patient nor obedient. It was a private expression that only I could interpret – a signpost to the secret, erotic territory that we shared – and it made my senses quiver.

Mannochie had arranged that I would give one interview and I retreated with Chloë, who was behaving beautifully, into a smaller room with the girl in leather trousers whose name was Lucy.

She set down a tape-recorder between us. 'How do you see the role of today's political wife?'

'It's developing . . .' I replied. In the sudden quiet, my exhilaration vanished, my bones almost burned with fatigue, and the weight of my broken nights hung like oil paintings under my eyes.

'So, not the traditional helpmeet, then?'

'Wives are different from the way they used to be.'

'Would you vote differently from your husband?'

'If I felt it was right.'

She looked extra sympathetic. 'Given that political marriages are, for obvious reasons, at risk, do you think you can hack it with motherhood and a career?'

I resented the implication that Will and I were doomed. 'I am not prepared to answer that question,' I said. 'As you will have noticed, my baby is still very young.'

From that moment, the interview limped.

Two days later, the article was published. The headline read: 'Sceptical and Independent, the Modern MP's Wife Votes against Her Husband'. The text read: 'Fanny Savage is one of a new breed: a modern woman with a career and a mind of her own. If she felt it was right, she would vote for the opposition.'

Pearl Veriker rang while I was still in bed feeding Chloë, and read the article out over the phone. 'That was so unwise, Fanny. A betrayal, even.'

With a sick feeling, I realized that Pearl's rulebook was more complicated than I had thought. 'Pearl, I am entitled to my own views, and this is hardly treason.'

But, as with the wearing of tights, it seemed that there was no room for negotiation. In the end, I handed the phone over to Will and listened to him finessing Pearl back into calm.

This particular mess *was* my fault. I knew it, and Will knew it. He slumped back on to the pillow. 'We discussed it so carefully,' he said.

I rubbed my hands over my eyes. 'She got me on the raw.'

Will swung himself out of bed, ripped off the T-shirt in which he slept and dropped it on the floor. 'We talked about that, too.'

'Could I point out to the Honourable Member that the first mistake was his?'

'And I've paid for it twice.'

I nuzzled Chloë's cheek. She smelt of milk and baby lotion, innocent, innocuous, ordinary, honest things. I visualized my culpability stretching out like a gauzy vapour trail through an endless sky. Had I ruined Will? Set a mark on him – *unreliable* – like Cain? 'I'm sorry. I forgot how hard it is not to say what you think.'

Will wrenched open the shirt drawer. 'Hasn't it been made plain enough to you? Never, ever say what you think.'

There was a long, odd silence as we each absorbed the implications of what the other had said.

'Will, don't you think it is slightly strange that, in order to appear honest and transparent, we have to pretend?'

Will picked out a blue shirt and examined the collar. 'I know.' He looked up at me, perplexed, and more than a little aghast. 'I *know*.'

My father was horrified when I rang up, almost incoherent with exhaustion and sobs, and reported on my latest lapse. 'I am coming over,' he said. 'Give me an hour to sort out some things.'

He arrived to the minute. 'You're coming back with me to Ember House,' he announced. 'I've phoned Benedetta and she's flying over to take charge.'

'You've phoned Benedetta? You've made up with her?'

A foolish smile spread over my face. 'Oh, Dad, I so long to see her.' Then I said, 'I can't abandon Will.'

'Will can come to Ember House at the weekends. It's simple.' He hugged me close. I hustled him into my cluttered, muddled kitchen and shoved a basket of Chloë's laundered clothes out of sight under the table with my foot. 'Sorry it's so untidy, but I'm too tired to tackle the cleaning.'

He threw his car keys on to the table. 'You're my daughter and you need help. You'd better come now. The house is ready.'

'All right.' I sat down with a sense of dizzy relief.

I rang Will and told him I was going home with my father. 'Just for a couple of weeks.'

'What do you mean "going home"?' He was offended. 'I thought home was with me.'

'Sorry. Slip of the tongue.' But it made heavy weather of our conversation and, not for the first time, I wished we did not have to discuss plans, issues, developments by phone.

'Do you mind? It would do Chloë and me good.'

'I notice you've just gone ahead.' But, in the end, he said, 'Of course you must go. Of course, you must have some help.'

I put down the phone and noticed the layer of dust that roosted on one of the ugly radiator cases. I was too tired to fetch a duster. I blew on it instead. The dust lifted and settled back. 'Go away,' I ordered it. 'Pack your suitcase and go somewhere else.'

*

When we arrived at Ember House, my father snatched Chloë from me. 'Look at her! Already a beauty.'

'And clever, Dad. She has us all running around after her.'

Chloë peered up at her grandfather. He sat down and propped her on his knee. 'I won't make the same mistakes with you.'

'You didn't make mistakes,' I said. 'You were the best father.'

He shrugged. 'There were times when I felt like packing the whole thing in and despatching you to your mother. But, of course, I didn't.'

I busied myself with a stack of Chloë's nappies. 'Was I in the way?' Suddenly, I was close to tears.

'Francesca, you haven't grasped my point. Once you arrived, I simply could not have been without you. I wanted you to be there and I strove to adapt in whichever way it took.' He stroked Chloë's chubby cheek. 'You'll find out.'

I watched the interaction between grandfather and granddaughter. I had already found out. I wiped my eyes surreptitiously and smiled at him. For a moment or two, the room was charged with love, the uncomplicated, unconditional sort that made me feel better and stronger.

Chloë opened her mouth and began to yell. My breasts prickled and seeped. Quick as a flash, my father handed her back to me.

Nothing had changed at Ember House. It was peaceful, solid, shabby and, above all, familiar. It allowed me to be sleepy and doe-like. It knew me, and I knew it. No surprises. No adjustments necessary. Father had been right. I needed this interlude and, with the arrival of Benedetta, a burden dropped from my shoulders.

'*Santa Patata*, you are pale,' she said. 'You must eat liver. I will cook it for you.'

Naturally she took charge, and it was as if the intervening years had not happened – and Benedetta had not been married and widowed, nor had I grown up. She issued orders in the foreground and fussed in the background – washing and folding Chloë's tiny clothes, making sure I slept in the afternoon, whisking Chloë away when she was fretful after her evening feed. 'You are my *bambina* Fanny, and I look after my *bambina's bambina*.' The inflections and rhythms of her voice roused many, oh, so many, dormant echoes of my childhood.

They were clever, my father and Benedetta. And generous. Despite their past, they united to give me the space and peace to concentrate on Chloë. I learnt that one kind of cry meant hunger, another that she was uncomfortable or bored. With Benedetta's advice, conducted in her broken English and my Italian, which had always required improvement, I learnt to anticipate Chloë's needs – when to feed, when to put her to sleep, when she might require additional soothing. Under Benedetta's tuition, I began to flex the muscles necessary to carry, lightly and gracefully, the weight of change and of motherhood.

10

The day before I returned home from that stay with my father was cool and blustery. I pushed open the sitting-room french windows and stepped outside. The smell of the garden never changed: damp earth, a sharp, acrid whiff of mould, the sweeter tang of the shrubs growing close by. The lawn was wet, the earth soft, and my feet left a predictable trail as I made for the beech tree. It looked the same and its sounds were familiar – the rustle of leaves, the whistle of wind, the fractured light shafting through the thick canopy.

I squinted upwards. The tree-house appeared to be intact still. I ran my hands over my hips, felt their extra fullness and softness. *Go on, Fanny.* Smiling, I placed my hand on the first branch and hauled myself up. Easy. Then I scrambled up inch by inch to the platform. Not so easy.

Yet once up there, queasily balanced on the now unsteady planks, I was, fleetingly, queen of all I surveyed.

The breeze released a shower of moisture from previous rain and I put my hand to my mouth and licked it. Clean and cool. Up here, I felt weightless, without responsibility, without the terrors that came wrapped up with a baby. Peaceful. Not precisely how I used to be, but good enough.

Gradually, my jangled feelings lightened and drifted away.

That evening, to cheer me up, my father held a little party.

It was quite like old times. My high heels felt strange from disuse and I squeezed myself into a tight black skirt, wincing at the pad of fat still attached to my stomach, and stood in the receiving line with my pelvis tilted forward and my toes pinched, and felt wonderfully normal.

The guests were wine people and I knew them all, including Raoul who was over for a short visit. We were often a little awkward with each other, but it tended to wear off. 'How's the nose?' he asked as he kissed me. As pregnancy was known to affect the nose, it was the first question he would have asked.

'I don't know,' I said seriously. 'I shall have to see.'

Raoul had olive skin, an interesting, sensitive face and liked to dress well. Today, for some reason, he had a scratch on his cheek which gave him a bold and buccaneering look.

'What happened?'

'I was hacking down some undergrowth back home and it hit me, but I haven't congratulated you,' he said. 'I hope when the baby is older you will make sure you pay us a visit. My family would love to see her.'

'I would love that, too.'

In France, passion for good wine was part of the national psyche – it is what makes the French consider themselves French, apart from their language. Thus the Villeneuves would consider it only their due that they lived in the most exquisite château I had ever seen.

He peered at me. 'You look a little tired, Fanny. I know it's hard after a baby to get back to normal.'

Again, I felt those treacherous tears and I looked away, down at the carpet that I helped to choose with Caro many years ago.

'My father will be retiring soon, and I will be taking over.'

How perfect, I thought. Raoul's life is now arranged like an immaculately set dinner table. Well off, position assured. Doing what he loves. Knife, fork, spoon . . . and wine glass.

'What's so funny?' he asked.

I told Raoul and he said he considered that the interesting bit in life would prove to be when one has worked through the *hors d'oeuvre* and was half-way through the entrée.

'We must discuss it when we get there,' I said.

Before I left for home, my father and I had a serious talk about the business and I began to understand more precisely my own limits. My new world. 'I think we should consider employing someone else to help me until Chloë is well launched. There's no hurry for you to come back. You need time.'

I was not sure if I was hurt or relieved. 'I can't imagine not working,' I said.

My father looked at me thoughtfully. 'I understand. But I think for the moment, you must put Chloë first.'

After a little struggle, I gave in. 'I want you to know I can cope, but you're probably right. It would be wiser for the time being. Why don't you ask if Raoul could come over and help out for a month or two.'

'I already have,' said my father. 'I can't put my granddaughter at risk. Nor your health.'

I digested his sleight of hand.

'By the way, he tells me he is going to marry Thérèse. Very suitable.' Thérèse, I knew, was the daughter of a fellow *negociant* family, also very well off. He smiled. 'So, it has all worked out, hasn't it? What's the matter, my love? Didn't he tell you?'

I wanted to go home. I missed Will and, now that I felt stronger, I needed to be in my own domain. The idea of it was growing clearer and more urgent: the notion of drawing the curtains, lighting the fire and tucking my daughter into a cheerful bedroom decorated with Beatrix Potter's Peter Rabbit.

'Now, you take care,' said my father, holding me close.

'Now, *you* take care.' I kissed his cheek, so familiar beneath my lips.

With his instructions about getting some help ringing in my ears, I got into the car and drove away.

The laurel hedge was still the same dispiriting colour and rooks dived over the beeches. No change there. I carried Chloë into the kitchen and slotted her into her bouncer. 'My best girl,' I told her, and her mouth split into such a lovely grin that I could not resist picking her up again. She smelt of baby, and was so small and trusting that I knew I would die to protect one tiny fair curl from harm.

On the Thursday afternoon, Elaine Miller dropped in on her way north to visit her mother. 'Amy thought you might need a helping word. Not a helping hand, mind. Just so we're straight.'

I gave her a kiss. 'The pastoral care can't be faulted.'

'Solidarity in numbers, Fanny.'

I served her shop-bought quiche and salad, and we scraped at the filling because the pastry was soggy. Chloë danced in her baby chair beside us and made ever-increasing eye-contact. Elaine's children rampaged in the garden.

Elaine asked for more, and filled my kitchen with energy and crackle. 'Listen, love, this is the worst bit. Once you're through it, you can take stock.' She cast her eyes over the battered old stove and the china stacked on the sideboard, which I had not got round to stowing. 'Could be nice here.'

Over coffee, she gave more advice. 'You'd better have something that's yours. An interest, your job ... otherwise ...' Now, she was serious. 'You don't know that yet, but you will.' Her mouth stretched in a taut, painful smile. 'Neil sleeps with his secretary. It happens. Some of 'em consider it part of the package. Don't worry, for me it's neither here nor there.'

'So you *are* a trouper.'

'So will you be. I can tell.'

Later, after Elaine had gone, Will surprised me by sneaking into the bathroom where I was bathing Chloë and slid his hands round my waist. 'Hallo, Mrs Savage. Please don't go away again.'

I twisted round to kiss him. 'I had planned to be all beautiful, shiny-haired and lipsticked for you.'

He swept the damp hair away from my neck and pressed his mouth on to the exposed skin and I gasped. 'Careful, I'll drop Chloë.'

Later on, we sat down to supper and Will produced a bottle of wine. 'I want you to approve my choice. I've been doing some homework.'

'Have you?' I felt extraordinarily pleased and excited. I raised my glass and sniffed. Rich and warm. Tannin and blackcurrant. 'Perfect, Will. Eight out of ten. No, nine . . .'

'It isn't *that* good.' His eyes danced above the rim of the glass. 'Not one word about politics, tonight. Promise.' He took another sip. 'So, first off, do you love me?'

We were half-way through our roast chicken when Chloë woke up with a touch of colic. When I finally made it back downstairs, Will was on the phone – deep in conversation with a colleague about an upcoming piece of income-tax legislation. I poked at my congealed chicken and listened in to a one-sided conversation about who in the party was likely to rebel, who would not, and the likely consequences.

Will was talking easily, rapidly, absorbed and intent. The lazy intimacy – the give and take of exchange, the delight in each other's company – of our supper table had vanished. By the time he had convinced his colleague that an extra penny on income tax was vital to fund a social programme, I was on a second helping of fruit salad.

Will yawned. 'Bed, I think.'

At this point in the evening, I needed no persuading. We lay with our arms wrapped around each other and, almost immediately, Will fell asleep.

It seemed no time at all before Chloë demanded her night feed. She was fractious and grizzly and when at last I backed away from the cot, hardly daring to breathe, I was chilled and shaking with exhaustion.

Will had turned on the light and was sitting propped up

on the pillows. He looked up and said, 'Fanny, I've had an idea which I've been mulling over. I meant to talk it over at supper.' Then he dropped his bombshell. 'I've been trying to think what's best for everyone. For us, and Chloë, and Sacha. And Meg. Meg has got to move out of her flat because the area is being redeveloped and she's looking for somewhere else. I know it's a really big thing to ask, a huge thing, but I feel it makes sense . . .'

'You're right,' I said, as the implications of his idea sank in. 'It is too big a thing to ask.'

He picked up my cold hand and kissed the fingers, one by one. 'Listen to me. I've worked it out. We could turn the scullery into a kitchen for Meg and give her the rooms above as a bedroom and sitting room. There's plenty of space in this house, and the alterations would be worth doing anyway. I can do some things.'

I had heard that before. 'Will, you know you won't . . . Anyway, that's beside the point.'

There was a lengthy silence.

Will broke it first. 'Families should help each other, shouldn't they, Fanny? Meg is miserable, needs a home. I thought that this might be a way to keep an eye on her.'

I let my hand rest in his. 'Will, I don't want *anyone* living with us. It's enough being with you and Chloë.'

'I know, I feel that too, but . . .' Up went a questioning eyebrow. 'You like Meg, don't you? She says she can talk to you.'

Meg had told me the story of her broken marriage, her battle with the bottle and her anguish when Sacha was taken away to live with his father because of her drinking. Meg had become estranged from all she cared about – her ex-husband ('a saint whose patience snapped'), and her son (who was only permitted to see her at weekends). I had felt very sad for her, and completely helpless.

'Of course, I like Meg,' I said hurriedly. 'I like lots of people. I *love* lots of people, but I don't want to live with them.'

Will pulled me close. 'Listen, Fanny. Here's a chance to practise what we preach. But not just for the sake of a cause, for the sake of my *sister* . . .'

'But Will, this is a marriage, not a . . . charity.'

I sensed he was struggling with the legacy of an old, difficult history. 'Fanny, when I really needed her, she was there for me,' he said simply. 'It doesn't seem fair for me to turn my back on her now . . .' He brightened. 'Also, we don't have much money to buy enormous amounts of help, and you need help. Meg can do her bit. You could spend more time in London . . . I think it will help our marriage.'

'No,' I said. 'No, I don't think it is a good idea.'

He looked down at our clasped hands and made a final appeal. 'She's losing her flat and she hasn't got a job at the moment; she can't cope. I owe her so much. In one way or another, her life has turned out pretty badly, and I can't help feeling that quite a lot of that is my fault.'

It was a long time before I got to sleep.

When I woke, Will was beside the bed with Chloë draped over his shoulder. 'She's hungry,' he said. 'I didn't know what to do with her.'

Everything had changed. The room swam and my heart pounded in protest. Every nerve in my body screamed with exhaustion. Downstairs, a basket of dirty washing required attention. There was not much food in the fridge, and dust still crusted the radiator. I pushed my hair out of my eyes, and pulled myself upright. 'Give her to me.'

Will laid Chloë in my arms and I put her to suckle. 'You win,' I said to Will. 'Meg can come and live here. But only for a few months, until everyone is straightened out. Just till I'm back on my feet and she's feeling better.'

It all happened very quickly, and while the house at Stanwinton was being altered to accommodate Meg (Will did not find the time to do any DIY), I flew with Chloë to see my mother in Montana. Father was dead set against the idea. 'Why bother?' he demanded, with a rare flash of bitterness. 'You can come and live here while the house is a mess, if that's the problem.'

'She has a right to see her granddaughter.'

'Nothing stopping *her* getting on a plane.'

Sally was waiting for us by the barrier at the airport. I had not seen her for three years, and it took me a moment or two to recognize her – she could have been any one of the middle-aged women dressed in tracksuits or capacious jeans and fleeces who milled around the concourse. Sad or funny? My mother was somewhere in that crowd and I wasn't sure who she was.

Finally I spotted her in a brown suede jacket with hair – frizzy and overlong – settled round a pale, freckled face innocent of make-up. Arms folded, she was leaning on the barrier and looked scared. Big, burly Art was beside her, smiling benignly as he scanned the arrivals. His baggy jeans and checked shirt were deceptive: he made a good living. Granted, property in Montana was not like property in New York, but there was plenty of it and more space.

'Hi!' cried Sally, in a voice from which all traces of her English origins had long gone. She kissed my cheek briefly, embarrassed, and turned to Chloë. 'Why, *hallo*!'

I relinquished Chloë and Art pumped my hand up and down. 'We sure appreciate this,' he said. 'Sally has been unreal with nerves for the past few days. Haven't known what to do with her.'

Out of the corner of my eye, I saw my mother give a tiny shrug.

Sally and I sat in the back of the station-wagon with Chloë between us while Art drove extra carefully through the town and out the other side. He did not say much but his was an easy silence. Sally did not say much either, except 'Hasn't changed much since you were last here. More houses, which is a pity.'

Paradiseville had been so named because at the height of gold fever it was thought a seam ran through the mountain foothills to the south and a cluster of tin and wooden shacks had mushroomed down by the river. It had grown from there.

Art gave a satisfied laugh. 'That's fine by me. Good business, don't knock it.'

'A person can comment,' Sally said sharply.

I had forgotten that the landscape of Montana was a spectacle on the scale of grand opera or a wide-screen cinema epic. Nature was big here. It was like walking into a great golden tidal wave into which red and ochre had been mixed. But the details were lovely too. Cobnuts lay on the ground and spilled their tender contents out of their husks, berries dozed in the hedgerows, and horses grazed against a backdrop of mountain.

I pointed all this out to Chloë, who took no notice.

To be honest, I remembered the house better than I remembered my mother. Constructed of clapboard, which had been painted off-white, it had a balcony that ran round it, and a swinging seat at the front, where I knew I would sit and rock Chloë.

Sally slid out of the station-wagon. 'I didn't know what stuff you needed so I asked Ma Frobber down the way. She put me right and lent me her stuff. She's had six.' Sally smiled a little anxiously. 'Hope it's OK.'

It was fine, except that Chloë was jet-lagged and refused to sleep for most of the first night. Naturally, in the small house, her crying was magnified and, as I strove desperately to pacify her, the light was switched on more than once in Sally and Art's room.

After breakfast, I sat on the swing seat with her. Sally plumped up a cushion which had a black horse embroidered on it and wedged herself beside me. 'I had forgotten,' she peered down at Chloë, 'how awful it is.' She rolled up the sleeves of her shirt, revealing freckled forearms. 'I was no good at it at all,' she confessed. 'I've got no advice or handy tips.'

'I'm not sure I've got the hang of it yet, either.'

'I reckon a person is given only one talent. Mine's for horses. I always thought if you could cope with horses, you could cope with the kids. But it doesn't work out like that.'

Chloë began to grizzle and Sally set the seat to rock, which seemed to settle her, and we sat there, talking of nothing much, until the sun slid round and hit us hard. Then we retreated to the kitchen. With one foot on the borrowed baby-bouncer, I drank bitter coffee and jiggled Chloë while Sally prepared a meal of stew and carrots for later.

I tried not to stare at my mother, but I couldn't help it. So much of her – how she walked with a little drag of her right foot, the mole on her arm – reminded me of myself. Could I edge closer and try to cross the barrier of time and our history? It was impossible. All we shared was a set of genes, and that was not enough.

Now I had Chloë I perceived my mother from a different perspective. I knew what it was like to hold a tiny person against my body and I knew that they depended on you absolutely. Thus, the question, *How could you have brought yourself to leave me?* trembled on my lips. But I did not ask it. A silence between a mother and a daughter should be (should it not?) an expression of years of mutual history. *My mother smacked me when I stole money out of her pocket. My mother made me wear a dress with smocking in coral pink silk. My mother promised me a hundred pounds if I did not smoke.* But there was nothing between Sally and me except a gap. Not a hostile gap, we did not know each other well enough for that, just an unfilled space.

Sally chopped vigorously at a carrot. 'How is your father?'

Sally would have had to nerve herself to ask the question and I was careful with the reply. 'I don't think he ever got over you,' I said.

She put down the knife and wiped her hands on her apron. 'Yes, he did. He knew perfectly well that we . . . did not suit each other. He wanted one thing, I wanted another. In the end, I chose for him.'

'You make it sound so simple.'

Sally switched on a gas-ring and slapped down a frying-pan. 'It was. If two people can't live together, one of them has to go. Anyway, I'd met Art so I went. It was better that you stayed with Alfredo.'

I bent over to check that the strap holding Chloë was tight enough. 'I used to search for you in the street. I made up stories about you and imagined you might fly into my bedroom at night. I used to try to stay awake in case you did.'

Sally went very still. 'That's a lot to put on a person.' She tipped the meat into the pan and the snap and hiss of frying filled the kitchen. 'I wish I could say I watched over you, but that's the way it is. Not all women manage what is expected of them, and I don't see why I should be guilty, Fanny. You had Alfredo, who loved you.'

'Sure,' I said.

'Pass me the casserole on the table.'

I got up and took it over to her. The phone rang and Sally answered it. I spooned cubes of meat and the carrots into the casserole, added some stock, and put it into the oven.

The next day I was awake early and stretched out in the old cotton-spool bed in the spare room under a patchwork quilt, watching sunlight slide like melted butter over the wall. Outside, a bird sounded in the larches, and a breeze rollicked through the branches. This was a wilder, wider place than home, with a bigger horizon. Sally had left my father for Art, a simple love triangle, but I reckoned, warm and sleepy in bed, that it had been as much to do with the wind in the larches and a horizon that marched out of sight as anything else.

'Come and see the horses,' Sally said, after we had had breakfast, and led the way up to the paddocks behind the house. There were seven of her shaggy-maned, large-eyed darlings milling around and, at the sound of her voice, they came over to us and jostled for attention. Rapt and confident, Sally talked to each one. 'Here, Vince. Here, Melly . . .'

Not sure about them, Chloë squirmed in my arms, and I longed to be as assured in my handling of her as Sally was with her horses.

Sally took Chloë. 'Go on. Make friends.'

I touched the hot, fragrant hides and soft muzzles. Chloë blinked and Sally guided her small hand towards a steamy flank. 'Nice horse, Chloë,' she said. 'When you're old enough, you must come and visit and I'll teach you to ride.'

A sour taste flooded into my mouth. With a shock, I realized I was jealous of my own daughter. I busied myself with Melly's mane and struggled to bring myself to order.

The moment passed.

Melly's neck was corrugated with muscle. I ran my hand over it, enjoying the feel of her damp coat. 'I wonder how Will is?'

'What sort of man is he?' Sally batted Melly's nose gently out of Chloë's orbit. 'Would he like it here?'

'I think so. But he hasn't time to come.'

Sally gave me back Chloë and swung herself over the

fence. Her horses swirled around her and she attached a leading-rein to Melly's head-collar, grasped a handful of the golden mane and swung herself up. In daylight she seemed older, but the thighs under her denims were toned and strong. 'Art gives himself plenty of time. That's the difference.' She turned Melly, then trotted her to the end of the paddock and back again. 'Just testing. We've had trouble with her hock. But she's fine.'

In the distance, Art's station-wagon was nosing down the track towards us. It slowed and he wound down the window. The sound of country-and-western shattered the peace. 'Thought I'd make a detour,' he said, 'to say hi to you ladies.'

He drove on. 'Now, that's what I call passing the test,' said Sally fondly. 'Most days he does that.' She slid down from Melly's back and leant against the picket fence. Once more, her horses closed in on her.

I felt the download of sadness, anger even, that my father had not passed Sally's test. 'You must get tired looking after the horses.'

Sally squinted into the sun, which emphasized the fan-light of lines around her eyes. 'You get tired of everything. The question is, what do you tire of least? My horses are easy and uncomplicated. They want feeding, grooming, and exercising, and they might, in return, love a person a little. But not too much. It's not their nature. I know that. And because I know that, it's fine.'

She climbed back over the fence. 'Do you want to know why your father and I didn't make it? He wanted to go too far, too fast. *That* tired me. I didn't want the big house, the entertaining and the wine snobbery. And I didn't want to sacrifice everything to make money. But it was hard, because we had known each other for so long.'

'He didn't become that rich. The business is hardly a gold mine.'

'I made a mistake,' said Sally. 'I didn't realize how a person could change as they grew older.'

On our last day Art minded Chloë, and Sally took me out on Melly. She rode upfront on the big, prancing Quincy and urged him along a track fringed by trees, which were turning every shade of yellow and ochre. The earth was moist underfoot and insects rose in clouds. In the distance the ridge of hills rose ragged and unpeaceful-looking in contrast to the warm landscape around the town. Sally pointed towards them. 'There's the ruins of a couple of mining buildings up there, if you look. Poor devils. They never found anything.'

Quincy's tail twitched and I tagged behind, fussing with Melly's reins and the angle of my foot. Every movement reminded me that I was not with Chloë. I knew she was perfectly all right, that she was safe, yet with every rustle in the undergrowth or shiver of the branches, I found myself listening for my child's breathing. With every thud of the horses' hoofs, I strained to hear her cry of distress, hunger or pleasure.

It was like that now, and there was nothing to be done about it.

After supper, I helped Sally to make gingerbread for the Rotary Club picnic. 'We take the station-wagons and head up into the mountains, sing a little, eat a lot. It's neat.' Chloë was asleep in the little boxroom and Art was watching television in the next room, surrounded by papers and beer cans.

Sally dug a spoon into the molasses. 'Since you've been here, my paperwork has gone to pot. Never mind – I've enjoyed it, Fanny. This has been good.'

The molasses had to be coaxed into the bowl.

'Friends?'

'Yup.' She flushed a harsh red. 'I wish . . . But that's my business.' She dropped the spoon and folded her hands across her stomach.

'I thought you had no regrets.'

'I don't and I do. That's natural.' She poured the ginger-bread mix into the tin. 'But I have to say it's mighty big of you to . . . Oh, what the heck, Fanny? What I did was for the best.'

'Hey,' I slipped my arm round her shoulders, 'I didn't mean . . .'

She looked up at me. 'I chose me because I figured I only had one life and I'd better live it.' She lowered her voice. 'In a manner of speaking, Art was incidental.' She gave a little laugh. 'Coincidental, more like, because he happened along at the right time. But that's our secret.'

I leant past her and ran my finger around the bowl. 'He's nice, Sally.'

'He's a man,' she said briskly. 'Is any of us nice? But we come in all shapes and his suited mine.'

I licked my finger. 'You got away.'

Sally offered me the bowl for a second helping. 'Like I say, I'm better with horses. And that's what I've stuck to. You need things, you know, to take your mind off the mess and muddle of eating and sleeping and being polite in the home. Men don't expect to think about it all the time. Why should I?'

Just as I was climbing into the spool bed for the last time Will rang. I wrapped a rug round my shoulders and went down to the kitchen to take the call.

'Can't wait to see you, Fanny,' he said.

We hadn't spoken for three days and I felt it acutely. 'Tell me what's been happening.'

He had several pieces of gossip. 'Listen to this. The PM liked the speech I wrote for him and used a couple of the phrases. "Tough care", you know, that sort of thing. Not very revolutionary but it seemed to do the trick.'

I told him about riding through the larch woods and the ruins of the mining buildings. 'They sat up there during the winter, freezing and dying.'

'They wanted a better life.' He sounded like the Will I had first known.

'If you come out here we can ride up into the mountains.'

'Yup,' he said. 'I'd like that.'

Arriving home in the airport in London, I spotted Will before he saw Chloë and me. He was deep in conversation with a girl with a blonde ponytail and tight leather trousers.

He was smiling and talking, and gesticulating, in the way that he had when he wooed a listener around to his way of thinking. This was Will at his most persuasive and the girl was listening intently.

Despite my burden of Chloë and the luggage trolley, I almost ran up to him. 'Will?'

He whirled round. 'Hallo, darling. Hallo, my poppet.'

The girl melted away. 'Who was that?' I asked.

'I've no idea.' Will hugged Chloë. 'She said she recognized me from television and admired what we were trying to do, so I was just explaining to her how it would work.'

I clung on to him. 'Am I pleased to see you. The last few days went so slowly.'

'For me too.'

Will handed back Chloë and took over the luggage and we made our way out to the car. 'It's good isn't it,' he commented, as he strapped Chloë into her seat. 'My face *is* getting known.'

All the way home, I kept looking at him, ravenous for every detail. 'Did you really miss me?' I asked.

He turned his head and looked at me and, for a moment, I thought I saw a shadow in his eyes, a wariness that I could not place. 'I missed you more than you can possibly imagine.'

I laid my hand on his thigh and let it rest there.

Back at Stanwinton, the brown leather diary was lying on
the hall table. Tucked into it were typed lists and invitations.
Bowling club tea. The single-parents' jumble sale. The
Ladies' Guild ball . . .

'Mannochie's been busy,' I said.

Meg came hurrying out to meet us. 'Welcome home,
Fanny. Are you exhausted? Oh, Chloë, you're such a big
girl . . . There's coffee and sandwiches in the kitchen. Come
and see what's been done.'

Along with the alterations to accommodate Meg, my
kitchen had been given an overhaul. It smelt of paint and
to my jet-lagged sensibility, it seemed to exude a fresh,
optimistic feel – if such a thing were possible. While we
were planning the alterations, Will suggested that we splash
out and buy a new oven. And there it was: chunky and
reliable looking. I showed it to Chloë, who considered it
extremely exciting when I banged the door shut.

Meg's tiny kitchen space sparkled with fittings and
equipment, and matching pink towels hung over the heated
towel rail in her bathroom. I touched one: it was soft and
expensive, and the colour matched the bath hat hanging
on the door.

Meg hovered behind me. 'Fanny, I haven't thanked you
properly . . . for agreeing to me living here.'

I turned round. 'You don't have to thank me. I'm glad we can do something.'

'I do have to thank you,' she insisted. 'I need somewhere safe and secure so that I can . . . beat . . . well, you know what I have to beat. I can't seem to do it on my own but I promise that I will be as helpful as I can, to make it up to you. I plan to find a job as soon as I can. Part-time, so I can help out with Chloë.' She smiled a little bleakly. 'I will try and earn my keep.'

I left Meg talking to Will, hefted Chloë on to a hip and went upstairs to our bedroom. I opened the windows and Chloë chuckled as I wrestled with the catches. She looked so gorgeous, so *edible*, that I caught up a fat fist and kissed it.

The rooks cawed in the trees. A curtain fluttered, and my inner eye caught the peaceful, supremely domestic vignette and settled it alongside all the other pictures and echoes stored in my mind. I sat down on the bed, held Chloë close and rested my chin on her curly hair. 'We're home, Chloë,' I said.

I had weaned Chloë in America, a process that had involved a few struggles on Sally's swing seat. I was giving her the goodnight bottle in the bathroom when Will came in. Chloë let go the teat and turned her head in his direction.

'Did you see that?' He was pleased. 'She knows me.'

'Of course she knows you.'

'You were away so long that she might have forgotten she had a father. Here, let me.' He hoisted Chloë on to his knee and gave her the bottle. Chloë fussed a little and then settled. He cuddled her closer. 'Fanny, now that we've sold the flat, how do you feel about renting a house in Brunton Street?'

With the birth of Chloë, we needed somewhere bigger in London to roost, and before I left for the States I had put Will's flat on the market. It had been snapped up within ten days.

'Why?'

'It's so close to Westminster.'

'But Brunton Street? It's full of narrow little houses that cost the national debt of most African countries.'

He had been gazing down at Chloë and now he looked up at me. 'I've learnt a few things, lately, Fanny, and taken soundings. We've got to entertain and make contacts, get our faces better known. Talk to ministers. I think you'll love it. Interesting people . . .' He shifted Chloë. 'Actually, I've been to see one with Meg, and she thinks it would be perfect.'

I threw Chloë's mucky dungarees into the laundry basket. 'She does, does she?'

Will said quickly, 'I was sure you wouldn't mind.'

I don't know why that tiny disloyalty stung quite so much, but it did. I took refuge in sarcasm. 'Would it be too much to suggest that I went and had a look too?'

Chloë finished her bottle. I winded her and we put her down in her cot. I wound up the musical mobile and we watched from the doorway as she drifted into sleep.

'Will . . .' I whispered. 'You are *quite* sure we can leave Chloë with Meg? We wouldn't be putting them both at risk? What would happen if Meg went on a binge and I was up in London with you?'

'Very unlikely,' Will replied, perhaps a little too quickly.

'Despite everything there was actually never any problem when she was in charge of Sacha. I know she would never let anything happen to one hair of Chloë's head.'

'I hope you're right, Will.'

He slipped an arm around my waist. 'I know that Meg would walk on water for Chloë.'

Meg appeared the following morning in the bedroom with breakfast on a tray. 'I thought you would be so exhausted.' She settled the tray on my lap. 'I've given Chloë breakfast and Will's playing now-you-see-me-now-you-don't with her. I don't know who's enjoying it the most.'

Meg had taken trouble with the tray. The marmalade had been put into a little dish and there was hot milk for the coffee. I thanked her and enjoyed my breakfast and felt extremely guilty that I wished she had not done it.

On the Monday, we left Chloë with Meg, and Will and I drove up to inspect the house in Brunton Street. Mannochie had agreed to meet us there, and the three of us looked around. I had been right: it was a narrow and gloomy building in a row of similarly narrow and gloomy buildings that had been previously occupied by a family from the Middle East.

Mannochie pointed out a tiny room off the hallway which would do as a perfect office for him when he was in London. I said, no offence, but I wasn't sure I wanted him let loose in our home, and he smiled and said in his wry way, 'I won't bother you. If you give me the key, I'm housetrained and I'll behave myself.'

So, the soft-voiced, soft-footed Mannochie would lie quietly in his basket until called. 'Don't you ever get sick of this, Mannochie? Do you ever stop to think what this life does to you – does to us all?'

He shook his head. 'I'm too busy to think. You could say I'm wedded to the business.'

It was astonishing, really, how willing Mannochie was to subsume his life into ours. Perhaps not thinking was an advantage, an effective weapon. Like the orphaned lamb draped in the skin of a dead one and presented to its new mother, Mannochie would take on our taste and smell.

Upstairs on the first floor, a narrow sitting room ran front to back and mirrored the kitchen arrangement in the basement. Up more stairs and there were two bedrooms. Then another flight, and a couple of attic rooms, mean and airless, with sloping eaves and high, barred windows.

Will went back downstairs to look at the sitting room. Mannochie stood on tiptoe to view the rooftops. He surprised me by saying, 'That's what our politics are for, to stop segregation in attics and basements.'

'I never heard you say anything political before.'

He said quietly, 'You never asked, Fanny.'

On the way downstairs, he ran over the forthcoming commitments. 'State Opening. The usual Christmas engagements at Stanwinton. Recess.'

'And what,' I teased, 'is the role of the wife in all this?'

He ticked off the points on his fingers. 'A perfect, smiling willing helpmeet who wears tights. Not so bad, Fanny?'

I grinned. 'Bit like childbirth, Mannochie. You read about it, go to the classes, practise the breathing, but the minute it happens you say to yourself, "Hey, there's been some mistake."'

After completing the inspection, we went back into the

street. Mannochie checked over a few things with Will and said, 'By the way, I need to talk to you about the traffic schemes. Small shopkeepers are organizing a protest. They want you on it.'

Will looked blank. 'Sure. I'll *listen* to what they have to say.'

'But not take sides?' I asked.

Will looked awkward. 'It's not sensible to take sides on local issues, is it, Mannochie? It's better to stick to the national ones.'

'You're learning,' said Mannochie.

We discussed the Brunton Street house as I drove Will to Westminster and agreed to take a decision that evening. I dropped him at the Houses of Parliament and continued on to the flat to begin the process of packing and clearing it out.

It was a mess, but that was no surprise. I did the washing up, watered the drooping house plant, threw out a month's newspapers and Hoovered the sitting area.

For diversion, I rang Elaine. 'Lovely to hear you,' she said. 'Let's meet as soon as poss. I want to hear everything.'

We gossiped for a good twenty minutes and Elaine described preparations for Sophie's coming birthday party. 'It's the party bags that are giving me a migraine,' she said. 'I'm trying to outdo Carol over the way. Rumour is there were plane tickets in hers. I've only got Smarties. Can I live with the shame? Am I harming my daughter for life?'

Still laughing, I rang Meg to check up on Chloë. 'She's fine,' she said. 'Just gone down for her nap.' We discussed the weekend when Sacha would be coming to stay. 'It's the

Giving Back I dread,' confessed Meg, and my heart bled for her.

'Oh well,' she added. 'I deserve it.'

'Meg, don't say that.'

'Come on, Fanny. What do you think happened? No husband. No son, no job as yet. If ever. Dependent on a brother and his kind wife. Hardly ruling the world. But all my own fault.'

I returned to the clearing up of the flat. In America, I had resolved not to let my mind stand idle and I listened to a current affairs programme which I would later discuss with Will. This stern objective was subject to a major diversion when I caught sight of myself in the mirror, and decided I needed I really *needed* some new clothes. The outer woman. This was the cue for longer-lasting debate with myself over the virtues of quality over quantity, and plumping for the latter. The easy, vibrant, well-informed, up-to-the-moment me required lots of clothes.

Will phoned. 'Just checking,' he said, ' . . . that you are there.'

I clutched the dust-pan brush to my chest. 'I'm here.'

'I'll be a bit late, but not too late.'

'Good.'

'Miss me?'

'Miss you.'

Next on the list in the flat was the bedroom. I switched the radio to a music programme which was playing Beethoven's Fifth, whipped the sheets off the bed and gathered them up.

Something fell to the floor.

My knees buckled and I sat down on the bed.

Lying on the floor was a plain, white silk camisole, and it did not belong to me.

When Will arrived – a little late, but not too late – I was waiting with a meal and an open bottle of wine. The flat was immaculate and the washing machine churned in the background.

I allowed him to kiss my cheek.

He was excited and wanted to tell me about the Bill they were pushing through the House. 'It's not perfect, Fanny, but it's a big step forward and we're in a hurry to get things done.'

That is what I had been. In a hurry to marry Will.

He poured out a glass of wine. 'Better still, there's a whisper of a vacancy in the whips' office, and my name has been mentioned.'

'And give up your independence?'

He ruffled his hair. 'It's the only way, you know. You can't do it by muttering on the back benches. To get things done, you have to be out front. And a way up is through the whips' office.' He slapped his hand down on the table. 'I'm starving. Can we eat?'

I faced him across the cutlery and china. 'Will, who have you had here?'

He started. 'Why?'

'Because I found underwear in our bed.'

Will went chalk white. 'What are you talking about?'

'You tell me.'

Did I want him to deny it, vehemently, convincingly, so that I could allow myself to believe him? Or would I prefer him to look me straight in the eyes and say, I have been unfaithful.

I did not know the answer. Each came with a terrible burden of pain or suspicion.

'Who is she?'

Eventually, Will said, 'It must have been Liz.'

'There's a choice?'

'She's a researcher and I said she could crash out here after she'd worked late one night.'

'Don't lie.'

He looked away. 'All right. No lies. No more lies.'

'When?'

'You want the details?'

I looked down at the floor which I had swept so blithely that morning. 'Perhaps not.'

Will put his hand over his eyes. 'What have I done?'

The sounds in the flat – the muted gurgle of a water pipe, the washing machine – seemed very loud. 'In *our* bed?'

'I'm sorry.'

'About our bed, or what you did in it?'

Will flinched. 'I deserve that.'

There was a long, long silence. 'I had a couple of whiskies,' he said. 'I don't know why. I, of all people . . . should know.'

There was a click. The boiler switched off and, with it, I felt something die in me . . . the trust, absolute and unquestioning, I'd had reposed in Will.

I felt so foolish, so naive, so ill-fitting.

'Will,' I whispered. 'Had you grown tired of me? We haven't been married that long.'

'It wasn't like that, Fanny. I can't explain. I have no excuse but, in a strange way, it was nothing to do with you.'

'How can we continue after this?'

He dropped his head into his hands. 'Please don't say that.'

'What am I supposed to say? What would you have said if it had been me?'

'I don't know,' he said. 'I just know I would have been desperate.'

'Well?' I moved in the chair experimentally, because every move I made seemed to hurt. 'It might have been different if we had been married for a long time.'

'No, it wouldn't,' he muttered.

'It was all so easy,' I burst out. 'I go away with your daughter, and you leap at the opportunity . . . to enjoy yourself.'

I got up and went into the bedroom and looked down at the freshly made bed. The images it conjured up were too much to bear, so I blundered into the bathroom, sat down on the edge of the bath, and tried to think what I could do. I looked into the mirror at an unfamiliar face.

I returned to Will. He was sitting on the arm of the sofa, still ashen and shaky looking. Our eyes met. I looked away first.

'I'm leaving,' I said. 'I'm going back to the house and Chloë, and I'll let you know what is happening when I've made up my mind.'

I was neither witless, nor an innocent. I knew about sex. I knew that lapses happened and people survived.

The world was built on temptation and Liz had been one of them. I pictured her hurrying busily though the corridors of the House. I saw her making telephone calls, working on the facts: smart and organized; the icing on the bun.

Maybe that was the explanation. Proximity – like that peculiar intensity of living cheek-by-jowl with Will in his flat. Those sweet, intoxicating encounters of body against body.

Perhaps that was true of Westminster?

I almost persuaded myself that if I'd worked where Will did, and watched the prowling men, I too might have listened to a serpent and eaten of the fruit.

But it was Will who had not kept faith.

Perhaps, if we had talked, he might have explained that he had been eased aside by the messy, cosy intimacies between baby and mother, and by a new and deadly priority: the need for sleep.

Maybe to give birth is to remind one of death, and the nudge is too sharp and shocking. I could understand that a tender-fleshed apple offers a moment of sweetness and oblivion. Then again, maybe something *has* to die when something else is born. If so, we should have shared our fears, for I felt their dark presence too.

I woke the next morning in our empty bed at Stanwinton.

What was I going to do?

Take refuge in motherhood. Take refuge in the slap and polish of running a house. *That* was what I would do. Give Chloë her breakfast. The heating? I'd adjust it. The morning post required sorting. Ordinary life flowed over the rocks and hidden pools and coasted over the dangerous shallows. In danger of drowning, I clung to it.

Somehow, the morning passed. These tasks accomplished, I held Chloë tight and, imagining that we were playing a game, she crowed with delight and looked up at me. Reflected in those huge, innocent eyes I saw a new version of myself: tall and strong, the one on whom she relied.

She bounced up and down and beat at my chest. Then, without warning, she regurgitated her lunch. She cried a little with shock and I took her upstairs and ran a bath.

Now it was the yellow-duck routine, the splashing routine, the song about the deep blue sea and the silly now-you-see-me-now-you-don't game with the towel.

Perhaps my distress filtered through to her because, after she was dressed, Chloë switched from the happy little madam into a tyrant who demanded extra cuddles. She fussed when I put her into her cot for her afternoon sleep and a thin, fretful wail followed me downstairs.

In the kitchen, I cast round for something to do and my eye lit on a mountain of baby clothes in the ironing pile.

With heat and steam, the iron battered the small garments into submission. If only it was so easy to batter a life into shape. If only I could iron into the white vests and pink tights the bright anticipation of yesterday. If only I could iron away a strange woman's underwear in my bed.

But I couldn't.

I heard a key in the front door. 'Hi.' Meg appeared in the kitchen. She looked flushed and pretty in a suede jacket and black trousers. 'Why did you come back last night?'

'No reason.'

'Didn't you trust me?'

I laid the iron in its cradle and switched it off. 'I want some peace, that's all.'

'Fanny! You do have some bite.' She looked at me sharply and unbuttoned her jacket. 'We all have our off-days, God knows.' She draped her jacket on a chair and I wanted to shout: *Take it away!* She pulled out another chair and dropped into it. 'You can tell me.'

'Go away, Meg.' This was the first time I had ever spoken to her in such a manner.

To her credit, she did not take offence. 'Have you and the darling brother quarrelled? Love's young dream sullied?' She propped her elbows on the table and rested her chin on her hands. 'You have my sympathy. Been there.' Her eyes followed me as I folded, tidied and stacked objects, anything to keep moving, to keep breathing. 'It's not worth it, you know.' She dropped the comment into the silence. 'Take it from me.'

Her mockery had a bracing effect and I caught the contradiction of love and hate that was Meg. 'You can't trust anyone,' she said. 'Not even yourself. Especially not yourself.'

Meg was right. There was not much to be said for it, yet pity for oneself opened one to pity for others. Despite my own torment, my heart ached for her as well as for me. I picked up the laundry basket with its burden of clean clothes. 'I'll make coffee, and then I want to get on with things.'

Meg cocked her head. 'Chloë's crying. I'll go and change her. See what she wants. By the way, I sorted out the cupboard with her stuff in. I noticed the other day . . .'

I trembled with sudden fury at her interference. I opened my mouth to say, 'It's none of your business', but exhaustion punched in. 'Oh, go and get Chloë.'

I had my back to the door when Meg returned. 'Fanny, I think Chloë's ill.' She spoke in a quite different tone. 'She's very hot.'

I whirled round and took the stairs two at a time. Chloë was flushed and her cheeks were burning. When I picked her up, she grizzled and ducked her head in an unfamiliar way.

'I'll hold her while you drive to the doctor,' ordered Meg. 'Now.'

'I'll ring Will,' Meg said.

She and I were standing over the cot in the hospital ward. I was shaking as Chloë lay in the cot, so small and ill.

'I know what you're thinking,' said Meg, more or less calmly, 'all sorts of dire thoughts, but she'll be fine. The doctor said they just wanted to keep an eye on her over-night. She's picked up a chest infection and a stomach bug, that's all, and they have it under control. All you have to do is take a grip.'

I grabbed Meg's arm and steadied myself. 'I can't.'

'Yes, you *can*,' she said.

The nurses were nice. They showed me where to fetch water and how to sponge Chloë down. They checked her pulse, wrote up their notes, spoke in professional terms. Meg was right, but I sat through the night beside the cot, my eyes fixed on the tiny figure of my daughter, not daring to look away once.

As instructed, every fifteen minutes or so, I dipped a sponge in water and squeezed it out. I lifted first one tiny stem that was Chloë's arm, bathed and patted it dry, then the other. Then I began on the pink assembly of minute bones that were her feet, then her little legs.

I sat down and, again, took up my vigil.

The nurse, fair hair twisted up into a tight pleat under her cap, checked on Chloë and the chart quivered a little at the end of the cot as she snapped it back into its holder. She sent me a half-smile and I could not be sure whether it was pity or reassurance.

Babies don't die, do they? I wanted to beg her. *Not now, not these days, especially if they're as round and rosy as Chloë.* Yet all through history they have died. The human race was known for it.

She must have sensed my panic. 'Shall I bring you a cup of tea, Mrs Savage?'

Around midnight, Will arrived. He was unshaven and looked awful. I refused to look at him as I spelled out the details. 'They say the antibiotics will start working within twenty-four hours.'

He bent over the cot and touched Chloë's cheek. 'Little one,' he said. 'You'll be better now.' He straightened up. 'I'll stay here with you.'

I fetched another chair and we sat, side by side, for the rest of the night only speaking to each other when it was necessary.

In the morning, it was clear Chloë was on the mend, and I told Will to go back to London.

Three days later, Meg and I regarded each other life-lessly over the kitchen table. Neither of us had slept much since we had brought Chloë home after that night in hospital.

Meg twisted a strand of hair around her fingers. 'We can relax now.'

No, we can't, I thought. I can't take anything for granted again.

I looked down at my hands, which appeared so white and thin that I hardly recognized them.

'Babies do this,' Meg offered. 'It's to test us.'

I managed a weak smile. 'I am grateful, Meg, for the support.'

She seemed pleased. 'For the moment.'

We sat in a non-threatening silence and drank coffee. Upstairs, for the first time in days, Chloë slept a tranquil sleep – which, at that moment, I considered the height of my ambitions.

'Will rang,' Meg said. 'Earlier. He's on his way.'

To the surprise of both of us, I dropped my head into

my hands and cried. There was a touch on my shoulder. 'Leave Will to me. You concentrate on Chloë.'

This was too much. I peeled my damp face away from my hands. 'Meg. Thank you for everything you have done, but you must leave Will and me alone.'

'Fanny . . .' Meg assumed her caring expression and I was never quite sure how to trust it. 'I've looked after him in the past. I know how to handle him.'

'No. It's fine.'

She shrugged. 'As you wish. But I suggest you have a sleep before he gets here.'

I was deeply asleep when Will shook me awake. 'It's six o'clock, Fanny.' I managed to drag open my eyes. 'Good girl.' He placed a cup of tea beside me and sat down on the edge of the bed. 'Meg has seen to everything downstairs, so we thought it best to leave you as long as possible.'

I lay quite still.

'Can I talk to you?'

'What is there to say?'

He looked marginally more kempt than in the hospital. At any rate, he had shaved. He looked down at the floor as he spoke. 'I have been a terrible fool. Liz is nothing to me. I am nothing to her. You are the person I love and with whom I wish to spend my life. I can't explain it further, without sounding beyond contempt.'

I tried to explain what I felt, and did it badly. 'Will, what we had was private and not to be shared. God knows, you share everything else with the world. Don't you see? That was the one thing that belonged only to us.'

He hunched over his clasped hands. 'Isn't it the other way round? It does not excuse me, I know, but – '

'I can hear Chloë, Will.'

'I'll get her.'

He reappeared with a pale, sleepy baby. 'Here.' He put her down in the middle of the bed and lay in his accustomed place.

Chloë gave a pallid chuckle. Will propped himself up and offered her a finger. 'Poor sweetie. Better now.' Chloë kidnapped his finger, pressed it into her mouth and bit. 'Ouch . . .'

He extracted his finger. 'Fanny, I know how bad it is, how bad it looks but, I beg you, don't make it more complicated than it was.'

'Will, what am I supposed to make of it?'

'I don't know,' he said, in a hopeless way. 'It was a terrible mistake. I will regret it to my dying day. I didn't stop to think, I didn't make comparisons. It was just for the moment, and I took it. I am sorry. I am so sorry.'

Deprived of the attention, Chloë shrieked, sounding much more like her old self. Will hauled her into his arms and pressed his cheek against hers. 'Precious.'

Chloë now bit his nose and Will yelped. 'When did she start doing that?'

'She's probably teething.'

I took a deep breath. 'I don't know if we can be married any more.'

Will reached out for me but I flinched. 'Don't touch me.'

'What can I say, Fanny? What can I do?'

I glanced at the clock. Six-thirty. I swung my leg out of

the bed. 'Get moving, Will, it's the Rotary Club supper. We won't stay late.'

His mouth dropped open. 'We're going?'

'Do we have a choice?' I opened the wardrobe door and dragged out the dress which I had earmarked. 'Can't let the Rotary Club down.'

'But what are you going to do?'

'I don't know, Will. Go to the Rotary Club supper.'

I pulled off my jumper and T-shirt and transcribed a slow, provocative circle in front of my husband. He swallowed and went pale. My body was still a little slack, breasts not quite settled back to their normal size; it was the body of a girl . . . no, not a girl, a woman, who had given birth, and I wanted him to see it.

That night, I glittered, or so Will reported. But perhaps he was filtering a new, rather terrible me through a guilty prism.

Oddly, along with my outrage and the still partly submerged pulse of grief, a peculiar kind of confidence had arrived, with the desire not to be beaten. I wanted to face this challenge, to be fierce and determined, to seize the competing strands of this situation and arrange them as I wished.

Will watched my every move surreptitiously as I donned the pink dress with the full skirt and a pair of high heels, for which I would pay later. I brushed my hair until it crackled and let it hang down over my shoulders. I made him wait until I was ready and Meg was summoned to take charge of Chloë.

I got into the driving seat, kicked off my shoes and

drove into the town in silence. I parked in the hotel car park and ran through a briefing. 'Pearl will be there. There will be an auction of books and things. A raffle. The usual. It's fund-raising to provide machinery for the new neonatal baby unit in the hospital. Got it?'

'Fanny. Stop this.'

'No,' I said. I gathered up my bag and shoved my feet into the high heels.

'If you want me to leave,' he said in a low voice. 'Tell me.'

'I don't know,' I said. 'I will think about it. Let's go in.'

Attired in a faded green dress shot through with silver, Pearl exuded a certain magnificence. 'Your father's here,' she observed. I glanced round. He was talking to a Knightsbridge blonde in black and pearls. He raised a hand and I waved back.

Pearl pressed a glass of indifferent champagne into my hand – I could tell by the colour and the general look of it. 'We must have a chat,' she said, and I could have sworn her eyes flicked over my legs to check that the tights were there.

By now I knew the form. We drank champagne in a reception room with tasselled brocade curtains and lots of gilt decoration. From there we progressed to dinner and were served chicken in a cream and mushroom sauce, followed by rubbery lemon mousse. Afterwards there was coffee with chocolate mints. I ate as much of it as I could and I answered the questions of the two men who sat on my left and right but, if I had been asked, I could not have remembered what we talked about.

I smiled politely as I lifted the cup to my lips, but I was struggling to make sense of it all. In a former life – so long ago – I had come and gone as I pleased, drunk coffee in the café on Saturday mornings, and read my wine books.

I looked up to encounter Pearl's unequivocal gaze. 'Are you feeling all right, Fanny? You've been very quiet.' The implication was that, by not chattering like a parrot, I was letting the side down.

'Chloë has been ill and I've been up several nights running.'

'Oh dear.' She brushed this aside. 'I've been meaning to ask, could I encourage you to do more in the constituency? The elderly, you know, and the children.'

Tact had never been Pearl's strong point. That was the secret of her survival. With some astonishment, I heard myself say, 'Would you like my life's blood? Would that be of use? Please bear in mind that I've moved house and produced a baby. I have a job to go back to but if I can kill myself for the constituency of course I will.'

The bullets bounced off Pearl, who did not even blink. 'That's the point, Fanny. The committee would prefer you not to have any other interests.'

In a strange way, I was enjoying myself. 'Do they live in an ark by any chance?'

By some miracle, Mannochie appeared at my elbow and said, 'Do you mind if I kidnap Fanny? There is someone she must meet.'

I followed him to an empty anteroom. 'You looked a bit at sea,' he explained. 'I thought you could do with a moment to yourself.'

I smiled gratefully at him. 'You're so nice, Mannochie.'

'It's not always easy,' he said.

'What isn't?' asked my father, gatecrashing this *tête-à-tête*. Mannochie muttered something about constituency matters and eased himself out of the door. My father commandeered a gilt chair and patted a second. 'First off, how's Chloë?'

I told him the details of Chloë's illness. At the finish, he said, 'Look at it this way, it's built up her immune system.'

I choked. 'That's good but mine's down as a result.'

He looked at me speculatively. 'I thought you might like to know I've got a new shipment coming over from the Margaret River. I think you'll approve. My bet is on the Semillon and Sauvignon blanc. Come over and try it.'

'I will,' I promised and, to my horror, felt tears spring to my eyes.

He searched my face. 'I think something is wrong. Can you tell me?'

But there was no chance to talk.

'There you are . . .' interrupted Will from the doorway. 'I've been looking for you everywhere. I thought you might like to know that I've rung Meg to check on Chloë. She's fine, and I want to take you home.'

I looked round. Will's features wore a mixture of chagrin and what could only be described as . . . jealousy. I was glad to see it, delighted to see it. I *wanted* to hurt him.

My father held out his hand. 'How are you?'

I thought Will might ignore the gesture, but he took it and answered without his usual easy charm, 'Fine.'

Will was never at his best with my father. Nor, it must be said, could my father have been less interested in what he considered an inferior occupation. Politics was for boys, business was for adults.

The atmosphere in the anteroom cooled.

'I've come to find Fanny.' Will abandoned his half-full glass on a nearby table. 'I thought she'd be anxious about Chloë and we should go home.'

My father put his hands on my shoulders and pushed me decisively towards my husband. 'Here she is. Come and see me soon.'

I squeezed his hand. 'Look after yourself, Dad.'

His look was so loving that it almost broke me. I blew him a kiss and he blended into the crowd of chattering men and women who were making their way towards the cloakrooms and their homes.

In the car on the way back home, Will asked, 'Have you been talking to your father about us?'

'Would it make a difference if I had?'

'Work it out for yourself.'

I disliked driving in the dark and my hands tensed on the wheel. 'Actually, I haven't. We were talking about wine.'

Will was not convinced. 'You talk to him about most things.'

'He *is* my father.'

The road curved to the right and the white line appeared to veer into the verge, as did my thoughts. My hands grew slippery. 'You talk to Meg all the time,' I threw at him.

'Yes, I do,' he replied. 'But I never had a father. Nor did she.'

Eventually I turned the car into our lane and drove up between the fields. 'This evening was a farce,' I said. 'One of many.'

'Possibly,' Will replied. 'But at your insistence.'

I parked in the drive, jerked on the brake and switched off the ignition. The interior of the car flipped into darkness.

'Now what do we do?' asked Will.

I struggled to control my panic and, with panic, came doubt. 'What I don't understand, Will, is that we hadn't had time to get bored with each other.' I removed the key from the ignition. 'Which means something was lacking. If it was, you should have told me.'

This situation was my fault.

As was his habit, Will sat upright in the passenger seat. 'You mustn't blame yourself, Fanny . . .' Silence. 'I can't possibly ask for more than we have and share.' Another silence. 'I'm not good at this, Fanny.' He twisted to look towards the laurel hedge. 'Nothing was wrong. It was a moment when I was offered temptation, and instead of refusing it I took it. How stupid was that?'

'That is one way of explaining it, I suppose.'

'Fanny – ' he began.

I cut him off. 'The bed is made up in the spare room.' I pulled on my shoes, got out of the car and left Will to lock up.

I lay awake, stomach unsettled, eyes wet, in mourning for a marriage as I had envisaged it. I was frightened by the violence of my feelings and by how savagely I had been thrown off course by an event so commonplace, so everywhere, so discussed.

I twisted and turned in the half-occupied bed.

At four o'clock, I got up and slipped into Chloë's room to check on her. I hovered in the doorway but could not hear anything and, with a shudder of apprehension, put my ear close to her lips and listened for the faint breath of my sleeping, alabaster baby.

On the landing, I paused by the Gothic window. Darkness. Nothing else. During the last few days my waistline had shrunk and I retied my dressing-gown cord so tightly that it bit into my flesh.

The spare-room door was open and I looked in. The night-light in the passage illuminated Will hunched over on his side. He muttered like a puppy, sighed and flung out a hand – just like Chloë. Drawn like a magnet, I tiptoed towards the bed. This side of Will, this sleeping, vulnerable, dreaming side, was private. It belonged to me and I would not share it.

His eyes flicked open. 'You were watching me.'

'You *betrayed me*, Will.'

'I know. And I betrayed myself, too. Double whammy, Fanny.'

'I don't know you one bit,' I said, and the cold crept into my bare feet.

'But you're wrong, you do know me.' He held out a hand. 'Come.'

As ever, my body obeyed him, and I slid into the bed, cold beside his slackened warmth. He did not try to touch me, and we lay like the marble effigies of the Earl of Stanwinton and his wife in Stanwinton church.

'You had a baby,' he confessed at last. 'It made a difference.'

'I did my best,' I said. 'I came back as soon as I could.'

'Yes, but half your mind is elsewhere.'

How could I deny it? The small-print department on motherhood had been careless, too, as to precisely what would happen, which meant that Will no longer took full possession of me – as once he had.

'I mourn the old you,' he said, and added miserably, 'I felt safe when you had only me to think about.'

That was as close as Will had ever come to admitting that his upbringing had laid a finger across his soul.

'I love Chloë beyond words,' he said, 'but it is different.'

I thought of the rooms of the spirit, and of how I had moved from a familiar one into another, as yet strange and unexplored. 'We change,' I said, for I was beginning to understand better. 'We can't escape it.'

I must have slipped into a doze, for I started when Will asked, 'Is it the not knowing me or what I did that's worse?'

'I think . . . I think it's that you didn't understand what *I* meant by us. Or, if you did . . . it didn't stop you bringing Liz home. Into *our* home.'

'I'm sorry, Fanny. Do you believe me? Please . . . *believe* me.'

'Does it matter what I believe?'

'And I'm sorry, too, for making you cynical. Cynicism's the politician's line.' His hand journeyed over the space between us and came to rest on my thigh. 'I imagined it would be different but it isn't, and you get caught up in the Westminster round,' he said. 'That's the trouble, and I know it's affected me. That's been a shock, Fanny. Finding out just how deep the cynicism is.' The hand on my thigh grew heavy. 'I've been wanting to tell you for some time.'

He shifted closer, wooing me with his own disappointments and frailties. I fought the impulse to cling to him and to weep until there were no tears left.

'I need to know what you're going to do. I'm not sure I can live with the suspicion that, every time you leave home, you might happen on another woman up in London.'

'But you won't have to.'

We must have slept for I awoke, stiff and feeling slightly sick. Chloë was practising her version of the dawn chorus and I stumbled out of bed and pulled on some clothes.

Sleepy and beautifully rosy, she cuddled against me and I carried her downstairs and fed her puréed banana and cereal. Frantic for some resolution, almost mad with exhaustion, I strapped her into the car and drove over to Ember House.

Alfredo swung Chloë up into his arms. 'Beautiful.'

Chloë nuzzled his cheek. 'And what's going on with you?' he asked, over the small, fair head. 'Don't bother to lie. You have circles under your eyes, you've lost weight and the atmosphere between you and your husband could be cut with a knife.'

'Can we go into the garden, Dad? Chloë needs a bit of fresh air.'

We walked at a snail's pace across the lawn towards Madame Mop, a bad statue of a woman holding what looked like a bucket but my father was fond of her. I narrated the bare facts and set Chloë down to see if she could take a few rudimentary steps.

'Bastard,' he said, and that shocked me more than anything, for my father never swore.

Between us we balanced the tottering Chloë, who shrieked with delight at the novelty. 'You'll need a strong nerve, Francesca, and cleverness. You've been badly hurt and I dislike Will for that. Very much. But you're not the first . . . or the last in such a situation.'

I listened to his beloved voice, which had seen me through childhood.

'At the moment, you imagine it is the only thing. Indeed, it is the only thing you can think about. But it isn't the only thing. The family matters, Francesca, very much.' He paused. 'It is a shock to discover that no one can expect serene and perfect happiness for always.'

'How can I manage knowing it might happen again?' I said.

'It may. Or it may not. We can never know. Part of the risk.'

Chloe's knees buckled and I bent down to pick her up. She crowed with delight and offered me a small dirty hand.

It was quiet in the garden, damp and cool. English weather. It was possible to think here.

'By the way,' he said, 'I think I should get a replacement for Raoul.'

'Are you sacking me?'

'I think I am. It will release you. I think it would be better. In a few years' time the picture will be different. Depending . . .' The last was delicately implied. Depending on the marriage, on Will's career, on . . . other children.

'I'm not giving up my work, Dad. I can't. I don't wish to.'

'It's a pity. But you must be reasonable and kind to yourself. Women are often not good at being kind to themselves. You have a lot to cope with. I'm getting older and I need more and more help, and you are not free to give it.'

That hurt. But my father knew what to say next. 'Your work is not dead, Francesca,' he said, 'only dormant. You can keep your hand in, if you wish, in a minor way. You can keep practising and learning and storing up knowledge. You are lucky.'

'No,' I said.

'Listen to me, Francesca, you have to be clever about life. I wasn't so clever, and I made mistakes. You have to put something together. I don't know what it will be, and you need to concentrate your energies on Will.'

'I'll think about it,' I conceded.

Madame Mop had grown a garment of green lichen. I held Chloë up in front of her, and she made tiny mouse-like marks on the grey-green with her fingers. 'Have you got a handkerchief, Dad?'

I wiped a protesting Chloë's hands. 'She's exploring,' said her grandfather fondly. 'Bold and brave. When she's old enough, I must get the tree-house repaired.'

Will was surrounded by the debris of fried bacon and toast when Chloë and I returned. 'Thanks for letting me know where you were,' he said. 'It didn't take much to guess.' Then he added nastily, 'I knew you'd run off to your father.'

I dropped the car keys on to the kitchen table. 'What are you getting at?'

'Just that.' He put his hands on the table and levered himself to his feet. 'We might as well acknowledge it, Fanny. This is not going to work. I've made a big mistake. Let's call it a day, pick up our lives and start again. I'll make sure that you're all right and we'll share Chloë as best we can.'

The strange intimacy of the night had vanished, replaced by a brisk, decisive, politician's blueprint for sensible arrangements and legal niceties. 'OK?' His eyebrows remained in a straight line. 'That's what you want?'

I felt faintness spread through my stomach and turn my

knees as soft as butter. 'I have to change Chloë,' I said.

I bore her upstairs to her room and laid her on the changing mat, which was patterned with fat yellow teddy bears and, for some reason, bells. She was tired by her outing, and from the excitement of seeing her grandfather, and was scratchy and grizzly.

I cleaned and wiped and patted. When I had finished, I put her into her cot and turned on the musical mobile. The wretched tune tinkled and the ducks embarked on a stately, circular dance.

'Gotcha,' they seemed to say.

Chloë's eyes drooped. I knelt down beside the cot. What was the truth? The truth was that now Chloë was here and well and safe, the luxury of choice had vanished. That was the deal with children. I knew. I *knew* about the chill of a child's lonely incompleteness. I knew inside out their bewilderment and the nag of unanswered questions. *A person has to choose.* But that was mind candy. There was no choice. 'I won't leave your father,' I told Chloë. 'I can't do that to you.'

Neither, I realized, could I do that to myself, for I loved Will. I hated what he'd done, but I loved him. I loved his passionate devotion to the idea of a better world; I loved the possibilities that beckoned in our future. I was not willing to give them up without a fight.

Chloë whimpered, and I stuck my finger through the bars and stroked her cheek. 'Weeping Eros is the builder of cities,' wrote a poet. I would weep and build my city too.

And rule it, and grow powerful.

I went downstairs to Will, who was waiting in the

kitchen. As I entered, he turned slowly and I saw how beaten and tired he looked.

'Fanny?'

'I've decided to give up working with my father,' I said. 'We agreed it would be better.'

I crossed to the dresser and picked up the diary, which shed its snowfall of invitations and reminders.

'OK.' I opened it up. 'Let's go through this. We have a busy month.'

Will sat down opposite me and dropped his head into his hands. 'Thank God,' he said.

A few days later, when I was lying in the bath and he was brushing his hair in the mirror, he asked, 'Do you really forgive me? Will you forget?'

I squeezed a sponge of water over my shoulders. 'I'll do my best.'

He abandoned the beauty parade, hunkered down beside the bath and kidnapped the sponge. 'I promise I will never, ever do it again.' His arm rested on the side of the bath. It was brushed with golden hairs that lay flat and silky over his skin. Underneath it the muscles were hard and different from my softer, yielding body. I reached out and arrested the hand that was trickling water over my shoulders. Will stared down at me and I returned his scrutiny more boldly than in the past.

I would do my best. I would clamp my mouth shut, stitch up my wounds, fight back and demand Will's sexual . . . loyalty. In return, I would place myself by his side: smiling, entertaining, supporting.

Yet in future I would be watchful.

I would reserve the right to inner immigration. When faced with the intractable, or the intolerable, people fled inside themselves. They studied, they dreamed, they learnt. My situation was hardly intolerable – I was neither oppressed nor abused – but my spirit had been dented. Nothing so terrible there either. Every girl . . . and every *woman*, the woman into which I would grow, required an insurance. That was mine.

'You will try?' Will bent over and kissed me. 'Will you try to forget?'

From its position on the shelf above the basin where I had propped it, a postcard from Benedetta of the church and a flower-filled piazza in Fiertino flashed in the corner of my eye. The red varnish on my toenails emerging from the water matched the scarlet of the geraniums in the photograph. An optimistic red. After a second, I kissed him back. 'Yes.'

As I say, to be good is not necessarily to tell the truth.

14

The years of children, politics and of a marriage slipped by.

There was no more talk of a house in Brunton Street. Instead we bought a mansion flat in a utilitarian-looking block in Westminster and it did us fine.

We settled in and Will came and went: to his chosen arena of deals and alliances, ambitions and ideals. There was less talk of ideas and ideals and more descriptions of personalities and who had done or said what, but his career flourished.

And I? I patrolled and marshalled a different world, but joined him as often as possible. Once a week, I sat down and did the paperwork for my father. Meg lived with us and Sacha came at weekends. Once or twice a man appeared on the scene, but he did not last. At odd intervals, she got herself a job, but they did not last either. And, in the later years, her drinking was not so bad. Months would go by without incident.

More often than not, the rooms in the house were full, there *was* the rustle and mutter of a family sounding under its eaves. Our marriage grew and deepened, went through troughs, blossomed, withered a little, blossomed again but it was never stagnant.

*

Before I had had time to catch my breath, Chloë had been gone for a week.

'How do you feel?' Elaine had rung up to commiserate.

'Like an arm or a leg has been chopped off but, and this sounds odd, I feel my energy returning . . .'

'Got you,' she said. 'Feeding and watering a household takes it out of a girl.' She drew in a sobbing breath. 'This household at any rate.'

'Have you been to the doctor as you promised?'

'Prozac,' she said. 'The caring wife's best friend.'

'Hey. I'm your best friend.'

'Fanny,' Elaine said sadly, 'you don't match up to the chemicals.'

Chloë's presence was in the house, in every room. If I loaded clothes into the washing machine, there was her favourite pink blouse. Her hipster jeans sat on the clean-laundry pile and I ironed them into shape. I picked up her sponge from the bathroom floor. Her copy of a *Harry Potter* book – 'Comfort reading, Mum' – had become wedged between her bed and the wall. I rescued it and placed it beside my own bed. The insurance loss-adjuster recorded her absence in toothbrushes and socks, in the silence when there had been words, in the hairs snagged in a hairbrush.

For the present, that would have to do. It was all I could manage in the way of coming to terms, and I closed the door on her room ('Izt bad,' said Maleeka, unnecessarily) until later.

'Mum,' she said, when she rang from Sydney, 'you never told me how exciting it would be.'

As I put down the phone, I caught a glimpse of myself

in the mirror. Expensively cut hair, waistline – well, *no* comment on the waistline – the correct lipstick for my colouring, long legs. Nothing new, nothing remarkable and yet I felt I *looked* like a woman in transition. Losing Chloë meant I looked back, and I'm sure Will did too. But Chloë would only be looking forward.

Meg and I were left to our routines. During the day, if I was at home, we kept our distance by mutual consent. After so long a time, we understood the limits for each other. But in the evenings – the dangerous time, the witching time – Meg often sought me out. She was my evening shadow, the reminder of the ties that earthed me.

At these times, because it was required of me – or because I required it of myself – I did my best and cooked light, nourishing suppers. Risottos, grilled salmon, chicken breasts in soy sauce. By now, these recipes had become second nature and I tossed them off easily and without much effort, and made a point of sharing them with her.

It was a sort of bargain struck between us – and we stuck to it fiercely: Meg because she knew she should have left our house long ago, I because . . . I had grown tough and strong inside. I had wept over Will and Meg and built my city.

On the day Chloë phoned, Meg and I shared a fish pie in the kitchen. 'Congratulate me,' she said. 'I haven't touched a drop since your anniversary.'

I murmured congratulations and Meg regarded me over her plate. 'I wish I could explain, Fanny. You're owed many explanations. You, of all people. I know what you've done for me. But I feel better and stronger . . . and I know that things must change.' She concentrated on spearing a piece of fish on her fork. 'It's like this. If this delicious pie was brandy I'd be the happiest woman alive. The terrible truth is, alcohol is so much more reliable than a husband or a son. Or love.'

I found myself laughing. 'Perhaps you're right.'

After we had finished, we moved into the sitting room and I opened the french windows. A moth flew in and attempted suttee on the lamp. I got up to rescue it and coaxed it out into the night.

'Better to turn out the light,' said Meg.

A tiny dusting from its wing had made a mark on the cream lampshade. I brushed it clean and turned off the light. We sat in the summer's dark, watching a bat swoop over the garden. Meg sat very still and quiet until she said, 'I will mourn Sacha when he goes more than you will mourn Chloë.'

'Why do you say that?'

'I'm not sure quite what I mean but because . . . because of what I missed. The law took Sacha away from me,' Meg shifted in the chair. 'The law, which is supposed to be fair and just and sane.' She shot me a look. 'OK. There were problems. But you had Chloë. You didn't miss out on anything, and she has a functioning grandparent, and I had years and years of watching you.'

This was unanswerable.

I *must* be truthful. It was Meg who had taught me how to wean Chloë on to solids. 'Scrape a bit of banana on to a spoon,' she said. 'Just a tiny bit.' It was Meg who showed me how to prevent nappy rash (use mouth-ulcer ointment) and coaxed Chloë to say her first word. Later, it was Meg who, when I was busy, went over and over with a truculent

Chloë the spellings, the times tables, the history dates, the physics problems.

A second moth flew into the sitting room and I got up to deal with it.

'Why don't we shut the door?' said Meg. 'It's getting cold.'

I did as she suggested, and turned on the light.

'Poor me,' she said in her ironic way, and hid her face with a hand.

Meg was correct. The law had – partly – taken away her son. But he had come back. Not long after Sacha turned sixteen, he arrived at our front door with two shabby tartan suitcases, and announced: 'I would like to live with my mum.' I don't suppose I'll ever again witness the same expression of pure joy that I saw on Meg's face when she heard those words.

Of course, Will and I welcomed Sacha. We had recently survived a major upheaval – in one sense – for in the previous election our party had been voted (temporarily) out of power, but Will had kept his seat with a decent majority, unlike some of his friends, who had been cast into the wilderness. Thus, the party was back on the opposition benches and Will had time to spare. He ran this way and that to arrange a school for Sacha and we made over a room for him.

Darling Sacha was no trouble, in many ways far less than Chloë. Even his music was bearable and the leather jackets and studs in his ears were offset by perfect cleanliness. He was forever washing and grooming – his hair was the cleanest I had ever seen. ('Trust you,' said Elaine, 'to inherit a paragon.') He fitted in with us so easily – perhaps that was a result of learning the hard way about adaptation and survival. Perhaps he was a natural chameleon.

I strove always to remember that.

The following morning, I drove over to Ember House. From time to time, I glanced in the rear-view mirror and was so pleased with my reflection (driving mirrors tend to cut off the jawline) that I hummed a tune.

I found my father in the study, writing up notes and making calls. Shoved into a corner was an opened case of wine, plus a stack of paperwork. Without looking up, he stretched out an arm and drew me close. 'Bear with me for a couple of minutes.'

The Fiertino expedition being uppermost, we discussed timetables, car hire and the necessity of bringing his anti-allergenic pillow. Benedetta had arranged where we were to stay and we compiled lists and talked over the practicalities sensibly. Yet I sensed a grand excitement in my careful father. He laughed and joked, whistled a snatch of Vivaldi's *Four Seasons* under his breath and fished out the photograph of the Etruscan couple. After Caro's departure, it had been relegated to the back of a shelf. 'We must visit the Etruscan museum, Fanny, and the tombs.'

Outside, the rain continued to dribble half-heartedly. My father got up to shut the window. 'I'm sorry Will isn't coming.'

'He's got the bit between his teeth. He hankers after the chancellorship and there's a hint, providing we stay in power, of course, that he's on his way. Last time we were out, I thought he'd go mad. But I did see more of him.'

My father peered at me. 'Self-pity doesn't suit you, Fanny.'

'Am I self-pitying? I don't mean to be.'

'Not really,' he said lovingly. 'Just a little dip now and again. Your husband is shrewd enough to know not to let up. He's in the game, and you can't expect him not to be down there with the best of them.'

My father was always fair.

'True.' I slotted a list into my handbag. 'He's tied up with the second-car tax project, which is touch and go. I'm not sure about it but he is.'

My father had an answer for that too. 'I understand,' he said. 'It's his chance to prove himself. Look at it this way, it's not as bad as selling arms.'

I peered at him. 'Dad, you look tired. The doctor is keeping an eye on you?'

'Of course,' he said, and I knew the odds were that he was lying to please me. I opened my mouth to insist that he make an appointment for another check-up, but made the mistake of glancing at my watch.

'Must go. Standing in for Will.'

I kissed him goodbye and sped off in the car to the opening ceremony of Stanwinton's spanking new sewage works. Here, I had to struggle to keep a straight face when the mayor referred to the reams of paper that had been necessary before the project had got under way.

During the night, the telephone tore me from sleep. I fumbled to turn on the bedside light and glared at the clock. Two o'clock. My first thought was: *Chloë*. The second: Mr Tucker.

'Look,' I said, 'if that's you, Mr Tucker, I'm going to be angry.'

'I'm calling from Stanwinton Hospital,' a voice said. 'We have your father here ... He's had a minor heart attack, and we think you should come in, Mrs Savage.'

I went into Meg's room and woke her. 'Meg, Alfredo has been rushed into hospital. I have to go.'

Frail and tousled, she pulled herself upright. 'Wait, I'm coming too.'

Like a mad thing, I drove through the night with Meg shivering in the passenger seat beside me. Please, please, let it not be serious, I prayed silently, and pressed my foot down on the accelerator.

Even so, we were too late.

The night sister, cool, slender and neat, materialized as we pushed our way into Intensive Care and took us aside. It had been peaceful, she said, and I knew she had rehearsed the words many times. Ten minutes ago. A second heart attack, but this time massive.

Meg gasped and began to cry. I fiddled with the strap of my bag, which was slippery with sweat, and the floor tilted beneath my feet. My first reaction was: *It's my fault, I should have gone with him to the doctor.* My second was: *I'll have to ring Benedetta and cancel the trip.* Then I thought ... but I don't remember what I thought except that I was grasping at inconsequential things. 'He should have waited until we got here,' I said stupidly.

The night sister put an arm round my shoulder, led us into the relatives' room and sat us down. While she fetched cups of tea, I sat on the stained bench and stared at an overflowing ashtray on the window-sill.

Meg pulled herself together and chafed my hands. 'I'm so sorry,' she said. 'Poor Alfredo. But better quick.'

I forced myself not to push her away – Meg was doing her best. It was the sort of thing I would have said but I knew I never would again.

The night sister's professional expression softened a trifle. 'Try to drink it, Mrs Savage.'

The tea tasted of leather and tannin.

'Mrs Savage . . .' The immaculate night sister braced herself visibly. 'Your father managed . . . he wanted me to tell you . . .' I raised my wet face. She checked herself and began again: 'He said to thank you. And sent his love.'

'But he didn't wait,' I cried out, in agony. 'He didn't wait for me. He should have waited.'

'He couldn't,' she explained quietly. 'But we told him you were on your way. We talked to him, even when he was unconscious. Hearing is the last sense to go, you know.' She laid a hand on my lap. 'He knew. He knew you'd get here as soon as you could.' She looked from me to Meg, who was sobbing by the window, and back again to me. 'It was peaceful.'

'But he was alone,' I cried. 'He shouldn't have been alone. I should have been with him. I know he would have wanted me with him. He would have minded – '

'I held his hand,' said the sister. 'I promise you, I did hold his hand.'

When we got home I rang Will at the London flat but the ringing tone went on and on until the answer-machine clicked on.

'Darling, it was an all-night sitting,' he explained, when I finally got hold of him. 'I'm coming down now. I'm just going to order the car and fling a few things into a bag. I'll ring Chloë and tell her and, if you agree, I will persuade her not to rush home. I'll tell her Alfredo would not have wanted that.'

At the back of my mind an old question rose: 'Are you lying to me?' I had grown used to it, and I had learnt to understand that it loved the limelight almost for the sake of it. It had become an automatic response to grief, shock and desolation.

My body felt stretched, weightless, attenuated. I realized that I should be making arrangements but I found it difficult to perform even a simple task like picking up the phone. I wanted to weep endlessly, but my tears were plugged now by astonishment that my father had allowed this to happen.

I pulled myself together and rang Sally. 'Oh,' she said. Then, 'I must sit down.' After a pause, she said, 'Go over it again.' A clink of china sounded in the background, and radio music, and other voices that belonged in my mother's life.

'It was a heart attack.'

'I won't come to the funeral,' she said. 'I don't think I could. I will think of him, though.'

At this, I wept down the phone. 'Listen, Fanny,' said Sally, 'you must remember that Alfredo considered you the best thing that ever happened to him. Remember that.'

It was the first really motherly thing my mother had ever said to me, and I wrote it down on the notepad beside the telephone, with the date scrawled at the bottom, because I wanted to make sure I had caught every syllable.

Mannochie came to the rescue. Organizing. Planning.

Cancelling appointments. Chloë was not to fly home – we talked her through what would happen and promised to call her every day. Where did I want the funeral? Burial or cremation? Which hymns? What music? I pulled myself together. Good wives were trained to make things take shape, to make events happen well, to smooth and soothe, and a good daughter followed suit.

Anyway, I had to keep Meg on the level, for she had taken my father's death badly. 'I loved him too,' she said.

'If you let us down now,' I told her, tight-lipped and hollow-eyed, 'then . . .' I didn't finish the sentence but it wasn't necessary. Meg understood well enough.

The funeral came and went. My father had left written instructions as to what he wished. With Will at my side, I sang the hymns and listened to a reading from Gibran's *The Prophet*, 'Open your heart wide unto the body of life', and shook hands with a great many people.

'Such a tragedy,' murmured one.

'So sorry,' said another.

But I did not pay them much attention.

Afterwards, the hearse took the body to be cremated. He had left further instructions that I should bury his ashes where I thought fit.

I did not know where was fit.

Afterwards Will dashed back to London, and in the evening Meg helped me to clear up. 'Fanny,' she said, more gently than normal, 'you'll have to think about the house. I take it you'll sell it.'

'Have you been talking to Will?'

She stretched clingfilm over a plate of leftover sandwiches. 'Maybe.'

'It's not his decision,' I said sharply.

'Have it your own way, darling.' She put cups and saucers back into the cupboard. 'By the way, since you've been so busy, I bought the socks for Will.'

'What socks?'

'He mentioned he needed some. I've put them on your bed. I thought it would help you.'

I stared at her. 'You needn't have bothered.' I could barely articulate the words.

'No.' She smiled brightly. 'But I did.'

I gathered up the plates in silence.

'I can see I've been naughty. Sock-buying is a sin,' Meg said, and added sadly, 'Fanny, did you know that your back can be so disapproving?'

'Can it?' I whirled round, a plate in my hand, and Meg shrank away. 'In the name of pity, can't you see you have Will, more than you should? Is that not *enough*?'

She held out her hand. 'I didn't mean – '

'Oh, yes, you did, Meg.' Then I heard myself say, 'Anything to keep your thumbprint on him.' And I wondered who this person was that I was turning into.

Meg gave a little gasp. 'Wrong, Fanny, so wrong. It's because it makes me feel useful. It makes me feel I have a place.'

The plate slid from between my hands. The sound as it smashed on to the tiled floor cracked through the kitchen. I crouched down to retrieve the pieces . . . and so did Meg. Our faces were so close and our fingers almost touched as we reached for the same shard of china. 'You're upset,' she said.

'For God's sake, leave me in peace,' I whispered.

Meg straightened up. There was an odd, terrible pause. 'I think I need a drink,' she said. 'A little nightcap. Want some.'

'There isn't any in the house.'

'Oh, no?'

I looked up at her. 'I don't want a drink. And you don't, Meg. *Please.*'

Again, the ghastly suspension of sound. 'Don't worry, I've got it under control. I can manage a little one, now and again. I'm lucky that way, not like the others. The doctor says – '

The sharp edge of the broken plate pressed into my hand, teasing the flesh. 'Meg, think. You've been doing so well.'

'Precisely.' Meg went in search of her contraband whisky bottle – her lover, brother, friend and child – and I did nothing to stop her.

I went upstairs to ring Will. With a shock, I realized that a primitive feeling of being protected had vanished with my father. He had left us to patrol the front-line between death and Chloë and it was a busy business.

Somehow, I had to pull myself together to make this family work. That was my business, and what was important. I had to . . . hold the family. That, and struggle towards resolution as he had.

I made myself walk back downstairs, through the kitchen and up into Meg's bedroom. She was sitting on the bed, staring at a photograph of Sacha. There was a full glass in her hand.

She did not offer much resistance. 'Where were you

hiding this and how much have you had?' I prised it away from her.

She looked up at me. 'Only a mouthful. I had a bottle in the wardrobe. It was my safety-belt.'

'Don't, Meg. I'll help you. I promise.'

She ducked her head. 'Why on earth should you?'

I set the glass on the bedside table and sat beside her. 'My father told me something once. He said, in so many words, that we should take life seriously.'

'Um,' Meg said, and tears trickled down her cheeks.

'He was right. We should take it very seriously. And laugh at it, too, but seriously.'

Meg's hand crept towards mine and grasped it in a desperate way. 'Oh, Fanny,' she said, 'and there was I thinking what a huge and awful joke life is.'

Will managed to rearrange his ministerial diary and, two days later, we drove over to Ember House. When it came to the point, I could not bring myself to walk through the front door. 'Will, I can't go in. Not yet.'

He put his arm round my shoulders and drew me close. 'Come on, we'll go round the garden.'

The grass was damp from recent rain, and the garden wore the drenched, drowning look that English gardens often do. I stopped to anchor a rogue spray of clematis by the wall and water showered down on me. Will brushed it off and kept his arm resting on my shoulders.

Soon it began to rain in earnest and he said, 'We can't put this off any longer,' led me gently to the front door and inside. 'Give me your hand,' he instructed, and held it fast.

It was strange but even in that short period since my father's death, the house felt quite different.

Will made coffee and I produced sandwiches. Will ate his hungrily but I only pecked at mine. I was thinking about the house, and how I could not bear to let it go.

'Will, what do you think about living here?'

He looked thoroughly startled. 'Live here? It hadn't crossed my mind.' He helped himself to an egg sandwich. 'Fanny, are you serious?'

I knew it was mad and totally illogical, but I whispered, 'It's my home.'

Will put down the sandwich. Too late, I realized the implication of my words. 'But it's not mine,' he said. 'And I rather thought our house was our home.'

'I don't want to sell Ember House.'

He held me by my shoulders and searched my face. He seemed puzzled by what he saw, which irritated me. Was it so puzzling to be grieving for my father? 'If you want me to think about it, of course I will. It's just not what we planned.'

'Oh, the *plan*.' I shrugged him off, and witless with misery, slammed the coffee mugs into the sink.

'Fanny, what *is* it?'

I stared out of the window and bit down on my knuckle. 'I can't get over the fact that Dad did not have me there when he died. It haunts me and I'll never forgive myself.'

Will stood behind me and put his arms around me. 'Hush, Fanny, hush.'

His mobile rang in the hall. Instinctively, he moved towards the sound. I leapt to my feet and blocked him. 'No. Just this once, Will. No phones. *Nothing.*'

The phone fell silent. Will put his arms round me. 'You think I don't understand, Fanny, but I do . . .' The old smile flashed, sweet and loving, and my sore heart lifted a trifle.

Now that I paid proper attention, I sensed a suppressed excitement in Will, a new tension. 'What are you up to?'

'This and that.'

'You'd better tell me.'

'OK.' He went and sat down again. 'Robert stopped me in the corridor. He said that in the next reshuffle the Exchequer was a definite possibility. But, Fanny, I have to get the car tax through.'

Just in time, I stopped myself laughing and pressed my hand to my mouth. I noticed it was trembling.

'The deal was that if I backed the government on the National Health Bill I opposed, then . . .'

'But as a minister you *have* to support the government. It doesn't matter what you think.'

'There's support and support,' he said.

Once or twice, Elaine and I had discussed power. What was it? In what sort of shape did it come? How did a wife fit around it? *Very snary*, we agreed. Power wraps a person up, as tight as liquor in a bonded store. *Very snary* are the courtiers, the adulation, the chauffeured cars, and the handing over of ideals in return for the commodity called power. Ideals are so much more uncomfortable than sitting warm and snug in the back of the limousine.

'Well?' He did not sound as sure as he looked. 'What do you think?'

I struggled to assemble my thoughts. 'Can we talk about this later?'

I abandoned Will and the kitchen and fled into the study. My father's fountain pen rested on the desk where he had last put it down. The red light winked on the answer-machine. I picked up a book from a pile on a chair under the window, *A Disquisition on the Grand Wines of Bordeaux*, and dropped it back.

I grasped the edge of the curtain between fingertips that felt numb. Years ago I had got it wrong. Grief was not like a blade slicing into flesh. No, grief was dull, heavy: it made your limbs drag, your head ache. It mocked those who drooped under its weight, for I could swear my father was in the room. I could have sworn I could hear his voice.

'After 1963,' he was saying, and we are talking Bordeaux here, of course, 'with its vintage of rain and rot and worthless wines, came 1964, badly undervalued because of the previous year. Nature, having taken away with one hand, now gave its lovely rich rounded elegant wines with the other . . .'

A tiny movement alerted me to Will's presence behind me. With my back to him, I said, 'There are so few people to whom one is joined, cell for cell, understanding for understanding. Far too few to lose or to betray.'

'Fanny, darling, we'd better check over the papers,' he said quietly.

We bundled up most of them, and conveyed them back to our house. Together, we worked through the obvious ones, stacking urgent bills and letters into one basket, less urgent into another. Finally, we came to a file with 'Francesca' written on it.

'I'll look at this later.' I let my hand rest on top of it.

An eyebrow flew up. 'I see.'

Will was not stupid. He invited me to share his work, his ambition, and I did not want to share the contents of a file belonging to my father.

Even so, I made sure that I opened the file in the privacy of our bedroom. I don't know what I expected – legal or financial instructions, perhaps – but certainly not a child's drawing of a house with a tiled roof, a large front door and pathway leading up to it. In front of the house were three figures: a stick man with a black hat, a stick woman with a bright red skirt and, suspended between them, a stick child with a bow in her hair.

It was a drawing I had done at nursery school.

The file also contained an essay written on lined paper. 'Show the effect on European foreign policy of America's isolationist stance during the 1930s, giving at least two examples.' The mark had been C. There was also a poem, handwritten on pale pink paper: 'Your absence grates on my skin/Which breaks into scarlet rubies/Until a red river slides towards the sea of my grief.'

I pressed my fingers to hot cheeks. The poem, a relic from a failed love affair – all right, *the* failed love affair with Raoul – was unutterably bad, but my father had chosen to keep it. Leafing through the remainder of the file's contents, I discovered a wedding photograph of Will and me, an invitation for my father and me to the Chevalier du Tastevin dinner, which, once upon a time, I had coveted above all else, and a tiny curl of baby hair taped on to a photograph of Chloë at six months.

Eyes brimming, I shuffled them back into order – those small, telling pieces from my past had been carefully assembled by my father, my unsentimental father. As I replaced them in the file, I noticed another piece of folded paper. It was a sketch, made roughly in pencil, not professional. Whoever had been the artist had been impatient, stabbing the pencil far too hard on the paper. But the shape was obvious enough. It was of a house planned round a central courtyard with a loggia at one end. Underneath the sketch were the words 'Il Fattoria. Val del Fiertino'.

Will was watching the television news.

'Will . . .' I sat down beside him on the sofa. 'Will, I've decided to take my father's ashes to Fiertino – as soon as I can get a flight. I know that's where he wants to be. I'd rather not wait till September.'

The newscaster continued to talk.

'Without me?'

'Without you.'

'And . . .'

'I would like to go away. Just for a while.'

'Of course you must, Fanny.' He did not look at me. 'If that's what you want.'

15

Early on the Monday morning, I was almost ready.

I was saying goodbye to Will. A plumber banged away at a dripping pipe in our bathroom. Maleeka's cleaning materials littered the hallway. The radio in the kitchen was at full blast. Will's car was in the drive and the driver had kept the engine running. Will had lost his wallet and was rampaging upstairs in the search. In short, everything was perfectly normal – except that the following day I would be driven to the airport to catch a plane, and the scent of an unusual freedom in my nostrils was almost unbearable.

Will clattered downstairs, his briefcase half open. 'Got it. What time are you flying?'

I tucked a copy of my flight schedule into the briefcase and zipped it shut. My husband's mouth was set in a tight line, but it was not anger. It was something deeper and more worrying. Will was bracing himself against my going. I kissed him tenderly but with an almost palpable sense of relief, and he kissed me back, almost angrily. 'Take care,' he said. 'You will phone?'

'Promise.' I brushed my fingers over the set mouth. 'Do your best.'

'For what?' he said, which was unlike him. 'Is it worth it?'

I placed my hands lightly on his shoulders. 'You know

what for.' As I had asked for comfort over my father, he had asked me to shore up his confidence and optimism. It was the least I could do.

His mouth softened, and he smiled down at me. 'I'm sorry about your father. I'll miss him too. I'm sure you will find the best . . . the appropriate place to bury the ashes.'

I watched Will trudge towards the waiting car, fling his briefcase into the back and climb in after it.

Almost immediately, the phone rang.

'Raoul, I've missed you.'

'I'm sorry, Fanny, that I did not make the funeral, but you knew why.'

'You were in Australia. Did it go well?'

'I've got a nice deal shaping up that I will tell you about at a better time.'

'How are the family?'

'Larger and much more expensive. Thérèse says she feels a hundred but she doesn't look it.' His laugh was full of energy and conveyed deep admiration. 'My wife is a beautiful woman.'

'If I was very nice to her do you think she would tell me her secret?'

'Living with me, clearly. We are going to Rome for a couple of years. Did I tell you?' Like the Rothschilds of old, the Villeneuves frequently despatched their family members all round the wine world to consolidate business contacts.

'Wonderful.'

He cleared his throat. 'I need not ask if you miss your father. I want to tell you that I will very much. He was a good friend and I valued him the more because he was from an older generation. One does not have many such friends, and I am grateful for the trouble he took with me.'

'Actually, tomorrow I'm taking his ashes back to Fiertino. I think that is where he would wish to be.'

To my surprise, Raoul did not endorse the plan – and, in the scheme of things, only Raoul, because of his friendship with my father, had the right to question my decision. 'Are you quite sure? Alfredo was a great romantic in many ways, Fanny, but his life was in Stanwinton. Perhaps ... you are right. It will give you time. Give yourself a moment to investigate the wine. I would like your thoughts on the super Tuscans.' He paused. 'I would like to talk to you about the business. Will you contact me when you feel better?'

I promised I would.

The plumber called me, and I went upstairs to find out the worst, which was nothing much, but he charged royally for it. I wrote him a cheque and ushered him out of the house.

I was searching in the chest in the hall for my passport and came across a bundle of out-of-date ones roosting under a selection of scarves no one ever used. I had a particular fondness for Chloë's old passports because I loved the photographs. The first was of a tiny minx with plaits. Then the half-formed teenager who glowered and sulked at the camera. Chloë had taken the up-to-date model with her, of course.

'If you want to be a real friend,' I begged Elaine, who had driven over the day before to console me over my father (Elaine had understood when I explained that, with my father's death, I had been ordered up from the rear to the front line), 'help me clean Chloë's room. Please I couldn't face it after she left.'

After lunch we went upstairs. As a pile of discarded clothes hindered complete access, I had to push hard on the door. I dumped them on the landing. Elaine surveyed the blasted heath. 'Seen it before,' she said. 'It's probably radioactive. Can't Maleeka do it?'

'She could, but she wouldn't emerge for at least a year.'

Elaine picked up one of the Barbies that had migrated into a Barbie gene pool on a shelf stuffed with childhood objects that Chloë refused to relinquish. This one had long blonde hair, cone breasts, a wasp waist and nothing on. Elaine manipulated one leg up above the head. 'I could sort of do that once,' she said wistfully.

I laughed. 'Chloë cherished great hopes of the Barbies, but they let her down. She never got over the fact that their legs wouldn't bend into ballet positions.'

Elaine leant against the window-frame and looked out across the sunny lawn and the border, in which a few opportunistic delphiniums raised their plumes. 'I am nearly forty-two,' she murmured, 'and I keep asking myself, "What else is there? Is this . . . me as I am now, is this *all* there is to life?"'

'All' is a big word and a foxy one. Ever since the Liz episode I had been wary of it. What did Elaine or I or Will expect from 'all'? I don't know. 'All' can mean soft, funny and silly memories placed side by side, like pieces of mosaic, which make up a picture that adds up to a great deal. They are precious, those memories. Chloë singing in her cot. Chloë winning the egg-and-spoon race at school.

My father holding a glass of wine up to the light and asking, 'What do you think, Francesca?' Will lying with his head in my lap, at peace and drowsy . . .

I dropped a kiss on the minx in the earliest passport and tucked it away under a dark blue scarf patterned with red cherries that Chloë had once treasured and pulled out my own.

A movement made me turn round, passport in hand. It was Meg. 'Fanny? Fanny, I've been thinking. Can I come too? I need a holiday. I wouldn't mind seeing this place you and your father talked about so often. This *special* place.'

I was checking my passport details, and not paying much attention. 'If you don't mind, Meg, I think not.'

'I wouldn't be any bother.'

'No,' I said, with only a hint of panic.

'I think it would be a good idea.'

I shoved my passport into my pocket. 'No,' I said. 'I have to go alone.'

'That's quite clear, then.' She pulled at a finger until the joint cracked. Her eyes narrowed and darkened.

To my astonishment, Will turned up at the airport. 'I didn't think we'd said goodbye properly.'

Weak with relief that I had got this far, I leant against him. 'Must be a first.'

'I've run away from school and the diary secretary was not amused.'

He felt warm, firm and, despite everything, reliable. The uncertainty had vanished and he was under control. Here was the embodiment of a successful politician who had come to see off his wife at the airport; the well-cut suit symbolized the fusion between his energy and achievements. It was Will at his most attractive and I never failed to respond.

'Go carefully with the car tax, won't you? Don't lose patience and make a muddle,' I said, then added, 'If that's what you want. If that's what you still believe.'

'I do.' His gaze fixed on the bookshop behind me. 'Why *are* you going, Fanny? Truthfully.'

'My father . . . I would like some breathing space. I want to get away.'

He frowned. 'Oh, well, then,' he said.

A family group, pushing two trolleys with suitcases wrapped in plastic sheeting, shot past us. Will stepped back. I watched as he detached himself mentally from me and what I might be feeling. That was the way he survived. The mobile phone shrilled in his pocket and, with obvious relief, he dived for it. 'Sorry, darling.'

I picked up my hand luggage. Inside, wrapped in bubble-wrap, Sellotape and one of my father's jumpers was the casket containing his ashes. ''Bye,' I mouthed, and moved towards Departures.

'Fanny,' he called sharply. '*Fanny.*' He clicked off his phone and caught my arm. 'Don't go. Don't go without me. Wait until I can come.'

'No,' I said, panic-stricken that I might be persuaded to stay, and guilty that I did not wish to. 'Please . . . let me go.'

And I shook him off and fled in a manner that – clearly – shocked him.

*

I was too tired to read on the plane and for the first slice of the journey I dozed and woke with a start from a dream where dank grass and grey mud clotted my shoes. I waded into a river of dead leaves, fighting for breath as the level went over my head. A little later, I found myself wreathed in a white river mist and its cold slid deep into my bones. In that dream, I cried out for the sun.

I woke and the Mediterranean coastline, vividly coloured and fringed by a bright blue sea, came into view and I breathed in deeply with relief. The stewardess dumped a tray of food in front of me. 'Enjoy,' she said.

I inspected a plastic lump, a roll attached to some dubious cold meat, drank the orange juice and found myself thinking of Caro. Her final words to me – her wedding present, which had been so crude and hurtful at the time – made better sense with experience. Nails screeching against the surface, wincing at the sound, Caro had attempted to wipe the blackboard clean of my father to begin again.

I could have explained how I felt to Will. I could have said: 'When I married you and I was swept up by the tempestuous emotions of early passion, of coming together in love, it was irrelevant (apart from the obvious physical mechanics) who belonged to which sex. It was a meeting of souls and minds. But once the marriage was made, the duties allocated, it mattered very much to which sex I belonged.'

What was more, when he had taken Liz into our bed Will taught me that to be a wife was separate and distinct from being a woman.

I looked down from the plane window at the green and

brown of the Italian peninsula. I wanted a rest from that part of my life.

As the plane began its descent, I uttered a silent thank-you to my father.

'Fanny ... *Fanny*!' To make up for not getting to the funeral, Benedetta had insisted on travelling from Fiertino on the train to meet me. She carved a swathe through the clumps of spectators gathered around Arrivals and folded me into an embrace. It combined the sensations of plump arms, sweat, heat, and a base note of garlic – and I was transported back to the child with plaits, wadded in a Chilprufe vest against the cold.

We queued for a long time at the car-hire desk. 'Let me look at you,' she demanded, and looked long and hard, laid a hand on my arm, touched my shoulder, caressed my cheek. The gestures were careful, loving and, like the best cough medicine, soothing and sweet.

Her English had deteriorated. So had my Italian, but some important facts were soon established. Her arthritis was bad, her son never wrote from Milan, where he now lived, much of the hillside surrounding Fiertino – which had been open and free – had been carved up by city-dwellers for summer residences, and you never knew who you would stumble across in the valley. But I was not to worry – she grabbed my hand: the house where I was staying was old, a strange preference she knew my father and I shared. For herself, she was happy in her modern bungalow.

On the drive out of Rome, past dusty oleanders and

fields of mass-produced tomatoes and courgettes, Benedetta chattered. Casa Rosa had been bought by an *inglese* couple who, failing to secure the money to repair it properly, had retreated back to England. Now it was empty, except for an odd letting or two during the summer. Not that the agent knew her job – '*Santa Patata*, she was born with no brain.' Anxious in the unfamiliar traffic, I listened with only half an ear.

Two hours later, Benedetta instructed me to turn right into a valley running from north to south and we drove between fields of corn and of vines. They were small and immaculate, cherished pockets of maize and grapes. Even so, it was noticeable that the machinery being used in them was elaborate and expensive.

Olive trees shimmered silver-white in the heat. The road wound through the valley and, on the slopes above it, the *crete sensesi*, the ridges on top of the hills, were dusty brown – 'old leather that has done good service,' said my father – and the river, which dropped into the valley, was a twisted ribbon of smoothed, burning rock.

The gearstick was slippery under my hand. I coughed a little and Benedetta clucked. 'You are low from Alfredo's death. It is to be expected.'

I turned and smiled at her. 'Probably. It was a great shock.'

'It is best for him,' she said, and tapped my thigh. 'Slow down, Fanny. We are coming to Fiertino.'

Stomach contracting a little with nerves, and frightened that Fiertino would not match up to all those years of thinking about it, I obeyed.

And ... yes, there was the church, and the piazza, hemmed by dusty-looking plane trees, and the jumble of narrow streets that radiated out from the centre.

And ... no. The Fiertino of my father's childhood almost certainly had no traffic, no garish adverts, or the sprawl of squat, modern housing that pressed for space up against the elegant architecture and stone of the old centre.

No matter.

We drove past the church and skirted the piazza, and Benedetta did not let up with her stream of information. The builders had cheated the *inglese* – anyone could have told them: the new wall they built developed cracks and fell down, and most of the plants in the garden died during an exceptionally hot summer. Her worst scorn was reserved for their sin of failing to ask the locals for help. 'They ran back home and, now, the house is in trouble.'

Casa Rosa was set back from the road about quarter of a mile out of Fiertino to the north. A dusty track sloped steeply upward and I was concentrating so hard on negotiating the rough surface that I missed the first sight of the house. This I regretted, for I would have known five seconds earlier what I knew the minute I got out of the car and walked up to the front door.

Painted a pink-orange, which had weathered in soft, subtle streaks, Casa Rosa was a flat-fronted two-storey house. Nothing magnificent, nothing special – except that it spoke to me in a manner that made me catch my breath. It said, *I should be yours*.

OK, I thought. At least that's clear. It's a little inconvenient since I live somewhere else, but at least it's quite clear.

It had long, shuttered windows on the ground floor and smaller echoes upstairs. The tiled roof had weathered as subtly as the stucco, and they matched each other for disrepair. There were ugly holes in the stonework, telltale scars from damp and missing tiles, and a plant grew out of the masonry by the chimney. Even the kindest eye could not ignore the raw, unfinished look, its air of desperation and need.

Benedetta shrugged. 'You need *la passione* to make it good.'

I shaded my eyes and counted the windows. It seemed a good thing to do, a *good* first thing to have under my belt.

The front door needed persuasion to yield. '*Allora*,' said Benedetta, 'it is the pig.'

As we went in, there was a rustling of insects and our feet kicked up dust. Benedetta clicked her tongue. 'Very bad. But no worry. I shall come and clean.'

'No, you won't.' I slipped my arm round her shoulders. I sounded proprietorial. 'I will.'

'No good,' said Benedetta flatly, when we inspected the kitchen.

'There is hope,' I contradicted her. If the cooker was both ancient and well used, it was clean; and if the taps were fur-encrusted, the sink was usable. A selection of crockery had been stacked on a shelf, and a box of matches with a saucer full of spent ones had been placed beside the cooker. A candle had been wedged into a Chianti bottle and the wax had splashed over the wooden kitchen table.

Upstairs, there were three bedrooms and a bathroom,

which was little more than a basin and a drain in the floor. The main bedroom was in a reasonable condition and the bed was positioned so that the occupant could derive full advantage of the view that swept beyond Fiertino to the other side of the valley.

My vision filled with the vividness of a blazing blue sky, the bosomy line of hills dipping into purple and brown, the sylvan grey-green of olive leaves and, to the west, the vines, which travelled in matching lines up the slope, and I caught my breath.

Benedetta took the state of the house as a personal affront and apologized with tears in her eyes.

I hefted my suitcase up to the bedroom and lifted my hand luggage carefully on to the bed. 'Benedetta . . .' I extracted the casket and unwrapped it. 'You will have to help me find the right place for my father.'

'Ah . . .' She touched the lid. 'Alfredo. Yes, we must think. That is important.' Her fingers rested on the casket. 'Perhaps the priest . . . I think Alfredo would prefer to be out on the hillside.'

'Perhaps,' I said, 'but I shall have to look carefully. I must get it right.'

Benedetta laughed a deep belly laugh. 'Your father was a wonderful man.'

16

'Poor you,' said Meg.

I had rung to report my arrival and thrown in a few details about the state of the house. There was no point in explaining to Meg that the state of the house was the point. Its quasi-dereliction and the suggestion of redemption suited my mood. No point telling Meg that Casa Rosa was the perfect outward setting for the curious inner landscape in which I found myself.

Anyway, there is nothing quite like running away. No points out of ten for this Girl Guide. *Not* a trouper. But I did not care. I tossed and turned in a strange bed, and yet I was perfectly, gloriously happy. Later, a hard, unEnglish light from the unshuttered window nudged me awake just after dawn and I uttered aloud into the cool air: '*Yes.*'

'Chloë rang,' Meg informed me, finally. 'She'd forgotten you'd done a runner. We talked and she's fine. Sacha had a long talk with her, too. Actually, Sacha's thinking of joining her for a while.' When I failed to rise to the bait, Meg plunged in the needle, as only she knew how. 'You know, Fanny, there *was* no need to hide the left-over bottles of wine from your lunch with Elaine. It just shows you don't trust me an inch.'

Weeping Eros might have goaded me into building a city, but when it came to the question of Meg, I suspected

I had never got past digging out the foundations. I glanced up. Through the doorway into the sitting room, light and sun pooled across the floor, and I thought, I am here and she is there.

'Enjoy yourself, Fanny,' she said, an admonition designed to make me feel worse.

I kept my eyes fixed on the sun and the light.

The phone was tucked into a niche by the front door, surrounded by an audience of dead insects. I brushed them on to the floor and rang Will. Our initial conversation was strained and difficult. Will was hurt by the manner in which I had shaken him off, and I was sorry – but not sorry enough to lie. 'I *love* it here,' I told him, but failed to add, 'I wish you were here.'

'That's what I was afraid of.' He sounded distracted and uncharacteristically low. 'Fanny, I've been asked on to *Newsnight* to talk about future plans. I'm in two minds. What do you think?'

'Any news on progress?'

'The wheels grind on. The car lobby is raging out of control. So, it's a case of I'm damned if I do appear and damned if I don't.'

We reflected on this for a second or two.

'The balance has shifted, as it does. I have an awful feeling that this one is going . . . pear shaped.'

My body was irradiated with warmth, right down to the tips of my varnished toes, and Will's distress was powerless to touch me. I felt almost insane with the novelty of stepping back. Should I tell the truth and say, 'Will, I'm off the case', and confess a great, burdensome distaste for the ins and outs, the double-dealing and the stratagems, the straitjacket of politics into which Will and I had been laced?

'Be honest,' Will begged. 'Tell me what you think I should do.'

I wheeled out the old tactics. 'What's happened to the man who said that a project should be fought over because it meant it had been tried and tested?'

'Perhaps I'm tired. Perhaps I've had enough.'

I wasn't fooled. Will's doubts and fear might be black, but he hadn't given up. He was still in there, sharp on the scent. 'Don't go on the programme,' I said. 'You'll be a hostage to fortune.'

'You think that's best?'

'I do,' I said – guiltily, for I did not care what he did.

Because I had neglected to close the shutters, the sun drove past the defences of the house and invaded, throwing a nimbus of light into the corner, a pretty crescent on the bottom stair, a diffuse, painterly wash at the top of the flight. Light-headed and dazzled by its splendour and novelty, I hurried round to close them and the interior was instantly shrouded.

The outer walls of Casa Rosa were built of thick stone. A beautifully cool passage, with doors opening off it, ran from front to back. I kicked off my sandals and, leaving damp imprints on the *cotto*, padded into the long sitting room, which I was convinced held faint traces of herbs and sandalwood. The windows gave on to a view that swept across the valley to the ridge of hills in the far distance.

The sunlight fractured into different colours and depths

on the walls and spilled on to the floor. A couple of faded and disgusting armchairs stood at either side of the fireplace. No doubt the impoverished English couple had sat here and mulled over their plans – *Let's take the wall down here, replaster there, can we afford central heating?* I felt pity for them too – in fact, I felt pity for anyone who had not had the luck to be in this house, in this country.

The fireplace was splattered with ash and cigarette ends, and on the shelf above there was an arrangement of dried flowers in a jam jar. I touched one, and brittle petals fell to the floor. I picked the jar up, padded out to the rubbish bin and dumped it. Then I found a dustpan and brush roosting in the back of the cupboard and swept up the ash and butts.

In the kitchen, the whitewash on the walls was stained and, in places, rubbed down to the original limewash. Grease rimed the ceiling beams, which had turned black. Bunches of dried herbs had been hooked on to them – a small offering to the kitchen god.

I dragged up a chair and took them down, which made the kitchen look naked. Arms folded, I stood back and took stock. How was it possible that, having escaped from all I resented, I desired nothing so much here as to assemble paints and an army of astringent cleaning tools? Byron wrote, 'I regained my freedom with a sigh,' and I thought he had been talking rubbish. Yet if this were my kitchen, I would love it so tenderly. I would make it glow with white and yellow, and the table would shimmer, bleached and virgin, under fresh herbs hanging from the beams, while blue and white plates sat on clean shelves.

On cold evenings, it would certainly be *the* place to make

Benedetta's mushroom risotto, and lash it into perfection with Parmesan and butter. On hot ones, when the sun had slithered down the horizon and the air panted with aromas of herbs and plants, it would be clever and cooling to rustle up grilled chicken and lemon, garnished with fresh basil, and take it out to the loggia to eat. I knew the place, too, where Mrs Scott's beaded cover would do its job: on a jug of fresh lemonade.

Upstairs, I would make up the beds with old, thick linen sheets, polish the floorboards with beeswax and tuck sachets of lavender into the cupboard – as the women who lived here must have done when Casa Rosa's fortunes were high and it sheltered a family.

In spring, no doubt, the shutters had been thrown open and the vegetable plot behind the outhouse planted with chard, spinach and potatoes. On cold days, a fire warmed the room with huge windows, but I dare say the family would have longed unsentimentally for central heating.

I would burnish and polish each room in Casa Rosa. Each would hold a special trove of things – books, a table, a picture. Each would have its smell, its different function. Each had its window that looked down on the landscape, whose intimacies would only be gradually revealed.

The loggia ran along the back of the house, and a wooden colonnade created a shaded area where it would be possible to sit for the whole day. I dragged a chair into it and sat down. The aspect faced away from the village and, apart from a large concrete building, the olive store, at the crook of the valley, and the road, which dropped over the furthest hill, it looked over an unimpeded sweep.

Sweat pooled at the base of my spine and soaked the back of my thighs. An ant ran over my big toe. The heat shimmered above the road, above the vines, above the hill. I felt warmth flow into my bones, fill my veins, irradiate me. I raised a finger and flicked it against the arm of the chair and told myself that that was all the movement I needed to make.

Forget that I was sensible and organized, forget that my life was arranged on practical lines. Forget the brown leather diary, the lists, the precooked meals stockpiled in the freezer, the clutch of sanitized topics I deployed at official dinners. Who was I now, this girl . . . no, woman, who smelt faintly of sweat? Fresh-sloughed of dull skin that had grown over me, still grieving – my father should be here – but filled, too, with a new and greedy curiosity and impatience.

Benedetta's bungalow was squeezed alongside ten others on the slope above the bridge at the southern quarter of Fiertino. There was no garden, just a rectangular plot that contained a row of tomatoes, which had been trained up bamboo stakes, a couple of olive trees and a plastic oil-storage tank. The houses, Benedetta said, had been built on the site of the old school, which, like so much in the valley, had been destroyed by the bombardment during the Second World War when the Allies chased the Germans north.

She introduced me to her dead husband's sister, a large woman quite a few years older than her, with false teeth and hair dyed almost purple. Her brother, Silvio, also put in an appearance and he sat and observed me with an unfaltering, gimlet regard, but it was impossible to take offence.

Signora Berto's accent was difficult and I struggled to follow. But I think I caught, 'Your grandmother was fine-looking. She was brave too. She worked in the fields, even when the guns were going, to bring in the harvest when there was no one else left to do it.'

'My grandmother did that? My father never mentioned it.'

'He was only a small boy. He could not know everything. We took good care to hide things from the children.'

My grandmother. Dodging mines, driving oxen, diving for cover when the shelling became impossible. *Tengo famiglia*, I muttered silently, to the shade of my father – which was as much to do with holding memory as with anything else.

The kitchen was tiny, the architect had followed instructions to be economical, and it was cluttered with religious pictures, church magazines, papers, tomatoes piled on plates, some with skins hardening and splitting from a scale disease. A Formica-topped table occupied most of the space but we squeezed round it and ate Benedetta's famed *spaghetti con verdura* and veal fried with sage in butter.

The valley was changing, they told me. For one thing, the olives were now big business and everyone was hurrying to put in for subsidies. For another, the English had invaded, snapping up the older, more picturesque houses. 'No matter,' said Silvio, whose son was working on a conversion of a big house on the Rome road. 'The English have the problems and pay the bills. We have the jobs.'

I told them I planned to walk up on the hills in the early

morning. Signora Berto looked alarmed. 'Be sure to wrap up warmly,' she said. 'You might catch a cold.'

The temperature in the kitchen must have been twenty-six degrees Celsius at least. I tried to catch Benedetta's eye, but she was agreeing with her sister-in-law. 'You can borrow my scarf.' She patted my arm. 'Tomorrow you will drive me around and I will show you everything.'

Benedetta was as good as her word. Talking non-stop, she piloted me around the village. I was shown the church, the piazza with its colonnade and fountain, and the ancient tethering stone where the merchant trains used to halt. Benedetta introduced me to the shop, which sold rosaries and prayer cards, the mini-supermarket, which operated from the ground floor of the bell tower, which was stocked with local olive oil, tubes of garlic pesto, dried tomatoes and out-of-date boxes of Baci chocolates, and the delicatessen, which sold bottled artichoke hearts and a mortadella sausage the size of a side-plate.

Afterwards we drove along the valley in bright, hot sun. 'There,' Benedetta said eventually, as I nosed the car between an avenue of chestnuts. 'There is the *fattoria* where your father's family used to live.'

'Oh,' I said, which was all I could manage.

The heat slapped at my flesh as I got out of the car. 'The *fattoria* was old, very old,' my father told me, 'and the brick was the softest colour you can imagine. Surrounding the house was a garden with a statue and a box maze. I thought it the most beautiful place on earth.'

So what was this ill-proportioned, mean-spirited building? Grimy net-curtain tongues hung out of the windows; there was no garden, and the outbuildings were of the same prefabricated material.

'Did your father not tell you, Fanny, that the old house was destroyed in the war?'

'No, he didn't.'

I circled the house. The sun reddened the skin on my arms while I considered the crude, blind execution. This was not the ancestral home of the Battistas but a substitute after war had done its worst. That was the best that could be said – this attempt to put a face, any face, on the violence and disorder.

I retraced my steps and my eye was caught by traces of a stone arch that had been incorporated into the concrete wall. A beautiful, graceful reminder of what had been lost.

Benedetta did her best to shore up my disappointment. 'The bombardment was very bad.'

'Who lives there, now?'

'Strangers.' Her tone was hostile. 'After the war, they came up from the south. We don't know them very well.'

'That was over *fifty* years ago, Benedetta.' I started up the engine and headed back to the village. After a while, I asked, 'Benedetta . . . do you think it would be possible to stay on at Casa Rosa?'

Benedetta's face creased into a big smile. 'Of course. We make the telephone calls now.'

When I discussed my decision with Meg to stay on in Fiertino for the rest of the month, she was her usual frank self. 'It's not like you to desert your post, Fanny. Will is quite upset.'

'He'd better talk to me, then.'

'I'm sure he will. I'm just repeating what he said. It's been tricky for him. He got blasted in the press for refusing to appear on *Newsnight*. Accusations of cowardice, et cetera.'

'Poor Will. I didn't know. But he'll survive. It's the silly season, and everyone will be on holiday.'

'I can't imagine what's keeping you out there that's so important.'

'A house,' I confessed, savouring my rush of pleasure. 'It's called Casa Rosa.'

'A house? I've never heard you express interest in a house before. If you had said *wine*, I would have understood. What's this house got that's so marvellous?'

'It has rooms,' I wanted to say, 'beautiful rooms, each requiring contemplation, my utmost attention, the seriousness of rapt observation.'

Meg signed off with 'I suppose I'll have to stand in for you.'

Will was not happy. He rang as I was preparing to walk down to the village square to eat, on Benedetta's recommendation, at Angelo's café.

I tried to explain to him that I had fallen in love with the Casa Rosa and tried to point out – gently – that some time off would be good, perhaps for both of us.

'You're probably right,' he conceded, 'but . . . Fanny . . . is there something I don't know, something we should talk about?'

'I'm sorry. I know it will be a bit inconvenient.'

'I don't really get it.'

'Try.'

'Why now? You can go back any time.'

I felt as though we were at opposite ends of a large room, straining to make ourselves heard, but I was not going to move.

'What's this house got that's so marvellous?'

'I'll bring you back photos and show you.'

'I've checked with Mannochie. There are a couple of things that you really should be at.'

'Does Mannochie ever give up? Get Meg to stand in for me. She would like that.'

He sounded doubtful. 'It's not ideal.'

'It's the first time, Will.'

There was an uneasy silence. 'Fanny, am I losing you?'

Then I felt guilty, and guilt generally succeeded in making me lose my temper. 'Will,' I hissed down the phone, 'I have looked after Chloë, run your house and . . . put up with Meg. I have smiled my way through endless charity functions, thousands of suppers, teas, meetings, and endless bloody surgeries. I gave up a job I loved to do so, not to mention my time, my weekends, and great chunks of my life. All I'm asking for is a few weeks off-duty. My father has died and I want to think about him. I *need* to think about him. I am tired and sad. I am missing our daughter.' I might have added, '*I am lost.*'

I heard the snap of the cigarette lighter. 'I didn't know you felt like that.'

'Well, you do now.'

When I was fourteen, the dentist had removed the braces from my teeth. For years, it seemed, my mouth had been weighed down with metal and every day the sharp edges had nagged another area of tender gum into an ulcer.

Smiling had been painful and never for one minute did I forget that I was ugly and awkward. The moment of release from their torture was to experience a miraculous airborne quality in my mouth.

I put down the phone, only to relive that miraculous airborne quality of pure release.

Of course I was sad, but the sadness was twisted into other strands – and to feel sadness was a part of being intensely alive. I sat on the stairs in the Casa Rosa and propped up my chin in my hands. How often do we have time to seek out our secret selves and bring them into the light? To examine and say, with delighted recognition, so this is what I am? This is what I might be? This is where I will go?

I had brought my wine books and embarked on a programme of study. I immersed myself in local history. I read about Punic wars, and of the chestnut woods which had supplied the timber for Roman galleys. Of Popes passing through, of civil wars, and of the pilgrim road – the *via francigena* – which connected Fiertino with the whole of Europe.

In the cool of the early morning, I walked the hills until I knew that Benedetta would be waiting to give me breakfast. In the evenings, I strolled along the road still pulsing with the day's heat, with the cicadas at full cry, and ate at Angelo's in the piazza.

By degrees, I explored the town, plunging into the noise-filled network of streets and houses where past and present muddled agreeably along side by side. In the church, modern stained glass sat uncomfortably in the fifteenth-century stonework and I went over to look at the frescos on the north wall, which were famous, and squabbled over pleasurably by art historians.

But if I had expected the glowing, gentle Christ of Bellini, or a massively reassuring Masaccio Divinity, I could not have been more wrong. The paintings depicted the erring human at the mercy of violent passions. A cauldron boiled a rich man and his wife. A stern angel speared a man in an obvious state of lust. Naked, screaming women clustered in the foreground. The corpses of children and babies were strewn upon the earth. A second angel bore down, sword in hand, upon a fleeing priest. Behind the scenes of retribution, this landscape of terror, an unforgiving desert stretched into infinity.

A notice on the wall informed the reader that the frescos, painted at the time of a plague visitation, 'depict God's displeasure for man's eternal state of sin'.

Definitely not a God of love, then.

I went out into the sunlight, in no hurry to return.

Thirstily, I absorbed the shapes and nuances of this landscape. It was strange to me but, yet, it took only a trick of light, a glimpse of a building out of the corner of my eye, a snatch of a song, and a shutter in my mind folded back . . . and I was in bed at Ember House, slipping deeper into sleep folding over me to the sound of my father's voice.

In the old days, Benedetta told me, the women beat their washing on the flat stone by the bridge. On St Anthony's day, the men brought in hay to church and asked the statue of the saint to make their crops yield and the perpetual Tuscan rose, *le rose d'ogni mese*, flourished unimpeded everywhere. 'It's not like that now,' she said. 'Obviously.'

Up in the churchyard, surrounded by the cypresses, lay generations of the Battista family, my family. They had names like Giovanni, Maria-Theresa, Carolina, Bruno, and I wrote them down in my notebook.

The week slipped by.

One morning I sat down to rest on the slope above Casa Rosa. The sun made me drowsy. I closed my eyes. From somewhere I could hear my father. *Once upon a time, there was a family who lived in a big farmhouse.*

I opened my eyes. For the first time, I noticed a line of pylons which marched through the farms and fanned out across the valley, then on into the distance. The heat haze shimmered above the house, giving it a trembling, insubstantial quality. I was afraid that, if I reached out to touch it, it would disappear.

It was going to be another scorching day.

I rubbed a sprig of thyme between my fingers, and sniffed, I saw a car drive slowly along the road and come to a halt outside Casa Rosa.

17

When I gave birth to Chloë, Elaine gave me her old baby clothes. A good quantity, to start me off, she said. They were a little worn, and stiffened from constant washing. The hem of one tiny dress needed mending, a button from a pair of dungarees was missing. But I loved that testimony to their previous life. In giving them, Elaine had welcomed me into the domestic pilgrim train. In time, I passed them on again.

It struck me then that, one way or another, the past has a way of keeping pace. Or, rather, it kept its hooks pretty firmly dug into the present.

Raoul, presenting himself at my front door, was definitely from the past. He did not offer any detailed explanations, saying only that he and Thérèse had been house hunting in Rome, Thérèse had returned to France and he had stayed on. 'So here I am, Fanny.'

He had changed very little over the years, except to become – naturally – more assured; he fitted, as the French say, into his skin. He had always dressed well and taken care of his appearance, but never at the cost of the important things.

'I'm so pleased to see you.' I kissed him on the cheek.

'I'm taking you to lunch,' he said. 'We are eating in a hotel owned by a friend of mine.'

We drove north towards Montepulciano. Raoul talked

knowledgeably about the wine, its history, and, more importantly, its future. The hotel was a modest house tucked away in the village of Chianciano. 'Don't be fooled by the paper tablecloths,' Raoul said, as we were ushered into a room filled with diners. 'This place is a local legend.'

We fussed pleasurably over the menu but there was no debate about the choice of wine. We ordered a Prosecco with the rocket salad and plumped for a 1993 ruby Brunello di Montalcino to accompany our onion tart. It was complex and almost flawless. 'The fruit of a perfectionist,' I said, after the first mouthful.

'But of course,' Raoul said. 'He dares everything; waits until the very last moment of ripeness before harvesting.'

Noses in our wine glasses, we paused. I breathed in summer and fruit, sun and mist – a voluptuous, lazy exchange – and searched for the words with which to describe it precisely.

There was a familiar concern in Raoul's eye. 'You haven't lost your zest for the business.'

I shook my head and grinned. 'I'm my father's daughter.'

'Who can predict what man and the elements can rustle up between them?' he said. 'Magic. And who could resist it?'

I put down my glass. 'Sometimes it's not the magic we seek,' I said.

He gave the smallest of frowns.

'Sometimes, I suppose, it is change. Diversion. A different way of looking at things.' I found myself telling him about Meg, and some of the more difficult moments at Stanwinton. The sun, the wine were loosening my tongue and it was not unpleasant. 'She once said she hated me for knowing when to stop . . .'

'Lucky you. Knowing when to stop is one of the secrets of survival, Fanny. And knowing when not to. Speaking of which, tell me about Battista's Fine Wines? What are your plans?'

'I haven't talked to Will yet. Dad's assistant is holding the fort for the time being, but when I get back . . .' I looked across at Raoul. 'I couldn't let his business go.'

'Are you feeling better?' he asked, carefully.

I took a moment or two to answer. 'You were right in one sense, Raoul; there is not as much of my father in Fiertino as I had imagined. I had all of him back home. But I find there is a great deal of me. I am beginning to feel much more happy and peaceful.'

'Not everyone can say that when they go abroad. Most of them discover bedbugs, bad stomachs and an extra dose of bad temper. You know, Fanny, I have often thought . . .'

'What?'

'Your father? . . .' He leant towards me. 'Forgive me if I am trespassing, but did he really want to come back to Fiertino? After all, he could have done so many times.' Raoul shrugged. 'He had such a strong ideas . . . and places change. They do not stand still, and your father was a clever man, he knew. It wasn't realistic to come back and to expect it to be the same.'

'Perhaps,' I said. 'Perhaps you are right.' I changed the subject. 'How is your wonderful family?'

Raoul took the hint. 'Getting older, but there is nothing startling about that.'

'And Thérèse?'

He frowned. 'She has no idea that I am seeing you. It is not a good position, but there it is. I did not mean to come here, in fact, but . . . well, as you can see, I am here.'

He gave the impression of having crossed some kind of mental Rubicon. I looked down at my glass. 'You mustn't lie for me.'

'That sounds very English.'

'And what does being English mean?'

'Never forgetting your manners.'

I started to laugh. 'I've always been perfectly behaved.'

'Not admitting that there is more to say. And we've had a long time to consider.'

The blood stormed into my cheeks and seeing this, Raoul took my hand. 'I am not going to take advantage, Fanny. We know each other too well for that.'

Now I was trembling – with surprise at being so propositioned, and delight as well.

I let my hand continue to rest in his. 'I have been faithful to Will.'

'I suspected that would be so. And I to Thérèse.' He poured the final glass of the Brunello. 'Some of my friends consider their . . . episodes . . . to be a little like wine tasting. You sample, you savour, but you don't take the bottle home.' He pushed the glass towards me. 'It was not my way.'

The waiter removed our plates and replaced them with fresh ricotta, a bowl of cherries, and a dish of tiny almond cakes designed to breach the sternest of defences.

'I have always been ashamed of how badly I . . . how badly I handled things when . . .'

I chose a cake and bit into it. 'I wasn't very kind to you.'

The dish had a border of faded blue and white – exactly what I would have chosen for the kitchen in Casa Rosa.

'I was only a girl,' I said, trying to put this part of the past into its proper place. 'I didn't understand. I was curious and, when it came to it, I was offended, because I did not understand. I hope you have forgiven me.'

'I know. Of course, I know.'

I traced the blue and white pattern with my finger. 'Raoul, what do you consider to be most vital when judging . . .' I raised my eyes and smiled, 'a wine?'

'You tell me.'

I mulled it over. 'You need independence. You need the courage, of course, to assess the bottle rather than the provenance or the pedigree. Maybe that's it; you just need courage.'

'Experience helps, I promise you.'

I swallowed the last piece of almond cake and raised my eyes again to his.

We explored the town and drove back to Fiertino as it was growing dark, a sumptuous, cicada-serenaded dusk. Raoul was staying in a hotel in Pienza and he dropped me at Casa Rosa, promising to return the following day.

I lit the candle in the Chianti bottle, made a cup of tea and took them out on to the loggia.

That night, the mosquitoes were deadly. I slapped frantically at my exposed flesh but, in the end, I was forced to draw up my knees and wrap my skirt around my legs.

Will was a long way away. It was unfair that he did not know quite how far away.

*

I saw Liz only once, at a children's party held at the House. I looked up from dabbing Chloë's chocolate-engraved face with a useless paper napkin and there she was. I knew it was her because, at that moment, someone called her name and she responded.

She was unaware of my presence, which gave me the advantage and allowed me to recover my equilibrium – and from my surprise. For Liz had nothing special in the way of beauty. She was dressed in a green corduroy skirt and black jumper, with her hair pulled back into a ponytail. Her figure was excellent, though, with a round curving haunch that must have been attractive to men. She was talking to a couple of the other wives and hugged a sheaf of notes to her chest.

'You're hurting me, Mummy.' Chloë wriggled out of my grasp and promptly fell over.

I bent down to soothe her smarting knees. 'It's all right, darling,' I said. 'Nothing terrible.'

Chloë snuggled into me and I lifted her up. As I did so, Liz turned and caught sight of me. She went white and, within a few seconds, left the room.

Chloë raised her face for a kiss and I gave one, passionately and with more love than I could possibly describe.

I have no idea what Liz made of that encounter, but I could imagine a little of her feelings. She would *never* guess my reaction. I did not hate her, nor did I despise her for taking Will (after all, I had taken him, just like that). Those emotions were redundant. No, what intrigued me was the realization that Liz had been instrumental in pushing Will and me further on. She had shown me that, for good or ill, I had left the fellowship of the single girls to which she belonged. My curved haunch was no longer an invitation to other men, for now a child sat snugly on it. A new set of templates had replaced the old ones. Unlike Liz, if I left a room, it was no longer an isolated gesture. Anything, *anything*, I did was connected to Will and Chloë.

Years and years of jumble sales, Rotarian dinners, evergreen outings. Four elections . . . and now I had arrived here.

I checked my notebook and, in the light thrown by the inadequate candle, reread my assessment of the Brunello. 'A clone of the Sangiovese grape, capable of great richness. Concentrated and brilliantly tannic.'

If I had not pushed Raoul away all those years ago. If I had not been confused, embarrassed, *aghast* at the business of sex, and at the desperate way in which he had helped himself to me, and my anguished, ignorant response, my life might have been different.

Something rustled in the clump of marjoram at the edge of the loggia. A mouse with dampened fur from the heat? A mosquito bit in the crease of my elbow where sweat gathered. I knew exactly what Will would say if he could see me writing up my notes: 'Wine is only wine. People's lives are much more important.' He truly believed it. Of course; and he had no reason to admire alcohol.

The phone rang.

'Are we not talking to each other?' asked Will. 'Why haven't you been in contact? What's happening?'

I scratched the mosquito bite. 'Plenty of winged biting things.' My voice sounded overbright. 'Are you OK?'

'OK-ish.'

'Will?' This was the moment to say: 'Guess who turned up? Raoul. He happened to be in the area.'

'You know politics, Fanny.' Yes, I did know politics. 'I can't persuade you to come home?'

I squeezed my eyes shut. 'No.'

His voice quickened with the anger that he had, no doubt, been nurturing. 'I don't know what's happening and it's probably my fault, but should the Stanwinton Glee Club's salmon supper, or whatever, suffer because you feel like playing truant?'

'You're the one they want, not me.'

'It seems so sudden,' he countered. 'You gave no warning. It was as if I had woken up and found I'd been living with someone I didn't know.'

This confession pleased me. It suggested that our lives were not quite so predictable and tame as I had thought. I slapped at yet another mosquito. 'Should keep you on your toes, then.'

'Stop it.'

'Will, the other day I worked out that I have spent approximately five thousand seven hundred and forty-five days of my life working for you. This was predicated on the assumption of one commitment per day of our marriage, minus two hundred and sixty-six days for child-birth and holidays.'

'As much as that?' he shot back. 'Doesn't time fly when you're enjoying yourself?'

Before I could help myself, I snorted with laughter.

'That's better,' he said.

*

226

Benedetta seemed tired and low at breakfast the next morning. I protested that I was giving her extra work, but she would have none of it. 'It's my son in Milan,' she said. 'I think he has bad habits. I worry that he spends too much money. Never saves. I tell him to come home. I tell him he needs his mama.' She spread her hands out in a gesture of appeal. 'He says he should come home to his mama. But how to do it?'

Che fare? A question we all ask of ourselves.

I sat at the table, drank her coffee and ate a hunk of bread and apricot jam. The sun speared through the kitchen window and illuminated the framed picture of the Madonna, the array of well-used saucepans on the single shelf. 'Benedetta,' I asked, 'how was the *fattoria* destroyed?'

Benedetta folded her hands on the table. 'It was bad. You don't want to know. There is no point.'

'Please tell me.'

She heaved herself to her feet. 'I must see to the tomatoes.'

I followed her outside. It was nine o'clock, but the sun was already like a power drill on the skin. Benedetta fussed away over the trusses and nipped out the leaders. 'Lucilla was your grandmother's sister,' she admitted at last.

'I didn't know she had one.'

Benedetta shrugged. 'When she was nineteen, she married a Fascist and went to live in Rome. I was still small, but the gossip . . . The Fascists made people volunteer to fight and they sent out people from Rome who beat you or put you in prison if you refused.'

By the law of averages, there's an awful similarity in war stories and I had a good idea of what might come next.

'This man arrived with Lucilla in a big car and demanded that all the men in Fiertino join up. None of the family would speak to Lucilla and we, the children, were forbidden to go anywhere near her. I remember coming down the road with my brother and she was standing outside the *fattoria*, crying and wailing. Eventually her husband put her back into the car and drove away.'

Benedetta harvested two ripe tomatoes from a plant and held one out to me. 'Eat, Fanny.'

The lush red was almost the colour of blood. 'Did they come back?'

'They did. Towards the end, after your grandmother and your father had gone away over the hills. The Germans had blown up some of the houses over there,' Benedetta pointed in the direction of the *fattoria*, 'to make it difficult for the Allies to get through on the roads, and they ambushed them when they took the route over the hills. Every house in the village had been damaged. It was bad. They came back because I don't think Lucilla knew what else to do. This time it was she who was driving the car. He sat in the back, very pale, very fat, hugging a bottle of brandy. She helped him out and took him into the *fattoria* to beg help from her sister, your grandmother. She didn't know she had left.' Benedetta flapped the material at the neck of her print dress to cool herself. 'Yes.' Sweat glistened in the folds of her neck. 'But it was the night when nobody was there, and nobody knows what happened. In the evenings, you see, we used to take shelter in one house or another, never in the same place.'

I had heard some of these stories from my father; they had been told to him by my grandmother. Stories are usually improved in the telling, but these had the directness and simplicity that came from having to face the worst. At night, the women piled the prams high with the hoarded provisions, and the children carried what they could to the safe house. It was a lottery. Often they picked the wrong house, and the shelling did its worst. 'By then,' my father had told me, 'we were used to secrets. Where to hide the oil, a ham, half a cheese, where the chickens had been taken.'

Having nipped the final truss, Benedetta levered herself upright. 'No one was willing to tell Lucilla and her husband where that night's safe house was. The Partisans sent word down from the hills that the Germans were planning to use the road running north of the valley so everyone made for the church. But in the end it wasn't the Germans. It was . . . A Partisan came down from the hills and demanded to know where Lucilla's husband was. No one said anything, for whatever her politics Lucilla was still one of us.'

'And?'

'It was me.' Benedetta spoke so softly that I almost didn't catch her confession. 'I heard the Partisan ask, "Where is this man?" and I ran up to him. "I know, I know," I shrieked, in my little-girl voice. "*In the fattoria.*"'

Back in the kitchen, Benedetta stood in front of her picture of the Madonna and crossed herself. 'I had been taught always to tell the truth. The next time we looked, the *fattoria* was ablaze. We could see it from the church . . . but they must have been already dead.'

I sat down. 'We must think so,' I said.

What seemed like an hour later, but was only a minute

or two, Benedetta added, 'Lucilla was a good wife, faithful unto death.'

Later, I walked up to the cemetery outside the village. The graves were a garish mix of coloured marble, white stone, plastic-embossed photographs and soiled plastic flowers. It took me a while to locate Lucilla's for she had not been buried with the other Battistas, her family. She had been laid to rest in the extreme edge of the north corner. Her stone was meagre, and badly carved, its inscription terse: 'Lucilla Battista. Born 1919. Died 1944'. Behind it a *Cupressus sempervirens* grew straight up into the brazen blue sky. There was no mention of her married name, or her husband, and no sign of his grave.

Raoul picked me up from Casa Rosa at ten o'clock. He was dressed in well-cut linen trousers and shirt, but there were dark circles under his eyes. 'We will eat in Cortona. Afterwards we will drive to Tarquinia and look at Etruscan objects.' He peered over his sunglasses. 'I know your father was always interested. Then I will bring you back to Fiertino and you can change. I will attend to some business in the next village. Then we will head up to La Foce where my friend Roberto will give us dinner.'

'Me?'

'He's expecting you.'

I could not help smiling at Raoul's presumption. 'You assumed?'

'I assumed.'

There was a trace of cumulus cloud as we drew into Cortona but it was hot. In a dim, shaded restaurant, we ordered antipasti and light, tangy pinot grigio. I ate and drank with a faint air of unreality, a sense that I had trespassed into a story where I recognized neither the characters nor the setting. But I was intrigued to know what would happen.

'Thank you for lunch, Raoul.' I tipped my glass at him. 'Do you know the best thing? Not having to think about a timetable.'

He looked at me with a question. 'Let me be honest, Fanny. I was hoping you might thank me for something else.'

The suggestion of sharp, sexual pleasure made my stomach lurch.

'I shouldn't be saying this, but it is unavoidable and I, at least, had better say it and you can think about it.'

At Tarquinia, we bought tickets to the fifteenth-century palazzo where the Etruscan artefacts were kept. Inside, we admired a pair of winged terracotta horses, a bronze mirror held up by a statue of Aphrodite, and a bronze of Heracles subduing the horses of Diomedes.

As I moved away, I happened to glance over my left shoulder and caught the image. I recognized it instantly. Behind the glass showcase, and beautifully lit, was the stone funerary carving. It was composed of a couch over which a tasselled cloth had been arranged. Stretched out on it were two figures, a man and a woman. She was young, with huge painted eyes and a trace of a smile on her lips. One of her arms was stretched across her breast so it almost touched her companion. His arm was round her shoulders and he was smiling too. The inscription read, 'Married couple, fifth century BC'.

But I knew that already.

I read out from my guidebook: '"They were the inhabitants of *opulenta arva Etruriae*, the opulent fields in which had grown wheat and vines. In the end, the plenty made them decadent."'

'They look so normal,' I commented to Raoul. 'So understandable.'

Raoul captured the guidebook. '"Etruscan women enjoyed the freedom to go out, to share feasts and to drink wine. The Etruscans honoured their wives and sought out their company."'

'Ah,' I said.

Raoul pressed on: '"Nor did they share them."'

18

Will had shocked me once by remarking that he reckoned MPs often had no idea as to what they were voting for: they just headed for where their whips were standing guard. He let this drop as we drove to Chloë's school for a parent-teacher evening. Chloë was fifteen and at a tricky stage: i.e. life was a production in which she took the starring role.

We were late. This was because Will had missed the agreed train to Stanwinton. *A deal in the tea-room.* He climbed into the car at the station and said, 'Don't say anything Fanny. Sorry, sorry.'

I let out the clutch. 'Last time, if you remember, we were so late we had to sit behind the headmistress on the staff chairs.'

'You should give thanks. It meant we only had to look at her back view, not the front.'

Will could always make me laugh. I reached over and laid my hand on his thigh. 'What was it this time?'

'That's it,' he said, sobering up. 'I must talk to you about it.'

If Will thought he could sneak unnoticed into the audience, he was wrong. As we entered the school hall, the headmistress bore down on him and whisked him into captivity with a posse of senior staff. I sought out an anxious-looking Chloë. 'Your father wants to know if there are any terrible surprises.'

Chloë looked rather pale. 'Only the sodding maths,' she said.

'Don't swear, darling.'

She looked even more pained. 'You don't understand, Mum. Our generation doesn't think of it as swearing. It's just words we use.'

'Could you not use them, then?'

She shot me one of her looks. 'It's as bad as when you try to lecture me about sex. We are the *informed* generation, you know.'

Not, as it transpired, *that* well informed. Chloë's maths was dire, so were physics and chemistry; and the geography teacher was not convinced that Chloë had grasped the nettle.

'At least,' I said to Will, back at the Stanwinton house, 'her Italian is forging ahead.'

'Good.' Will dumped a pile of washing on the kitchen floor.

I groaned. 'There's a laundry basket over there.'

Will achieved a look of utter surprise. 'Oh, of course.'

I watched him stuff the clothes into the basket. 'Fanny, can we talk?' He draped his jacket over the back of a chair. 'I don't suppose there's a drink anywhere? You haven't hidden a shifty bottle?'

'I wish.'

'No. No. Of course not.'

Will and I had stuck to our decision not to keep drink in the house as it was unfair on Meg. The place to enjoy wine was London. It was no great deprivation, we agreed. But there were times . . .

'It's the vote on fishing and shooting.'

'I thought that had all been sorted, that our side were to vote for banning them.'

'That's it,' said Will. 'I would *never* fish or shoot, but to forbid them makes me uneasy. It is to ban a fundamental freedom, and I am not sure I should agree.'

I tied on my plastic apron, a present from Chloë, with its picture of a cat spatchcocked over the seat of an armchair while its owner looked on crossly, with the words 'Never give up' written underneath, took out of the fridge a cheese and mushroom quiche I had made that afternoon, and put it into the oven to warm. 'But you have to. You're a whip.'

'No, I don't *have* to. I could vote against. After all, it *is* what I believe in. It's a question of conscience.'

I handed him a couple of tomatoes – the cold, round English type. 'Could you slice these for me, Will?' I fetched a lettuce from the pantry, to give myself a few seconds to consider. 'You'd lose the whip.'

Will sliced away, if not with skill, with diligence. 'Chuck in the wrath of the animal-rights people, too,' he said.

I froze in the act of shredding the lettuce into the salad bowl. That was different. 'You can't, then,' I said flatly. 'It might endanger Chloë. They'd find out where she goes to school. She'd be a target. We'd be a target.'

Will deposited the tomatoes in the bowl. 'I don't think Chloë would be in danger. They would choose better targets.'

'How do you know?'

Will ignored that. 'Fanny, I'd be cast out. There's no question of that. Permanent backbencherdom. But I can't quite bring myself to sell out.' With a little jerk of anxiety, I saw that we had come to an unexpected crossroads and Will wanted me to choose for him.

'Will . . .' I heard myself say, and wrapped my hands in my apron. 'Please don't do this. Don't sacrifice all you've worked for. The figures suggest the Bill is going to go through whether you vote for it or not. It would be . . . a wasted gesture.'

Will said quietly, 'You've changed your tune.'

I turned away before shame got the better of me. 'The quiche is ready,' I said.

Later that night, when we were in bed, Will asked, 'Is that your last word?'

I grasped the edge of the sheet and drove the point of the corner under a nail. 'Yes, it is. You're making your way, and that's what you want and what I want for you. And there is Chloë. I *have* to think of Chloë. So do you.'

'And conviction and principle?'

I wanted to say that the question was bigger than me. I wanted to be a coward and protest that I was confined to the business of stacking sheets and moving food from the oven to the table, and that some questions were impossible to answer. I wanted to say, too, that it took only the merest hint of a threat to Chloë to make me take the stand.

It would not do. If I still possessed a shred of honesty, those excuses were not the whole truth. Of course – passionately anti-hunting – I minded about the fish and the birds. Of course I would have died for Chloë. Yet, somewhere along the line, I had grown accustomed to the up-and-coming politician who was my husband. Painfully and slowly, yes, but I had adapted to fit the mould and learnt to relish his role and mine.

He rolled towards me. 'Come here.'

I obeyed. Will used me roughly, carelessly and without finesse but, because I deserved it, I made no protest.

The following week, I joined Will at the mansion flat in Westminster.

He was sitting on the sofa. It was growing dark but he had not turned on the light.

'You'll have seen the vote, Fanny. But I don't think I did the right thing.'

I sat down beside him and took his hand. 'I don't know what to say, Will, except that we have to make our way, too.'

'You could say I'm a fool. A fool, furthermore, who has given in.'

There was no point now in not sticking to my guns. 'Or is being realistic.'

The sofa was covered with a cheap, rough-textured slub cotton and I picked away at it. Will disengaged his hand and got to his feet. 'It was my call, my decision, Fanny. Nobody can make me vote one way or the other.'

I swallowed, tasting the acid of compromise.

'I wouldn't know,' I answered, but that was not true either. I did know.

Will stuck his hands into his pockets. He was already adapting to the situation, making the best of it. 'That's that,' he said, and his smile was ironic. 'These things come up. You deal with them and then you move on. We'd better get dressed for the reception.'

If I listened carefully, I could trace both mockery and disappointment – in himself.

And in me.

And Will was right.

Back at Casa Rosa, I stripped to the skin and washed at the basin by the window that overlooked the valley. The water ran down from my shoulders to my toes, cool and sweet, and I thought of Lucilla's sufferings – my unknown great-aunt – and of the terrible things that had happened to her. Poor Lucilla: she had imagined that in marrying she was satisfying her private desires. Yet on account of her husband's politics they had become a public matter.

The towel crunched against my shoulders, which were a little tender from the sun. I rubbed cream into my legs and arms and bent down to clip my toenails. Their rims were white against my brown skin.

Raoul knocked on the door at precisely eight o'clock. 'May I come in?' Tonight, he had changed into a formal linen suit.

I stood aside. 'Yes. Yes, do.'

Without further preliminaries, he stepped into the house and took me in his arms.

I let him.

'Don't look so worried,' Raoul ordered, holding me close.

'But I should be,' I replied.

He touched his finger to my lips. 'Shush . . . I know.' He twined his fingers through my hair and tugged until my scalp rippled. 'I have wanted to do that for a long time. Never cut your hair, will you, Fanny? So thick, and dark.'

'When I'm old, I'll have to.'

Raoul bent over and kissed me. His lips were dry, and there was a faint trace of wine on his breath and the smell of his expensive aftershave – a hint of unspoken and mysterious pleasures. I placed my hands on Raoul's chest and pushed him away gently. 'Won't we be late?'

He released me. 'Fanny, what I love about you is your innocence.'

Astonished, I looked up at him. 'But I'm not innocent,' I protested. 'Not in the least.'

Raoul and I returned in the small hours to Fiertino, having dined lavishly *en famille* at La Foce and sampled wines from the golden year of 1970. The talk had been almost exclusively of wine: new methods, new production, the use of oak casks . . . The Italian slipped from me easily and fluently now, and the language of wine gave me no trouble.

The melon we ate was perfumed with summer. The meat was so tender that it fell apart at the touch of a fork. The grapes that accompanied the cheese were dark, and bursting with juice.

Raoul was at his best. The elegant rooms and furniture provided a setting that suited him. Every so often he sent me a look or touched my shoulder. Look, he was saying, at how seductive I can make seduction. Please enjoy it. This, here, tonight, is a taste of what we will have. Light, joyous, civilized, and full of sensual pleasures.

Helped by the wine, I talked and laughed, relished the

feel of my linen dress on my skin, the fall of my hair on my shoulders.

I described my father's interests to my host, and imagined being woken by Raoul. Still drenched with sleep, I would be warm, face washed smooth by unconsciousness, naked, and I would allow him to do what he wished. It would be a moment of pleasure and sensation: to be tasted, savoured and noted. *Exquisite. Complex. Flawless.*

My hostess offered coffee in tiny brittle cups and I told her about my daughter. She was clever, she would be beautiful . . . and, suddenly, I was gripped by a terror at how easy it would be to destroy Chloë's optimism and trust. As easy as it would be to drop and break one of my hostess's coffee cups.

We drove back over the hills in bright, intense moonlight. The cypresses pointed dark fingers up into the sky. Raoul parked the car outside Casa Rosa. 'I'm asking you again, can I come in?' He leant over and brushed back the hair from my hot face. 'I can't not ask. I don't *want* to ask. I am desperately afraid, but I have to ask.'

Again he kissed me, and I was startled by how different it was. With Raoul there were no accustomed pathways that had been followed across the years, no previous knowledge, except for what I now saw was an imperfect memory of what happened in the tree-house. Had it been so very bad?

'I have always loved you,' he said. 'It has been a long time. That doesn't mean that I don't love Thérèse. I do, and she would die if she ever knew what I was saying to you, and I would never harm her. Am I making sense?'

I touched his cheek. 'Lovely sense.'

It was an extraordinarily intimate moment.

The interior of the car was growing very hot and I opened the door and climbed out, conscious of the arrangement of my arms and legs, of the texture of my dress, of the sweat on my body.

I looked up at a night sky sprayed with pinpoints of light. 'I can't get over what a difference a few hundred miles makes,' I said to Raoul, who was standing beside me. 'You never see sky like this in England ... nothing so beautiful.'

'Has it been worth it, Fanny?' he asked.

'Who knows? A few years back I would have said yes, but I don't know any more.'

'That sounds quite healthy. As nothing is certain, we might as well own up to it.'

'Uncomfortable, though.'

Raoul was not looking at the sky. 'It took me a long time to get over the tree-house,' he said, and we had arrived at the point of the evening. 'It haunts me. It also amazed me how sex can destroy something so quickly. Just like that.'

I let my hand rest on his arm. 'You know ... I knew nothing about sex, or not much, and I was frightened by the experience.' I smiled. 'But I got over it. It took a little while, and by then you had gone back to France. Life went on in a different way. It was bad timing.'

Raoul took my hand and we wandered towards the house. In the moonlight, Casa Rosa appeared larger than it was, mysterious, and its windows glinted darkly in the moonlight.

'Are you unhappy, Fanny?'

'I came to bury Alfredo's ashes. I can't quite decide where yet, but I don't think he minds waiting. I think he would want me to take my time. And . . . I suppose . . . I came out here to escape, for a bit, and to think. I have been unhappy, but I don't think significantly so.'

I touched the wooden column by the front door. 'Even the wood is hot.'

Raoul pushed me up against the column. I felt beautiful, mysterious and elated. I felt like a bird climbing into flight. And why not? Once, Will had betrayed me. Why not I? Uncertainty, mystery, playfulness . . . could be mine. I could take them and bundle them up into an area marked 'Private', and Will would never know.

Raoul placed one hand on my breast, the other at my waist and pressed his fingers into the curve of my back. It was a confident gesture. 'Second time luckier, Fanny.'

I stretched out my neck and waited for my surrender. *Willing* my surrender.

The past dug in its hook. What was it I had promised myself so long ago? *If I worked where Will did and watched the prowling men, I would have fought to keep the faith, to cherish a perfection.*

And then I thought of Will, clearly and properly, and I knew that if Raoul and I went into Casa Rosa together, that would be the moment at which our marriage died. And what would remain? A man and a woman living under one roof, and the rooms under that roof would be empty and echoing.

'No,' I said sharply. 'Raoul, I've made a mistake.'

'Fanny . . .'

'I wish I hadn't, but I have. I can't get away with it.'

'Yes, you can.'

'Not in that way. *I* can't get away with it. With what's in my head.'

'Could I point out, Fanny, that at this moment I'm not interested in what is going on in your head?' Raoul's hand tightened on my flesh and fell away.

'I'm very sorry. I don't expect you to understand.'

'That is beside the point,' he said, and moved away.

While we had been talking, a figure had stepped round the side of the house. It was a woman dressed in a cotton skirt that adapted itself smoothly to the lines of her body as she moved.

'Hallo,' said Meg. 'I've been waiting for you to return. I wasn't sure that the taxi had dumped me at the right place. Then I spotted a wine book on the kitchen table.' She moved forward and the moon outlined her in a sharp, silver light. 'Hallo, Raoul, I haven't seen you for a long time. Fanny always keeps you to herself whenever you come over.'

Raoul did not miss a beat. He went over and kissed Meg's cheek. 'Fanny did not mention . . .'

Meg submitted to Raoul's embrace. 'That was nice.' She touched her cheek. 'We should meet more often. Come to that, Will didn't mention that you were here.'

'Will doesn't know,' I said.

Meg looked from Raoul to me. 'Oh, well,' she said.

Raoul laid a hand on my shoulder. 'I will be in touch. Maybe we can all have dinner somewhere before I go home.'

All three of us knew this was a fiction.

'Oh, yes,' said Meg. '*That* would be cosy.'

19

'Just what are you doing here?' I demanded after Raoul had driven away.

'Arriving in the nick of time, it would seem,' she said drily.

There was no answer to that.

Meg followed me into the kitchen and dropped her suitcase on to the floor.

'If I said, Fanny, that it seemed a little greedy of you to have all this space in a lovely house in Italy and not to share it . . . or I could say, that I missed you. So does Will. He does love you, you know. And . . .' She bit her lip, but spoke with her usual mockery, 'I love whoever Will loves . . .'

Her eyes shifted away, and I knew she was frightened as to my reaction.

Meg commandeered the single chair in the kitchen, leaving me to stand. 'He was nice. My darling brother is always nice to me. But he made it plain that he didn't wish me to appear at his side. He said . . .' She grimaced. 'He said it was your place, not mine. But before you go all dewy, he had probably calculated that if I stood in for you people would talk.'

'Meg – '

'Will never gives up. When he dies you'll find "percentage swing" engraved on his heart.'

'Who taught him to be like that in the first place?'

'I suppose it might have had something to do with me.' Meg nudged her suitcase with a foot. 'I'm sorry to have surprised you, Fanny, it was not nice of me, but you can make room. We've lived together long enough.'

My energy had returned and I knew I had to confront Meg. The compromises were over. 'Go home,' I said. 'I won't have you here. This is *my* breathing space.'

Meg's lips quivered. 'Don't be nasty, Fanny. I'm not sure I can bear it.'

'Try.'

'I have tried, and I need you.'

It was close to midnight. It was hot, I was bone tired, the airport was miles away and, as usual, Meg had brought her baggage of the funny, the sad and the monstrous with her, and there was nothing much to be done.

We cleared a space in the second bedroom. Inhaling camphor, I knelt down by the chest of drawers in the corridor and searched among its contents for extra sheets. Eventually, I found a pair with embroidered initials, MS, at the corner and we made up Meg's bed.

'Clearly, this was meant,' she said.

Heated with the effort of dragging furniture around, we went outside and walked up the road.

'What will you do with me in the morning?' she asked.

'I don't know.'

Our feet stirred up a wake of white dust as we passed. Cicadas sang in the undergrowth. The darkness was scented – basil and marjoram, a hint of lemon – and far, far removed from the cool, rain-laden, sodden air of Stanwinton.

I broke the silence. 'I've been out of touch. Is there any news?'

'The polls show that support is slipping,' Meg sounded troubled, 'but what can you expect? Everyone needs a change. People get fed up with continuity and good intentions.'

We walked past the clump of olives and the vineyard where the vines grew straight and disciplined. At the end of each row there was a rosebush.

'Nice detail,' observed Meg.

I pinched a leaf or two of wild thyme between my fingers and sniffed. 'Smell this. You'll never buy herbs in a bottle again.'

At the point where the road divided, we halted. One fork led down into Fiertino, whose lights, a bright contrast against the dark sky, were strung in a necklace of brilliants. The other snaked up past Casa Rosa and over the hill. Meg pushed back her hair. 'It's hot.'

'That's its point, to be as different from Stanwinton as possible.' I spoke more passionately than I'd intended.

'Poor you, you've got it bad.'

'I have. But I've sorted out a few things while I've been here.'

'If you call Raoul sorting out,' she said.

We walked on. 'Raoul and I are good friends. I knew him long before I met Will.'

'If you say so, Fanny.' Meg scuffed at a stone with a sandalled foot. 'I have been good, Fanny,' she said. 'I'm as clean as a whistle. I *have* tried.'

I was touched by the halting admission.

'I wish I'd been different, Fanny. I wish I'd *done* things

differently. I would never have ended up so . . . wanting. So under the spell of a substance.' Meg tugged at her hair so hard it must have hurt.

I sighed deeply and Meg heard. She gave a bitter laugh. 'Drink destroys. A girl fetches up with no friends, no husbands, no lovers. Only . . . only a son, and he has grown up and gone away. That leaves you and Will.' She paused. 'You managed it better. As you *always* do, Fanny . . . the good Fanny.'

'OK, Meg,' I said. 'We've had this conversation before.'

Meg did a swift volte-face. 'Two old lags, then.'

'Less of the old.' In the moonlight, Meg's face looked odd, strained. 'What's wrong?'

'I'm trying to frown. I've had Botox shots. I reckoned if I couldn't frown, life wouldn't seem so dreadful. But I keep forgetting.'

I found myself standing – an adulteress *manquée* – on the dusty, moonlit road with the lights of Fiertino blazing in the distance, helpless with laughter.

'You should have some too, Fanny,' Meg suggested, when she could get a word in edgeways. 'You're getting a few lines.'

I tucked my hand under her brittle elbow. 'Meg, why don't you consider doing that university course you once talked about?'

She froze but did not draw away. 'I'm not clever enough for that.'

'Actually, you are.'

We walked back up the path to Casa Rosa. 'I'm frightened of not winning my particular battle,' Meg admitted, in a rush. 'For the rest of my life, I will be on twenty-four-hour watch. But the demon will try to slip under my defences, in the dark, when I'm sleepy and sad. It will try to outwit me in the sunshine, and the boredom of the day when nobody minds if I'm there or not.'

'Sacha minds. Will minds . . . I mind.'

'Sacha is . . . a son. Not a husband, or a lover, or a companion.'

During the night, I heard Meg call out. I threw back my sheet and felt my way across the room over the cool floor. Meg was hunched on her side and the sheets were twisted and bunched. I bent over her and she muttered something unintelligible: a troubled, sad sound. Inadequate to console, and guilty that I did not want her here, I did my best to straighten the sheets. 'Meg?'

Her eyes flicked open but she looked through me, and beyond.

After she had quietened, I went downstairs and took out the two bottles of wine – Vigna L'Apparita (the merlot grape) – which had been given to me by our host at La Foce, from where I had racked them in the kitchen. These were worth dying for, and I hid them under a cache of cardboard.

Upstairs, I searched for aspirins for my aching head and upended the contents of my handbag on the bed. My new mobile phone dropped out and I switched it on. A text message flashed up: 'I LV U Mum Cxxx'.

I sat down and wept tears for my father and Chloë's absence. Tears of confusion and – more than a little – of regret.

The next morning I left Meg, still asleep, in Casa Rosa.

It was market day in Fiertino, and the square was choked

with vans and stalls selling cut-price kitchenware, mounds of vegetables and raffia baskets. I bought a bucket from a stall and rubber gloves, a broom, disinfectant, cream cleanser, descaler and polish in the supermarket.

'Signora.' The dark-eyed woman serving me spotted the red bumps on my arm and tossed a tube into the purchases. '*Per i morsi*,' she said, with a smile. '*Gratis*.'

I thanked her and trudged back to the house in the now broiling sun. I tied a scarf round my head, boiled water and began the cleaning.

I scrubbed the table. The kitchen floor. The bathroom. I brushed every nook and cranny of the house and the dead insects piled into heaps. I cleaned the windows, chipped away at the fur-encrusted taps, washed the walls, erasing with scourer and chemical the stain of doubt on myself.

Perhaps, in life, one regrets more the things that one did not do than those one did?

What would my father have thought?

Surely what was important was the affirmation of passionate feeling? The resolve never to have an empty heart?

The chemicals and the immersion in water puckered my fingers into pink prunes. My back grew stiff from stooping, and I was soaked with sweat from head to foot. To clean Casa Rosa properly was a hopeless task, but I was going to do it.

'Looks to me like a bad conscience,' Meg commented, when she eventually appeared. 'Scrubbing away the sins. Don't ask me to join in.' There was a red mark on one cheek where she had slept on it and her fair hair was mussed. 'Any hot water?'

'I've used it up.'

Meg looked thoughtful. 'It's very frontier,' she said. 'Still, if that's what's required, Fanny, I'll wash in cold to join you in spirit.'

From where I knelt on my hands and knees, I said, 'Ring up the airport, Meg, and book a flight home.'

'Please Fanny. Let me stay. *Please.*'

'Why is *she* here?' Benedetta whispered to me when, later in the morning, I took Meg over to see her. 'To make the trouble?'

'I hope not.'

Benedetta opened her dark eyes wide and I saw how beautiful they still were and remembered how my father had once loved them. 'Big nuisance, Fanny.'

Meg was on her best behaviour, but she was not offered a fresh tomato from Benedetta's crop and I took the hint.

Strangely enough, Meg was still *in situ* at Casa Rosa the following morning and we ate breakfast at Angelo's.

'*Amore!*' Maria, who was busy at the coffee machine, called.

'That's what mothers call their sons in Italy,' I informed Meg.

'A mummy's boy?' Meg smiled winningly at Angelo, who blushed, and watched his well-covered form as he hastened inside to answer his mother.

'No more than Sacha.'

Meg tried to frown and failed. 'Sacha does not always obey his mummy.'

Meg's brioche had been reduced to crumbs, but not

much had been eaten. 'You should eat,' I said. 'Eat break-fast like a king.'

'Funny how we repeat the same things. I used to say that to Will. He was bullied at school and it took away his appetite.'

'Will? Bullied?'

Meg seemed surprised. 'Didn't he tell you? No, well, I suppose he wouldn't. He'd probably die rather than admit he'd been frightened. But he was.'

'Go on.'

Meg wet the tip of her finger, picked up a crumb on it and put it into her mouth. '*I* was frightened of the grandparents. Not that they were evil or anything, but just so old and boring, and they preached all the time. I was always terrified I'd go home and find two dead bodies. That's why Will always waited for me after school. That was one of the reasons he was bullied. *Loves his sis.*'

'And the others?'

Meg sounded impatient. 'There were so many.'

A horn tooted. It was Raoul. He parked under a tree and walked over to join us. 'I've come to say goodbye. As it turns out, I can't stay.'

Meg searched in her bag and produced a lipstick, which she proceeded to apply. Its dark pink glistened on her mouth.

Raoul's departure did not surprise me. There was no point in his staying. We both needed a polite gap and to make the readjustments. I thought with a flash of bitterness and regret of how I would miss our conversations.

When Raoul got up to go, he bent over and kissed me. 'I will be in the UK later in the year,' he said pleasantly.

'I will ring you. I would like to talk to you about the business.'

'Have you decided where to bury Alfredo's ashes?' Meg watched Raoul's car negotiate the traffic around the piazza and vanish.

'No.'

'I thought that was why you came here,' she remarked innocently. Her attention was now drawn to a van unloading pallets of spinach and melons. 'Are you planning changes, Fanny? I didn't *quite* buy the burying-my-father's-ashes story. Especially when I saw that Raoul had put in an appearance. This little escape is more of a not-waving-but-drowning gesture, which must be to do with my brother.' She paused. 'Perhaps you're thinking that the marriage has run its course. Marriages do. You start out full of good intentions, the *best* intentions, and life gets in the way.' She flicked me a look. 'You're well rid of Raoul. What's it worth for my silence?'

'I'll tell Will. Of course.'

'I wouldn't if I were you,' she said.

I fiddled with a packet of sugar. 'I bought myself some time.'

'I'm sorry I cramped your style.'

'No, you're not.' I gave Angelo the money for the bill. 'Go home, Meg and don't interfere.'

'Consider me warned.' Meg got to her feet. 'Other people's lives are just that. Other people's lives. And a complete mystery.'

*

Meg did not go home after a few days. Of course, she didn't. Initially, there were difficulties in changing her ticket. Then it appeared there were no available seats to London for a couple of weeks. Then she said. 'Look, I might as well stay on until you leave. It's only one more week.'

Each day that I spent in the valley, I grew more detached from my former life. I looked back at it, dim and blurred, through the glass, without nostalgia, only half remembered, imperfect in detail. An inner sleepiness folded around me, almost smothering, and I was happy to sit and do nothing as the light deepened, turned brassy and the heat set in.

I thought about Chloë, the thick rope of feeling that bound me to her, and how, after she was born, I was no longer a separate person. I thought of Raoul, my first lover, from whom I had fled – for a second time. Of Will, my great love. The shapes of our lives and the spaces between them.

When Meg woke, we walked into Fiertino, took a table overlooking the piazza at Angelo's and ordered coffee. Sometimes, the piazza was almost deserted. Sometimes, summoned by a mysterious force, there was an influx of the puttering vans the Italians favoured, and fumes mixed with the odour of coffee and vegetables from the supermarket next door.

I drank my coffee and worked through my wine books while Meg read a novel or gazed at nothing much. I liked it there, and I think Meg did too – she seemed content. Our only major expenditure of energy was to move our chairs into the shade as the sun shifted.

'You know,' she said, 'Will would like this.'

'Will?'

'Don't you see? He's never had a chance to sit and do nothing. He has always been so driven. Right from the word go.' She cupped her chin in her hands. 'My brother's a brave man and it's not his fault that the world is so difficult and awful. Anyway, Will wasn't going to let it get the better of us.' The eyelids closed on the dark eyes. 'See?'

Each day, from either the shop or the market, we selected a different vegetable as the main ingredient for lunch. Tomato or aubergine? Zucchini or big fat mushrooms? I did the chopping. Meg confected the dressings. (She had a knack for balancing the balsamic vinegar, oil and mustard.)

In the afternoons we took a siesta, and in the early evenings we braced ourselves to get into the car and do some sightseeing. More often than not, we drank iced coffee in a nearby village.

I took Meg to the museum in Tarquinia and asked her if she recognized the couple. 'Oh, yes,' she said, 'of course I do. The happy couple.' She peered at the inscription. 'They died so young that there wasn't time for hatred and boredom.'

'No,' I said.

Then I took her to see the frescos in the Fiertino church. She stared at them for a long time. Finally, she moved away – 'Too hellfire for me,' she said.

After that, by mutual agreement, we dropped the cultural trips.

20

Instead, Meg and I were perfectly happy to shop. When the sun dropped behind the hill, and it grew cooler, we browsed through boutiques and markets, tried on neat Italian jumpers, discussed handbags. We bought pretty straw baskets and silk scarves for Meg.

Maria tipped us off about a shoe-shop tucked away in a street behind the church. 'All the shoes from Rome,' she said, and winked. 'But not the prices.' Meg and I agreed that we had a duty to shore up the local economy.

The shop was in the medieval quarter of the town. Hot, dark and womb-like, its interior smelt pleasingly of leather and varnish – a craftsman's smell. We spent a good half-hour hunting through the racks. Meg pounced on a pair of cunning high heels and I hovered between delicious red-leather sandals, which spoke to me, and a utilitarian black pair with 'Stanwinton' written all over them, which did not.

Meg slotted her feet into her shoes and turned a full circle. She seemed excited, alight with joy, almost a girl again, and I could see why Rob had fallen in love with her. Rocking on the heels, she said, 'Will bought me my first pair of nice shoes. He took a job stacking supermarket shelves and saved up. He wanted to say thank you to me. I kept them for years.'

Our stay in Fiertino had had an unexpected consequence: it had loosened Meg's tongue. She had dropped quite a few bits of information into my lap. 'Take them,' she appeared to be saying. 'They are my present to you.'

She was trying to tell me about the unknown Will: the one who had existed before I knew him. Scratch me for the facts, and I could tell you that Will's favourite breakfast was fried bacon. I knew what kind of shirts he favoured, the way he turned over in his sleep and flung an arm over his head. I knew that he loved his daughter, that he had been unfaithful to me. I knew we had had many years together.

But I was ignorant about the slice of his life when Meg had held the reins in hands that must have trembled often – with fear and anxiety.

I replaced the red sandals on the shelf. 'It's too hot in here. Another time.'

'More fool you,' said Meg, and paid for hers.

At the end of the week Will rang. 'Fantastic news, Fanny. Chloë's got her results. Two As and a B. I phoned her and she was so pleased.'

A lump sprang into my throat. 'Clever, wonderful Chloë.'

We discussed her university plans and which of her friends had got what. While we were talking, I entertained a vision of Chloë, now properly grown up, graduating in a black gown, getting married, coming home with a trio of grandchildren. Time was slipping this way and quickly, and I had to catch up with it.

'Did you send her my love?'

'Of course. How are you both?'

'Practically comatose.'

'Good.' He cleared his throat. 'The house seems very empty. But I have been in London quite a lot. The flat's a bit of a mess, I'm afraid. I'm sorry you were invaded by Meg. I know you wanted a bit of a breathing space. But these last few weeks have been hell.' He continued in the same vein. Dreadful weather. Tedious boxes. Finally he said, wistfully, 'You seem a long way away.'

I brushed a dead fly on to the floor. Did I miss it in my cleaning frenzy? 'Guess who turned up? Raoul. We went out for a marvellous dinner with his friends and talked vineyards and vintages.'

'How nice,' he said guardedly. 'By the way, there's a stack of papers from the lawyer waiting for you here.'

'Yes, I know.' I made an effort. 'Tell me what's happening.'

'The polls are gloomy,' he said, 'but perhaps that's to be expected . . .'

While Will talked, I stared out of the window at an olive tree which grew precariously but defiantly on the slope above the house. The undersides of its leaves appeared white in the sun.

I heard the rustle of a cigarette packet. 'Fanny . . . as I feared, the second-car tax is to be dropped. It's too sensitive. With an election coming up . . . so, very politely, I've been told to bugger off, keep my head down and someone will fling me a bone if I am very good. End of story. I suppose, after all this, I don't care very much.'

This would not be true. 'Then we needn't waste any more time on it, Will.'

'I thought you'd be a bit more sympathetic.'

'I am sympathetic. Very. I'm sorry you've been disappointed, but it's over.'

In the hall of the Casa Rosa, I turned myself round and the telephone cord twisted across my leg, but I wanted to look at the vines the other side of the road. How curious. Why had I had failed to notice that a pylon sat precisely between two cypresses on the hilltop?

'Fanny, when are you coming home?'

I heard myself say, 'I don't want to come back. I feel at home here.'

Meg was not stupid and she had cottoned on that Benedetta did not like her. 'Look,' she said, later that evening, as we prepared to walk over to her for a pasta supper, 'on second thoughts, I'll leave you two to talk over old times. I'll have something to eat at Angelo's. I'd prefer it.'

It was agreed.

Dressed in her best print frock, over which she had tied a lace apron, Benedetta was in a cheerful mood. Radio Vatican provided a background commentary. 'My son,' she smiled broadly, 'he has phoned to say that he is coming in the winter.' She handed me a knife. 'Make the salad, please, Fanny.'

Red and luscious, the tomatoes fell away from my knife. I snatched up a piece and crammed it into my mouth. It tasted of sun and earth. I arranged the slices on a plate, and scattered basil over them. The Madonna smiled down from her vantage-point on the wall. Cramped and cluttered it might have been, but Benedetta's kitchen was a comfortable place, far more comfortable than my kitchen in Stanwinton, for all its modern conveniences.

We carried our food out on to the back porch, and while we ate we talked about my father.

Benedetta pressed another slice of her apricot tart on to my plate. 'He never forgave himself that your mother left.'

'Why do you think he would never marry again? I never understood.'

'And give you a stepmother? No. Alfredo told me he *never* wanted that for you.'

Best not to pursue the subject.

Back in the bedroom at Casa Rosa, I addressed the casket that held his ashes. 'Where shall I put you, Dad? Where would you like to be? Will you tell me?'

An hour or so later Meg returned, and I sat on the stairs in my nightdress while she chatted away to me from the kitchen.

'Tea?' There was a clatter of water as she filled the kettle. 'I had a good meal.' The gas popped and she appeared in the kitchen doorway. There was a faint colour in her cheeks and her hair looked soft and shiny. 'Sure you don't want some tea? Angelo's is fun at night, full of young bloods who make a lot of noise. I enjoyed it, even picked up a word or two of Italian, so you don't have to worry about me.'

On the loggia the next morning, I was dreaming over my first cup of coffee when Benedetta puffed up the road. I sat her down and fetched her a glass of iced water. She drank noisily. 'Fanny, you must be aware that foreigners in particular are noticed. And there are many eyes in Fiertino.'

'I'm not a foreigner,' I protested. 'Not exactly.'

'*Santa Patata*. I lived for ten years in England and I was still a foreigner.'

I took a sharp breath and picked up her hand. 'You were my mother.'

Benedetta rubbed her finger over my wrist. 'I was and I wasn't.'

'How have I sinned?'

'Not you. Meg. She was seen by Angelo going into the Bacchus with a couple of the younger men. Bacchus is not a good place. The women don't go there. You must tell her.'

By the time Meg woke up Benedetta had long gone. I tackled her at once. 'You've been spotted.'

'Oh, for God's sake.' Meg slapped at an ant on her arm. She was pale and groggy with sleep, and her hair straggled sweatily over her shoulders. 'It's none of your business where I end up. I had a peach juice, that's all. I just wanted some company. Is that so odd, or wicked?'

'No, but why didn't you mention it?'

She gave me a level look. 'Think about it.'

My own hair felt hot and heavy and I scraped it back. 'Angelo's nice. He just wanted to warn you. It's probably nothing much but they know things that we can't. We are, as Benedetta has just reminded me, foreigners.'

Meg's ravaged face was unreadable. 'Angelo thinks I'm worth bothering about?'

'Obviously.'

'It's just a bar with a few chairs, and a naughty picture stuck up on the wall.' Her mouth tightened disagreeably. 'Who cares?'

She was willing me to say, 'I care'. But I could not bring myself to say it.

Meg's curious, hopeful expression faded. 'Perhaps your behaviour doesn't bear too much examination either, Fanny.'

Perhaps it didn't. There was no answer to that.

'OK,' she said. 'Point taken. But I'm not promising anything.' She looked down the valley. 'I suppose it *is* a very small town. *Very* Dark Ages.'

'It was just a friendly warning. Benedetta was concerned.'

'Yes, dear.' She shot me a look. I didn't know what it meant – except that I was uneasy, and the knot that tied Meg and me together was as tight as it had ever been.

We patched things up and decided to go to Siena. We swept the floors, brought in the washing from the garden and went round the house closing the shutters.

Meg was wearing a red skirt and a white blouse and huge sunglasses. I put on the dress which I had worn to the dinner in La Foce. She linked her arm in mine. 'We do credit to each other.'

In the car, she asked me. 'Did I really interrupt something with Raoul?'

'I had already sent him away.'

'But why?'

I glanced at her. Her hands were folded in her lap and she was looking straight ahead. 'I don't need a lover.'

'You don't *need* a husband.'

'Ah,' I replied, 'but I have one.'

She turned away abruptly but not before I spotted tears running down behind the large sunglasses.

When I married Will, I thought only of him: my hunger to know him, my delight and pride in his ideas and ambition to help, and my excitement that we had chosen to be together. He felt the same. Only later did I understand that I was required to pick up other lives and carry them as well as my own.

We spent the afternoon exploring the city, and wandering the streets to no great purpose. We bought salami, olive oil and raffia mats, and Meg insisted on presenting me with a blue and white plate for the kitchen at home. 'A corner of a foreign field,' she said, 'for Stanwinton.'

We agreed that the cathedral looked like a black and white humbug and decided to give it a miss, heading instead for a café on the edge of the piazza where we ordered pistachio ice-cream and coffee.

'This is nice,' said Meg, softly. 'Pity Will isn't here.' I made no comment. 'You know what I think? I suspect mid-life crisis with my brother. It happens, and Will would never say. He's not like that.' She dug down into the frozen mixture: pale green, glossy and grainy with the nuts. 'I might tackle him.'

At a stroke, the peace and accommodations between us were ruptured. An old jealousy caught me by the throat. No doubt Meg was right. But I could no longer bear – *I could not bear* – her prowling around my life. The inner, intimate life, which, for all its tatters and tears, for all its precariousness, belonged to Will and me.

Meg spooned ice-cream into her mouth and swallowed. The sun had shifted. A shadow lay across the piazza. Birds wheeled around the campanile uttering shrill cries.

'Meg,' I said, 'when we get back to Stanwinton you *must* find somewhere of your own.'

Her spoon clattered against the metal ice-cream bowl. 'Christ,' she said, and went pale under her tan.

'I think it would be best.'

'I can't,' she said calmly. 'I'm no good at just me.'

'You don't have to go far away. You tell me that you're managing to keep on track.'

She shook her head. 'That's not the point.'

Meg stumbled to her feet. 'I've just thought of something.' She picked up her leather bag, swung the strap over her shoulder and disappeared into the nearest street opening.

'Meg! Come back.'

Angry with her, furious with my ineptness, yet relieved in the way one feels after a boil is lanced, I sat for five minutes or so, and I thought: this is an end.

I paid the bill and set off in search of her. The via Duomo was lined with boutiques selling beautiful objects – scarves, leather handbags, pearls of a size and whiteness that were startling in the comparative gloom of the narrow street. In one shop I admired a particularly lustrous string. Beside them, there was a large ruby and diamond ring balanced on a velvet cushion. It struck me that it required a home.

And Meg required a home.

On the opposite side of the street there was a shop whose long glass doors were thrown open to reveal rows of shelving stacked with hundreds of bottles of wine. I slipped inside, breathing the familiar smell of wooden crates and the must that grows on the bottles. The wine was arranged by continent and country: Chile, Italy, the US ... The reds glowed with dark greens and browns. The whites reflected a spectrum of pale yellow, gold and amber.

An expert hand had made the selection: Château de Fonsalette Cuvée Syrah, Monte Antico Russo and, incredibly, a Beringer Private Reserve from the Napa Valley in California, a personal, idiosyncratic choice by a wine lover who had honed discrimination to the finest pitch.

I ran my hand along a shelf. Years of thinking, tasting, making mistakes were racked up in these shelves. A lifetime of inching forward towards true understanding, true knowledge, true feeling.

I wanted to do the same.

A movement behind me made me turn round. Leading off the main shop was a second, even more dimly lit room with no window. A woman was holding a bottle – carefully, almost tenderly.

It was Meg.

'A good one,' she held it out for my inspection, 'but not outstanding. I think that is what your father would conclude.'

I glanced at it. A 1988 Pomerol. 'I disagree. This is outstanding.'

'Oh, no,' she said. 'Trust me. I *know.*'

How can I trust you, I wanted to throw at her, when you step so carelessly on what is mine? My husband, my wine, even my daughter. How can you trust a trespasser?

Meg raised an eyebrow. Even *that* was Will's.

I turned away. In the street, the tourists plodded up and down, clutching plastic bags with interesting bulges. They were taking home olive oil and local pottery and, some of the better-off, jewellery. They would take with them the scent and taste of Italy. Afterwards they would go to a supermarket or shop, hunt out inferior oil or *sugo di pomodoro*, take it home but it would not be the same.

Behind me, Meg was saying. 'Your father was right about most things. Would he have advised me to find somewhere else to live?'

21

On the way back to Casa Rosa, Meg and I spoke only when necessary. I went to bed early.

After the day's heat, the sheets were a cool, fresh contrast. I read, I made notes and, occasionally, I glanced up at the wooden casket on the shelf. Would my father approve of what I had done? I wasn't sure. Maybe he would have felt that you have to hang on to the bits and pieces of a family, whatever the cost.

I put out the light and settled to sleep. I felt the relief of the patient who, after illness and incapacity, has taken a first step.

A noise on the stairs followed by a cautious footstep on the path outside made me sit up. I swung my legs out of bed and pushed open the shutters. 'Meg?'

Moonlight streamed into my bedroom and illuminated the thin figure on the path below. Meg had twisted up her hair into a sexy caramel knot and she was wearing her new high heels. The light played tricks, for she looked so young and pretty that I caught my breath. She raised an arm and the bracelets on her wrist emitted a faint, high shiver of sound.

I leant on the sill. 'Don't go,' I begged, for I had a good idea where she was heading.

She laughed without humour. 'Jealous?'

'I so am jealous.' I mocked Chloë's vernacular.

She shook her head. 'Not convincing, Fanny. You'll have to do better.'

Her voice was husky with excitement. I clutched at my nightdress. 'Wait. I'm coming down.'

The cotton flapped round my legs as I ran out on to the path. Meg was searching in her shoulder-bag and I grabbed at the strap. 'It's not worth it. Stay.'

'But you've told me to go. You have made . . . everything quite clear.'

In a final effort, I tugged hard at the strap and Meg swayed a little on her high heels. 'But it doesn't mean you have to throw everything away. Don't be silly. Please, please, stay here. We'll talk . . . I'll listen to you . . . whatever.' Meg shrugged and I threw in quickly, 'Think of Sacha. Think of Will.'

'I am thinking of them,' she said. 'Very much.'

'I was unkind.'

'Go back to bed,' she said, an adult addressing a troublesome child. 'I'm going out for a little diversion. I know *exactly* what I'm doing.'

'Do you want me to go down on my knees? I will, you know, if that's what it takes.'

Meg fiddled with her bracelets. 'I must make you understand, Fanny. It's all right. I'm in control. But . . .' she seemed to be searching for an explanation, 'I'm not the only woman to have fallen from grace, and to have inflicted these wounds upon myself. But, at times, I've felt so alone. That's what makes me so crabby and selfish, I guess.' She nodded her head. 'I appreciate the knees bit though, Fanny. I know what it would cost you, and I'm tempted to take you up on it.'

I forced Meg back into the kitchen and made her sit down. 'Talk to me. Come on. You can talk to me.'

She seemed both surprised and gratified. 'I've tried.' Her mouth tightened and she fiddled with the bracelets. 'OK. Confession time. I've tried very hard to absorb myself in other things. Clothes. Part-time work here and there. An occasional lover. Charity, or whatever those women do who have too much time on their hands. But apart from Sacha, and you and Will and Chloë, nothing burrowed very deep. My mind had been blown.'

'I'm listening.' I put on the kettle and the gas-ring glowed and bubbled.

Meg seemed fixated by the glow. 'But you are right, Fanny, it is time to make changes, and to think differently. When we go home, I will look for somewhere else to live.'

'Close to us,' I said.

Her eyebrow flicked up. 'No need to go mad.'

'All right, at a decent distance.'

She smiled at me. A car drew up outside the house. Its engine revved, its door opened and shut. Meg gathered up her bag.

'You're not going?'

'Sure, I am,' she said. She got up, put her hand on my shoulder and kissed my cheek, a light, cool touch. 'We're quite good friends really, aren't we? In the end? I like to think so, Fanny.'

I kissed her back. 'Of course.' Then I held her tight, and the breath of her forgiveness stole over me.

'That's straight, then. That's *something*. Go back to bed, my good and watchful Fanny.'

'Shall I come with you? Why don't I? Give me five minutes.'

'No, Fanny. I am on my own now. Remember?'

Defeated, I went back upstairs. I heard voices, doors banging, and the car accelerating down the road.

I opened the shutters wide to let in the night.

I meant to wait up until she returned but I fell asleep and was woken by a light pulsing through the room.

There was an exchange in Italian outside on the path, followed by a knock on the door. I reached for a T-shirt and pulled it over my nightdress. With each step down the stairs, my heartbeat accelerated.

Italian policemen, I noted in a stupefied way, were always immaculate, even at that time of the morning. The male one had a perfect crease on his shirt sleeve and an equally perfect one ironed into his trousers. His belt buckle gleamed and his hair was brushed and beautifully cut. 'So sorry, Signora,' he said. His female colleague had long blonde hair and a tiny waist. She stepped forward and took my hands in her tanned olive ones.

'Where did you find her?' I asked eventually.

'Outside the church.' The policewoman was calm and professional. 'We think she tripped and hit her head on the tethering stone by the fountain. But we are not sure if that is what killed her. The doctors will tell us.'

The woman paused, then asked, 'Did the *signora* have a history of illness?'

I bit my lip. 'In a way, yes, she did.'

Later, about ten minutes or so, when I had brought my knees under control and fought my way into some clothes, they escorted me down the path and handed me into the car.

A hush fell as I was led through the police station to the morgue at the back. The policewoman touched my arm. 'Hold on to me if you want to,' she said.

My nails dug into my skin.

At the policewoman's nod, the sheet over the figure on the gurney was pulled back.

My first thought was, It's all right. Meg's sleeping. Only sleeping.

Her cheek had a faint flush, and her hair fell back naturally on to the rubber sheet beneath her head so that the wound was concealed. Her mouth was peaceful and there was not one line on the smooth, youthful forehead.

The policewoman knew, all too well, the many ways in which the bereaved reacted. One was to refuse to believe.

'The *signora* is dead,' she said gently. 'No doubt.'

'Don't bother to grieve,' those peaceful lips might say. 'I've had enough. Battle over. Eh?'

The policeman consulted his notes. 'She had been drinking in the Bacchus. Too much, according to the reports, and she was asked to leave at approximately half past two. She was seen walking down the road towards the church and knocking on the church door. The witness said he was worried because she was unsteady and he went after her, but by the time he caught up she had fallen.'

I leant over and touched the untroubled, line-free forehead. Then I picked up her hand and smoothed the fingers with their tiny, pearly nails, one by one. Already they seemed waxen, doll-like. 'Oh, Meg,' I whispered, and hot tears ran down my cheek. 'I'm sorry. I'm so sorry.'

As I left they handed me a packet of her things in a plastic bag with a list. One ring, gold. The bracelets. One leather purse, empty. One cotton skirt. The black high heels. And, finally, one cross, gold. Surprised, I held it up between finger and thumb and, caught in the electric light, the chain glimmered. 'I can't stand religion,' Meg had protested more than once. 'So bossy. So pointless. So vulgar.'

I returned to Casa Rosa and made the first of many phone calls.

Some time later, I'm not sure when, I went into the kitchen. There was the chair in which Meg had sat. The bottles of oil and balsamic vinegar she had used. The coffee machine, which she had taken over.

I touched them. Implements and objects that, only a few hours ago, Meg had also touched.

I did not believe she was dead.

Still later, as the heat shimmered above the tarmac and the geraniums in the pots outside the houses drooped in the sun, I walked past Maria and Angelo, who nodded at me sorrowfully, skirted the tethering stone, with its iron ring for the horses' bridles, and entered the church. The gloom in the interior was a cool bath, and I swam through it towards the frescos. Instinctively I knew Meg had been trying to get into the church to see them. I reckoned she had felt that you knew where you were with them. Stupid with drink, she had forgotten that the church was locked at night to protect the paintings.

I unclenched my fists, felt pins and needles lick up my arms, and tried to make myself understand. Meg *was* dead.

Dead . . .

Then I got into the car and took the road to the airport.

Sacha was in Meg's room next door and I could hear him moving about restlessly. Will lay on my bed with his arm over his face.

I sat down and took his free hand and held it.

He dropped his arm. He had been crying and he was white with shock and fatigue and he had bitten his lip. It had left a rough, sore patch. 'I suppose it was bound to happen, one day.'

I climbed into the bed and took him in my arms and held him until he was calmer. Then I made him take some aspirin and stroked his hair.

'Do you want me to tell you what happened, or would you rather wait?'

He nodded almost imperceptibly. 'Tell me.'

Without camouflage, I described our visit to Siena, our conversation there, and the exchange back at the Casa Rosa. As I reached the end of the story, I felt myself grow hot and cold with shame and regret. 'Until last night and our quarrel, she was under control.'

'That was something.' Will was eager to latch on to anything positive.

'I'm afraid it was my asking her to find somewhere else to live that set her off. I did try to stop her, Will. I promise you, but I feel responsible.'

He took a while to absorb all the details. 'Not even you could predict a fatal blow to the head on a tethering stone outside a church in an Italian town.'

'Even so.' I looked at the floor strewn with clothes in

my haste to get dressed when the police arrived. 'In the end we were friends. And she knew that you loved her, and Sacha.' I bit my own lip. 'I'm sure she knew.'

The bedroom had grown very hot, and the bed was rumpled. I asked Will to get up and led him into the bathroom and made him wash.

I remade the bed, pulling the sheets tight and smooth. I threw open the shutter and let in the night air. I folded clothes and closed drawers.

I went downstairs and put the kettle on to boil. I poked at the tea bags in the mugs and the water turned from amber to brown — the brown that Meg had so despised.

Oh Meg, I thought, with a wild and terrible sense of loss. *Oh, Meg.*

'Sacha?' I shook him gently. 'It's seven thirty and things are done early here.'

He turned to me with big, hot-looking eyes. I swooped down and felt his forehead. 'You're ill.'

Sacha was clearly feverish and I ordered him to remain where he was, then went down to take charge of Will, who was wrestling with the stove. 'Poor Sacha. He'll feel he's letting Meg down.'

We drank our coffee on the loggia. Unable to sit still, Will paced about. 'I like it here, and I like this house. We should have come here with your father.' He looked away. 'But I would have invaded the private club of two.'

Surprised, I looked up. 'You minded. I'm sorry.'

Will decided to view Meg's body alone, and emerged composed. We negotiated with the police and struggled to short-cut delays. Once the suggestion of foul play had been eliminated, the doctor signed the relevant certificates and we made arrangements for the body to be flown home. Then, it was a question of waiting for the authorities to release it.

Meg was to be buried at Stanwinton. As Sacha pointed out, it had been her home. Working together, Will and I shared the endless phone calls back to England. Mannochie. The funeral director. The vicar. Will had a knack of dealing with emergencies, but with this one he was too tired and sad. Once or twice I had to intervene when he lost the thread.

Will also phoned Chloë and, having told her the news, passed the phone to me. Chloë was almost incoherent. 'You won't die on me, Mum, will you, or Dad? *Promise*.'

I did my best to calm her, and wondered if we should encourage her to get on a plane, but Will anticipated what I was thinking and shook his head.

'Poor, poor Sacha,' cried Chloë. 'I can't bear it for him. Tell him I love him.'

'He'll ring you,' I said, 'when he's feeling better. I promise.'

Rob rang several times and Sacha staggered downstairs to talk to his father. Will and I retreated out of earshot. When I broached the subject of his father, Sacha said only, 'He's left it all up to me. He says he doesn't feel he should interfere.'

I urged him back into bed and dosed him up. 'Your father's trying to make it easier for you by not getting in the way.'

I reported this conversation to Will, who went straight upstairs and spent over an hour talking to Sacha. When I took up more tea, I discovered him sitting on the edge of the bed and a red-eyed Sacha propped up on the pillows. Both of them looked dreadful. I stood over them, and fussed and bullied them into drinking it. After a couple of mouthfuls, Sacha grimaced. 'Give me the stuff the spoon will stand up in.'

In the morning, Sacha was better but still weak, and agreed without too much argument to remain in bed. I fed him more tea, made him change out of his sweaty T-shirt and insisted on brushing his hair.

'Thanks,' he said, leant back on the pillows and closed his eyes.

The police told us, 'Only two days.' But this was Italy and two days stretched into three, then four. Meg would have appreciated the joke.

The convalescent Sacha was content to sit it out on the loggia at Casa Rosa. 'I need to get my head straight,' he said, and it was clear that he preferred to be on his own.

In contrast, Will was restless, had not eaten much and was sleeping badly. I said to him, 'There's something I would like to show you if you'd like to come.'

He showed only a polite interest. 'Let's do it, then.'

We left Sacha well supplied with iced drinks and a cold pasta salad. Armed with maps and guidebooks, I drove Will to Tarquinia. The car skidded a little as I forced it up the slope leading out of the valley and down the other side, past poppies, clumps of herbs, wild lavender and the olive trees, their bases plastered with summer dust.

Will slumped back in the passenger seat and wiped his sunglasses. 'Italy's too hot.'

'You get used to it,' I said.

'For God's sake,' he said, and fell silent.

The museum in Tarquinia was cool and almost empty. We did not linger over the exhibits – I suspected Will's concentration was not good. Eventually, I led him up to the funerary couch. 'There. Do you recognize it?'

He looked blank. Then he said, 'It was on your father's desk. He was very fond of it.'

'The real thing is better.'

'She's no beauty.'

I nudged him gently. 'Nor is he.'

I went to inspect an exquisite bronze candelabrum, worked with bunches of grapes and vine leaves. 'Will . . . come and see this.'

But Will was rooted in front of the funerary couple, eyes narrowed, his face a mask of distress.

We returned to the car and consulted the maps, for I was anxious to visit the Etruscan tombs. Chloë and I always teased Will about maps but, truth be told, his skill had got us places. Now I waited for him to say that women have no spatial awareness and for me to reply, 'Women are better team players.' But he didn't and I didn't.

On his instructions, I drove far up into a *maquis* of rock and scrub. Here the land had a blind, bitter, cussed feel. Yet the books reported that, all those centuries ago, the Etruscans had made it fertile and fruitful with trees, pasture and crops. Their lovely Paradise. Their Elysium.

We drove into a clearing and parked close to the remains of an Etruscan town, which didn't amount to much – a hint of a mosaic pavement and the suggestion of a stone wall running at an angle up the hill. Drinks were being sold under a cluster of umbrellas, and an overflowing rubbish bin was sited next to an ancient brick arch. Otherwise the scene had an abandoned, desolate quality.

We followed the track up into the hills. The going became precipitous and it was very hot. In my sandals, my feet grew slippery with sweat, and Will was panting. An arrow indicated a steep incline and a second pointed yet further up. The heat seared into our backs.

'Over there.' I pointed to a dark opening, partly obscured by vegetation.

Will smiled grimly. 'This had better be worth it.'

He pushed back the vegetation to let me through, and we found ourselves in a large rock chamber lined with stone shelves on which the Etruscans had laid out their dead.

There was no mistaking an odour of semi-stagnant water and rock that never saw the sun. The smell was the essence of extinction. I laid a hand on a cold shelf. The ghosts of the Etruscan dead were locked into this place, far, far removed from the banqueting and harvesting, the wine, lovemaking and married love depicted in their painting and sculpture.

'I don't know why we make such a fuss about the afterlife,' said Will. 'Once you've gone, that's it. Meg has gone, so has your father. What's left?' he reached for my hand.

But I fled from the tomb and scrambled back down the path. I heard Will come after me and, by the time he caught up, I was breathless. I gasped for air and the heat whistled painfully into my lungs but I welcomed it. Far better to be here in the open, burning hot but alive.

I lifted my face to the sun. To emerge from the dark

cave into the light was to know that I was free.

On the way back, Will asked, 'Alfredo's ashes . . . have you decided?'

'No. Silly isn't it?'

'You can't put it off for ever.'

'I know.'

Over supper of grilled veal chops and roasted peppers, Sacha told us that he would be moving on. 'To Manchester. I think,' he said. 'I've got a couple of gigs lined up. After that . . . well, I'll go and see Chloë in Oz. Hitch around a little. Take a look.'

'That would be nice.' I kept my voice neutral.

'I miss her,' he said simply.

'So do we.' Instinctively, I glanced at Will and our eyes locked. '*Don't*' was the message in his. A mental nudge, I suppose.

After supper, Will said to me, 'Fanny, go and get your father's ashes.' I stared at him. 'Go on.'

I went upstairs, retrieved the small wooden casket and carried it down to the loggia. 'May I?' asked Will. I nodded and he took it from me. 'Now we'll find a place for Alfredo.'

Holding the casket under one arm, he propelled me out of the house with the other.

We walked up the dust road, and the residual heat cradled our feet. 'I should have paid more attention to the descriptions of Fiertino,' Will said, in a conversational way. 'Then I would know where I was. Where did your father's family live?'

The moon was as bright as burnished silver as I pointed

down the road to the ugly replacement *fattoria*. 'It was burnt down at the end of the war,' I explained.

'I see.' Will considered. 'I don't think that would be right. Nor, I think, is the churchyard. I think your father would prefer to be free.'

I blinked back tears. 'Yes, he would.'

At the fork in the road, Will ignored the route into the village and we picked our way up the rise where the cypresses and chestnuts grew in clumps and the vines swept past them down into the valley. It was a mystery to me how anyone slept in the deep, perfumed Italian nights, and I said so to Will. He smiled.

'I don't believe you said that.'

Down below, the lights of the village were tucked into the slope of the hillside under a starred palanquin. The moonlight worked its usual deceptions and Fiertino seemed to spring out of the landscape, untouched and complete. 'I love this place,' I confessed.

'I know you do. But, Fanny . . .' He was hesitant. 'You do know you're only a visitor?'

It would have been so easy to say, 'No, I belong here.' But that would be to ignore many particulars and the evidence against. I *was* a visitor – a special one, but a visitor. I knew that now.

'Your father never liked me,' Will remarked, in the same conversational tone. 'I wish he had.'

'He didn't say that,' I replied. 'You were different. You use politics to deal with difficult questions and difficult problems – how to conduct ourselves in society before death and . . . extinction. Dad thought it was a waste of time. He relied on himself.'

'But I liked him.'

'So did I,' I said, with a half-sob.

Will gestured towards the vines. 'What's the grape?' he asked.

'Sangiovese.'

'Was that a favourite?'

'He admired it.'

'Why don't you settle him among the vines?' Will offered me the urn. 'Don't you think he would like that?'

I knew he had got it right.

I picked my way between the swollen grape trusses and came to a halt. With a little painful thud of my heart, I upended the casket and watched my father's ashes drift towards the earth.

His *terroir*.

By the time I returned to where Will waited, I was shivering with emotion and he held me very close.

The following days were waiting days. When it got too hot, we retreated to the loggia at Casa Rosa and ate green bean and tomato salad from Benedetta's harvest for lunch and grew sleepy on a glass of Chianti. At night we ate at Angelo's, and Sacha sometimes remained to drink coffee in the square. I was glad to see a little colour returning to his face.

Naturally, Will was preoccupied, and very quiet. I waited until we were alone in our bedroom at the Casa Rosa before I finally coaxed him to talk.

'Meg's death has pulled everything into focus. What's so important as that? Nothing.' He sat down on the bed. 'I can only explain it as a loss of nerve,' he said. 'I find I'm not so sure any more. Facing things and fighting battles feels more difficult to me now than it did at the beginning. I used to be so certain about the things we needed to achieve. Now I wonder whether we do any good at all.' He looked up at me ruefully. 'I don't know why I should feel that now, at the grand old, battle-hardened age of forty-eight.'

I looked at him and saw for the first time that it was only after blazing desire has turned to tenderness and familiarity, that true knowledge – the knowledge which I sought – was possible. And I thought with a little flutter of nerves of the degree of risk which I had taken. Not that I regretted it, but it was worth considering the destruction of what might have been.

'Go on,' I said. 'What else.'

'You disappeared out here and seemed so absorbed in a quite different world, and I didn't think I could catch up. I thought you would vanish. Then I thought I had kept you against your will. No, I don't mean against your will exactly, but caged, and when you had the first chance to fly away, you did.' He gave a rueful laugh. 'I suppose I was jealous of Fiertino, and of you in Fiertino.'

I felt a pang of sympathy. 'So the minute I go away you develop a first-class case of nerves?'

'I wouldn't put it like that exactly.'

A little later, he said. 'You really love this place . . . the Casa Rosa, and the town. Don't you?'

'Yes, I do. It's in my bloodstream. But that is not to say it is my father's Fiertino. That was different.'

Will stood by the window and looked out across the valley. 'I wish I didn't have to go back.'

I did not have any illusions. I understood perfectly that once Will got back within sound and scent of the Westminster arena, his ears would prick up and his nose would twitch.

'Listen to me,' I said and came and stood beside him and gave the gentlest of nudges. 'You are fine. Absolutely fine.'

He bent over and kissed me.

The following day, I went to the priest and arranged for a small stone to be placed, with my father's name and dates, among the rest of the Battistas. And then I turned my face homeward. We spent the last few hours at Casa Rosa setting it in order. I swept floors, stacked china, dusted the bedrooms. Together Sacha and I packed up Meg's things and talked about her.

When evening came, and the sun flooded the valley with shadows, I sat by the window of the bedroom and drank in the last moments until Will called, 'Fanny, please come.'

I loved Casa Rosa, and never more so than when I was saying goodbye to it. The last task was to fasten the shutters and I had insisted that I did it.

Will and Sacha waited in the car. I gave it a final, lingering inspection before we drove down to Benedetta, who had a present for me. It was a small, blurred photograph of a house whose roof had fallen in and whose blackened beams pointed burnt fingers to the open sky. I could just make out a fountain in the garden, which was filled with rubble and churned-up earth. I turned the photograph over: on the back was written, '1799–1944'.

'The *fattoria*,' she said. I put it into my handbag and kissed her goodbye. '*Santa Patata*,' she said, 'you will be back.'

I looked back only once as we took the road for Rome, and the view shimmered into a brilliant radiance of olive tree, scarlet poppy and vine. I thought of Meg.

How cross she would be that she was not here to climb into the hot car and say, 'Poor me, I've got the worst seat.'

I pictured the vines pushing their roots deep into the *terroir* and the sun on the grapes. 'Allow the sun to shine on the grapes,' my father would say, 'until the last possible moment, and it will seduce the fruit into such richness and flavour.'

22

We brought Meg home and buried her in the Stanwinton churchyard. Will said he wanted time to think about a gravestone and I was to leave it to him. So I did.

Reclaimed by the charity suppers, the good works and the regular journeys to London, I went back to work. Mannochie had almost – but not quite – forgiven me for my defection. 'Train tracks, Mrs S,' he whispered into my ear at the Glee Club's annual fund-raising evening when I had the misfortune to laugh after an excruciating rendition of 'London's Burning'. The eyelash-dye appointment was booked the next morning.

I was glad of it when, a couple of days later, I blinked back tears as POD artists in clowns' motley wooed the children in the cancer ward into laughter. 'Look,' said a mother, who was standing beside me, pointing out her bald daughter. 'She's laughing, she's really laughing.' She pulled out a photograph from her bag and showed it to me. 'Carla used to have the longest plaits,' she said.

'So did mine,' I replied – and I was the lucky one: the lucky, lucky mother.

Elaine rang up. 'So you didn't leave Will,' she said. 'I had an idea that you might.'

'I did think about it,' I said.

'I'm leaving Neil,' she said, 'and setting up my knitwear business. Will you wear my jumpers, Fanny?'

I breathed in deeply. 'Always.'

Probate for my father's estate came through. There was little money and it was clear that there was no option but to sell the house. As for the business, I had plans for it. As I explained to Will, I would have less time for his side of things but I would do my best not to let him down.

He listened quietly. 'I don't have a problem with that,' he said.

I touched his cheek. 'Nor should you.'

He flashed his old grin at me. 'It's your turn. And while you are at it, Fanny, do you think you could make us some money?'

I rang Raoul and told him I was taking over Battista's, and could we still do business his end?

'Of course,' he said. 'I look forward to it. And, Fanny . . .'

'Yes?'

'I'll see you soon.'

'Yes.'

Armed with cardboard boxes and cleaning equipment, Maleeka and I drove over to Ember House and began the task of packing up my father's things.

'Izt good mans,' she said, as she cleared out the saucepan cupboard. 'I know.'

As always, Maleeka was oddly comforting. 'I know, too, Maleeka.'

It took us several days, and as the furniture – except for the pieces carefully chosen for Chloë – was removed, Ember House assumed the peeled, denuded aspect of a dwelling in which life had gone away somewhere else. I went through my father's papers and sorted out the business files. The rest I burnt – letters from my mother and

285

Caro, tax returns going back twenty years . . . anything. I was keeping his desk, the blue and white fruit bowl, the framed photograph of the Etruscans and a selection of books.

I rang my mother and asked if she wanted anything sent over. 'No,' she said. 'I left it all behind.' She was coughing. 'A cold. I've been quite sick with it.'

It struck me that I could do more to breathe the mother–daughter relationship into existence, but there did not seem any point. My mother had made that choice years ago. 'Get better soon.'

Sally protested. 'And a person could die of coughing here before they get any sympathy.'

'Art not paying you enough attention?'

'Ouch,' Sally exclaimed. 'He's just pinched my butt.'

After the final session at Ember House, I returned home exhausted and filthy. Sacha insisted on making supper. I watched him boil up the pasta and open a bottle of ready-made sauce. 'Sacha, I want you to know that you're wonderful.'

He placed a heaped plate in front of me and sat down with his. 'This looks disgusting.'

I ate a mouthful, then a second. It *was* disgusting, and I was hit by such a longing for Benedetta's fragrant sauces, for wine, olives and sun, that I almost cried out. Sacha stared at his plate. 'I wish Mum was here.' Then he pushed away the plate and cried.

I waited until the storm had died down. 'It will get better, I promise you.'

'At least you don't say, "It'll be all right."' His voice was muffled. 'I couldn't bear that. It'll never be all right. It was awful, horrible. Mum's story, I mean, and she's left behind such complicated feelings and muddle.'

This was the closest Sacha would ever come to criticism of his mother, and I loved him all the more for his loyalty. 'It's not complicated for her any longer.'

'No.' He raised his drenched face. 'But I feel . . . as though she didn't love me enough to stick around.'

'Oh, Sacha . . .' I got up and put my arms round him. His hair was wild and – so unlike him – in need of a wash. I kissed his wet cheek. 'Meg loved you better than she loved herself.'

Sacha thought about it, then asked, 'Is life so exhausting all the time?'

I shook my head. 'Not all the time. You'll have moments of great joy, I promise. And contentment. And pleasure in small things.'

He ducked his head. 'I wish.'

'But you have to make up your mind to look for the moments.'

'You think?'

I said, as steadily as I could, 'It's taken me a bit of time, but I do think.'

'Fanny, you're not going to leave Will, are you?' He stumbled over the words.

Shocked, I stared at him. 'What makes you ask that?'

He shrugged. 'I don't think I could bear it if you did. And it would kill Chloë.'

'*Chloë?*'

'She said as much to me.'

*

Sacha left to go up north before I attempted to do anything with Meg's things. Before he left, he gave me permission. 'Please . . . please will you do it? I trust you.'

Meg's bedroom smelt unused and stagnant, but the mess was as if she had walked out just a few seconds ago. Not surprisingly, her presence felt stronger here than anywhere else. I picked up a scarf from the floor, bright pink silk, one of her favourites. Traces of her scent lingered on the fabric – and I sat down, abruptly, on the bed. We had been so mixed up, Meg and I, so entwined. She had been part of me: the dark, tangled side but something else, too.

I pleated the expensive silk this way and that.

The door to Meg's cupboard was partially open, revealing her clothes bunched up like anxious spectators. A photograph of Sacha in his leather jacket grinned down at the empty bed. A book lay on the bedside table and I picked it up: self-help psychology, with a message that to feel the fear was to defuse it. A postcard marked Meg's place. It was from Chloë in Australia. 'It's cool,' she wrote. 'Hope you're well. Looking forward to seeing you.'

I longed for my daughter. For her mess, her occasional rudeness, the glimpses I caught of Chloë's private, inter-esting inner life. Her 'Oh, Mum, you're so sad.' I hated to think of her so far away and, no doubt, feeling left out of the family business.

Sacha had owned up to the mess and muddle of his own feelings and I should do so too. When it came to Meg, mine were as painful and as disturbing as his. They always would be. Yet, I must do my best not to remember her in a negative way. Nor should I for, in her own way,

Meg had struggled so hard not to allow the negative to overwhelm her.

Her room transformed – clean, aired, sterile – I twitched back the curtain and said aloud, 'I'll miss you, Meg. Do you believe that?'

I was folding up her favourite cotton blouse, ready for the charity pile, when Will walked unexpectedly into the kitchen. He was dressed in his dark grey suit and immaculately polished shoes and he was carrying – of course – the red box.

'Fanny, the election is on. It's battle stations.' I tucked the blouse into a bag and spread tissue paper on top. 'Can I count on you?' He dumped the box on the table, moved too abruptly and knocked over a carrier-bag with a clunk. 'What on earth . . .?'

'Her lifeline bottle. She always kept one.'

When everything had been sorted and stowed, Will suggested a walk.

It was fresh up on the ridge and a breeze shook the leaves in the trees, like impatient strokes of a hairbrush. Rabbit spoor peppered the rough grass on the slope and, under the beeches, there was a faint imprint of deer tracks. We traversed the ridge and dropped down alongside the hedgerow, which still bore the scars of a recent swiping. Tucked under the blackthorn was the tiny body of a fledgling. It had been dead for a long time, and had dried and stretched almost out of shape.

Will walked on ahead and I watched him.

I was trying to puzzle out what, in the end, I was doing here, with Will.

Then I remembered.

'Mama . . .' whined three-year-old Chloë, during the sermon of one of the innumerable church services we had had to attend, 'Mama . . .' I was tired, so tired that I felt almost dead. Will swooped down, picked up his troublesome daughter and held her close. Enchanted, Chloë ran her tiny hands over his face, exploring every plane, every angle of his chin and poked at his eyes. And Will, gazing with pure love on his fair-haired, minxy daughter with an expression that was as far removed from ambition and striving as it was possible to be, let her do so.

That was what it was about.

Will waited for me to catch up. 'You will be able to spare time to climb on the battle bus,' he asked anxiously.

There was an edge to his tone – a reprise of the doubting Will of the Casa Rosa – and I knew, for certain, that they were all frightened that they would lose.

'I can manage without you,' he said. 'But I'd rather not.'

'That's something, after all these years.' I would have liked to have raised a smile, at least, if not a laugh. 'It's that bad?'

His reply was dragged out of him. 'It's that bad.'

I braced myself mentally. 'I'd better get going then, hadn't I?'

The tea-and-cake session for the party workers was, of course, well attended. There was nothing like an election for galvanizing the sheep and the goats, the supporters and the detractors, even if the press had already rushed to print its doubts about the party.

Mannochie came over. 'Glad to see you back.'

He was holding a mammoth sheaf of papers. I looked at them. 'Are they all for me?'

'Not quite.' He sounded cheerful at the prospect of the fight. Someone had to. We commandeered a couple of plastic chairs and ran through the staggering list of commitments. Coffee mornings. Suppers. Press calls. Mannochie had excelled himself. 'I'm counting on Will to wheel in some big guns. The Chancellor . . . or even the PM. Nothing like the big cheeses to make us feel we're on the map.'

A little later, I got up to make a rally-the-troops speech. I knew I looked the part – unremarkable skirt, slightly more elegant black jacket, discreet jewellery. The uniform of the model political wife.

I surveyed the faces. They were good-natured, expectant, and wishing to be told that all was well. I had the choice as to whether to be honest – and the speech would run along the lines of it was going to be hard and bumpy, there were no safe harbours and no safe outcomes – or . . . I smiled. 'Ladies and gentlemen, I know Will would have liked to be here, and he will be just as soon as he can. Meanwhile, he sends his thanks in advance for all the work he knows you'll be putting in during the next six weeks. None of it will be wasted. We have the right policies, the right team and, if I may say so, the right person to represent you and lead you to victory. I live with him . . .' pause for a ripple of laughter ' . . . and I know he spends every waking minute thinking about the constituency . . . even when I reckon he should be thinking about me.'

More laughter.

'One of the things that I know concerns Will in particular is, as a minister, how much time he has to spend in

Westminster, but that does not mean that his constituency of Stanwinton is not engraved on his heart. I hope you feel that he has always considered your views and put your interests at the top of the list.'

I sat down to enthusiastic applause.

'Very graceful,' said Mannochie. 'Thank you.'

I was sitting in front of the mirror rubbing cream into my face and getting ready for bed when Will placed a hand on my shoulder.

'Fanny, I must ask you. I *have* to ask you. When Raoul came and saw you in Italy. Was that . . . was it?'

I knew exactly what Will was asking, and I knew he must have thought it over very carefully before he broached the subject. If it had not been for Meg, I am sure he would have tackled me earlier, and the long interval between my telling him that Raoul came to visit and this moment must have given him pain, for which I was sorry.

I continued to smooth the cream into my cheeks and neck and I watched my reflection performing this little everyday routine.

I had it in my power to square an old circle, to redress a balance. I could choose to tell Will the truth. I could say that Raoul offered me sweet and civilized delights, a moment of pleasure and sun, where I was not a wife, but myself . . . and I could add that I wanted very much to accept.

Or I could tell Will that I had taken Raoul as a lover, but he was not to worry. It was a terrible mistake and certainly was not going to affect our marriage. He would know what I was talking about.

Or I could say that I had thanked Raoul, and replied that I would bear his offer in mind for the future. Keep it stored in the attic, so to speak, and drag it out every so often to dust it off.

I encountered Will's wary expression in the mirror and put down the tube of cream. It struck me that the politics of a successful marriage involved never asking too straight a question, and in never answering it fully, always leaving that tiny margin of unknowing. It was enough to know that each loved the other, and the rest had to be done with smoke and mirrors and more than a little trust.

I stroked in the final dab of cream. The mirror bore the double burden of me looking at it and being looked into at the same time. My skin gleamed with its expensive lustre and my hair was satisfyingly smart and chic. A girl had grown into a woman who, among other things was a wife and mother. Making sense of what you turned out to be was as much to do with that faith and determination of the will. And, above all, I had my inner room into which I could retreat and draw breath.

I got up and turned round to face Will. 'It was business.' I kissed his nose and drew a heart on his chest with my fingertip. 'Only business.'

'I've had an idea,' Will said, as he threw back the covers and got into bed. 'If there's any money left over from your father's estate, I think you should make inquiries about buying Casa Rosa. We could do it up. I'll help you. I like DIY.'

I slid in beside him, and plumped up my pillow. 'There won't be enough.'

He smiled conspiratorially. 'Did I tell you Meg has left me a small amount? You can have it. You *must* have it.' He reached out and snapped off the light. 'That should do.'

23

I had been on the stump for four hours. My feet hurt, and my wretched rosette kept falling off. Our last but one stop was a block of flats down by the river where the concrete walkways were streaked with damp and corridors were littered with . . . best not to inquire. I knocked on a door that had once been bright blue.

A woman in a plastic apron stuck her head through the window. 'What do you want?'

I launched into the spiel and she frowned. 'You lot never talked to us.'

'But I'm talking to you now.'

'That's what you call it.'

Behind me, the junior party apparatchik trailing in my wake sniggered and I gave up. 'Fine,' I said, and tried to stuff a leaflet through the letterbox, where it stuck.

I stifled a yawn, as well I might: I had been woken at five thirty a.m. by Mr Tucker, who had demanded to know if my spirit was in good working order.

Good question.

Next up was Mrs Scott, my special assignment, who, I knew, would have spent most of the afternoon preparing tea for my visit.

The apparatchik and I squeezed into her sitting room, where a tray with legs had been laid with a lace napkin and a jug with a beaded cover. In the corner, a television with the sound turned down winked and blinked. 'I hope you use yours.' She whipped the cover off the jug.

'I do, Mrs Scott. I'm very fond of it.'

'Mrs Savage and I are friends,' Mrs Scott addressed the apparatchik, 'she sits in for the minister.'

I glanced around the room. After much tussling, the council had replaced the glass in the front door after the violent neighbours had bashed it in. There was a patch of new plaster, too, where the window had cracked and the damp had got into it. 'I am glad Will was able to organize to get the repairs. It's been rather uncomfortable for you, I'm afraid.'

Mrs Scott did not see it this way. 'If those buggers hadn't bashed down my door, I would never have got to meet the minister.'

Polling day dawned stormy. I climbed out of our warm bed and pulled back the curtains. The rain rattled across the field, and welled into puddles on the road.

'Sod it,' said Will from the bed. 'No one will go out to vote.' He picked up the phone and rang Mannochie. While I dressed, a conversation ensued in which my name cropped up. I knew what it meant.

'Mannochie's ordered transport for the elderly,' Will lay back on the pillows, already looking exhausted, 'but we could use the second car and a driver.'

I picked up my election skirt, not a garment of great beauty but it made me look reliable and approachable, and put it on. 'I know my duty.'

The polling station was the primary school, where, as

the roof leaked, voters dodged around buckets – which, it occurred to me, was not a good advert for Will.

He and I voted, and I set myself to pilot the aged, infirm, and those with small children to and from the polling stations. Every so often I checked in at one of the twenty committee rooms scattered over the constituency for an update.

The day vanished and, after a snatched supper of a banana and yoghurt, the order came: the MP's wife's call to arms.

I went home and changed into a dark grey trouser suit, a silk camisole and a pair of pink, soft leather flat shoes. I was, of course, wearing tights. I looked in the mirror and checked my eyelashes. A girl . . . no, a *woman* had to consider her strategies. If it was victory, I was primed. If it was defeat, I needed to be at my feminine best. I wanted to go to the death scented, lipsticked, hair in place.

I hid the shadows beneath my eyes with foundation, outlined my mouth in lipstick, blotted it and reapplied a second coat, then brushed my hair until it fell obediently on to my shoulders.

Mannochie caught up with me as I threaded my way through the army of helpers at the party association headquarters. He looked grim, and his hair was lank and unbrushed. 'Exit polls don't look so good.'

'For the party, or for Will?'

'Hard to say,' he said, 'but it's possible that Will is going to cop it.'

'Grief, Mannochie.' I froze on the spot. 'I thought it might be better on the day.'

'Politics isn't a science, but hunches are pretty good too.'

Defeat would come hard to Mannochie as well as to Will. They were linked together like a horse and carriage.

'We've been through it before,' I said to Mannochie. 'We'll survive.'

'It's not as though there's a real reason,' he said miserably. 'The economy's OK. Inflation's under control. Public services are ticking over.'

I am told that sea-changes in the earth's composition take place underground in secret. We don't know about them, but they happen, and it is not until later that the scientists can work out exactly what has happened. Meg had been correct: people get bored and they crave change just for the sake of change. There is no rhyme or reason for it, and it is bad luck on anyone caught by the short-fall.

Will broke into a smile of relief when I pushed my way through to him. 'Thought you'd done a runner.'

Like minor royalty, he and I stood side by side as people came up to discuss, take orders, make a point. Every so often, Will felt for my hand and pressed it. Out of the corner of my eye, I spotted Matt Smith making a beeline towards us.

Will whispered, 'Could you smile at Matt, Fanny?'

'You ask me to do such terrible things.' I forced my lips into the appropriate shape.

And so . . . on to the torture of the count. Keyed up and fatigued, the bystanders wandered around and made aimless conversation. The activists were best at keeping up the semblance of mad activity and, with respect to the drones, it was those from the opposite party who appeared happiest and more diligently occupied.

The ballot boxes arrived, were emptied, the papers sorted, bundled and placed in lines on the trestle tables. I knew now to watch the lines. Sometimes they creep . . . sometimes they rocket along and you can tell from the way the tellers glance in your direction which pile belongs to whom.

No one appeared to be looking in Will's direction.

'See?' said Mannochie, in an undertone. 'Not good.'

'I know.'

I helped myself to coffee from a Thermos. It was stewed but at least it was hot. Anyway, it gave me something on which to concentrate. No need to get the bad news before it was necessary.

At four o'clock there was a final altercation with the Natural Earth candidate over spoilt ballot papers. That sorted, the returning officer made his way to Will and me. 'I'm sorry.' He spoke directly to Will. 'You win some and some you don't.' Will swallowed. The gaze of the returning officer drifted towards the winning candidate. 'I'm sorry,' he repeated.

Will stood on the platform, as upright and unflinching as he had trained himself to be, and I was proud of him. The final figures were read out and he did not falter, not once, not even when he heard how his majority of 7,005 had been wiped off the face of the earth.

The victorious candidate bowed, grinned, and made a speech in which he individually thanked most people in Stanwinton.

Then Will took the microphone . . . and we were back

to the beginning. He spoke about change, the need to rethink and recharge, and how he had fought to hold on to his ideals. He thanked his supporters and told them that nothing had been wasted.

Every word drained him, I could see that, and I willed him to the finish in this gladiatorial death. At the end, head bowed, he listened to the applause. Then he raised his eyes and sought mine.

It did not end quite there: we had to speak to so many people who required to be reassured and reminded that there was a tomorrow and it would come.

On the way home, Will said suddenly, 'Stop the car.'

He wrenched open the door and stumbled out. I followed him.

Then he was sick.

I held him until the bout was finished. 'Sorry,' he managed.

After he had got his breath back, I made him walk with me as far as the oak tree at the corner of the field. The sun was just poking above the horizon and, after the heat and frenzy of the town hall, the air was fresh and cool. We leant on the gate and looked across the field to the dawn, where the light was picking out the pattern of leaves on the hedgerows. The birds were stirring in the beech trees.

Will laid his head on his folded arms. 'I always wondered how I would deal with it when it came.'

'The answer is, fine. In fact, more than fine.'

His voice was muffled. 'We will have to think again about everything. How we live, all that. What we do.'

Back at the house, I made him tea which he drank

thirstily. 'Let's see what's happening on television,' he said.

But I stopped him. 'No, that's finished for the moment.'

The dark eyes were dull with misery. 'I suppose you are right.'

Although I knew he had not had any dinner the night before, he refused to eat anything, and I led him upstairs. He submitted obediently as I unbuttoned his shirt and peeled it off. His body was soaked in sweat and, every so often, he gave a shuddering sigh.

In bed, I eased myself close and held him.

After a few minutes he fell into a twitchy sleep, but I kept on holding him until my arm grew numb. When I could not stand it any longer, I detached myself from Will and went downstairs to phone Chloë.

It took a bit of determination to track her down but, eventually, I got through. It was very late at night for her, and she sounded terrified when she came to the phone. 'Mum? Nothing bad has happened?'

'Nothing so terrible, but Dad did lose his seat last night. He wanted me to ring you.'

'Oh, poor Dad. Is he very upset?'

'Yes. He's sleeping at the moment.'

Once Chloë was reassured that, basically, her family hadn't been wiped off the face of the planet, she sounded quite cheerful. 'He can do something else. Tell him lots of people do. It's the spirit of the age. It's good for you to have a change. Tell him he's lucky to have another chance of doing something.'

'Darling Chloë, I do miss you. I want to tell you about a lot of things and what I saw in Italy.'

It struck me that it was time I talked to Chloë about the family and its history.

'Oh, Mum, I miss you too . . .' She chatted on for quite a time, and it was only towards the end of our conversation that she dropped in the following information: 'Mum, I've met someone . . . His name is Paul . . .'

I surveyed my domain. I tidied the kitchen, checked the food and wine supplies. Without a doubt, Mannochie and the team would be coming over in droves and they would require feeding in defeat as much as in victory. I would cook bowls of pasta and open bottles of wine and we could sit round the table and go over what had happened until it was shaped enough to consign to memory. Then we had to move on.

I picked up the diary and leafed through it, resisting the temptation to score through the dozen or so pre-Christmas constituency engagements. That would be to snatch too small a victory from the jaws of defeat.

'Fanny?'

I looked up from the diary. Will was in the doorway. 'I'm here,' I said.

'Good,' he said and, unable to resist, disappeared next door to switch on the television. The nation had spoken. The party was out. The other one was in and everyone was either licking wounds or looking smug or pious, or both.

We discussed what this would mean for various colleagues, and by how much this pushed back Will's dream of the Chancellorship. Privately, I knew that it was unlikely Will would ever realize it now. But it was not the moment to say so.

'I've rung Chloë. You'll be pleased to know that she thinks you should look on this as an opportunity for a second chance.'

'Cheeky monkey,' he said, and dropped into a chair, smiling wryly. 'But she's right.' He frowned painfully. 'I'd give anything to see her.'

'Do you want more tea?'

'No.'

'Neither do I.' I bent down to inspect the bottles in the wine rack. 'I never want to drink tea again. Lots of lovely wine instead.'

Now that Meg was not here, I felt I was at liberty to say that sort of thing.

Will went quiet.

We were both busy with our thoughts – and mine were principally preoccupied with how I was to shore Will up until he felt better.

'Will,' I said gently, 'you never know, you might like being free for a while.'

He shrugged. 'Easy to say.'

It was not as though he lacked courage, Will had masses of that. It was just that, at the moment, he was used to thinking along one set of lines. I would have to persuade him that trying out another set would be uncomfortable, but intriguing and perfectly possible.

He tied and retied his dressing-gown cord several times. 'What did Italy do to you?' he asked. 'And can I have some of it? At one point, I wondered if you were going to stay there.'

I replaced a bottle of claret – a disappointing 1997

Haut-Marbuzet – in the rack and straightened up. 'I might have done,' I said. 'I thought about it.'

He ran his hands through his hair, as if in search of the old Will, the one who had been so full of optimism and vigour. 'I would have gone mad,' he said, 'or taken to the bottle.'

'Not a good joke.'

'Not a good joke,' he admitted.

'After I'd got over the relief of being on my own, Will, I realized I wouldn't like being without you either.'

'Good.' Will got up to check the latest figures on the television. 'That's very good.'

I picked up the full rubbish bin and carried it outside. Daylight was well advanced and a shaft of light fell on the garage door. With a curious half painful, half pleasurable squeeze of my heart, I perceived a suggestion – a hint – of the texture and colour of the Casa Rosa.

'Francesca,' said my father. 'You live here in Stanwinton, of course, but you are a Fiertina.'

Well, I was, and I wasn't. I cherished his metaphor, and the story of making the hillside bloom. From bare hillside to the lushly fertile – 'my grandfather's wood, my father's olive-grove, my own vineyard' – in three generations, went the saying. But even he would have to concede that he had been talking about a time that was long ago. My father had not been in Fiertino when the workmen rolled up the road in the mechanical diggers and constructed the row of pylons which marched up the slope. Nor had my father been sitting in Angelo's where the talk was of olive subsidies and of house conversions.

But I would not think about Casa Rosa now. Not yet. I

walked across the lawn. The house was behind me, an emptier house than it had been for years, in which the movement of things and people had dwindled. My territory. After all, after everything, I had grown used to its spaces and awkwardness. We had rubbed along together, it and I – the ugly windows, the laurel hedge, the kitchen that never quite gelled. Even the kittens on the tapestry stool and I had come to an understanding. Like it or not, the house had been the *terroir* in which Will and I had conducted our marriage and made the effort to shape our lives. And, yes, I too had grown powerful within it.

I went back inside and folded up clothes and tidied papers and unopened post. As I moved through the rooms, I listened out for that elusive trace, that tiny echo, of the presences that had once filled them.

Will had gone back to bed and I discovered him huddled on his side. I slid between the sheets, pulled my mother's quilt over us and put my arms round him. He felt cold and lifeless. I kissed his cheek and my hair fell over his face, and I whispered to him that we would survive, it would be all right, and that I loved him.

'I was thinking about Meg,' he said. 'And what more I could have done. How do you think she would have felt? I know what your father would have said. "Look at it this way."'

I laughed.

After a moment, Will turned back to face me. 'I like it when you laugh,' he said.